Judgment

NORTHWESTERN WORLD CLASSICS

*Northwestern World Classics brings readers
the world's greatest literature. The series features
essential new editions of well-known works,
lesser-known books that merit reconsideration,
and lost classics of fiction, drama, and poetry.
Insightful commentary and compelling new translations
help readers discover the joy of outstanding writing
from all regions of the world.*

David Bergelson

Judgment
A Novel

Translated from the Yiddish by
Harriet Murav and Sasha Senderovich

Northwestern University Press ✦ *Evanston, Illinois*

Northwestern University Press
www.nupress.northwestern.edu

Printed in the United States of America

10   9   8   7   6   5   4   3   2   1

Library of Congress Cataloging-in-Publication Data
Names: Bergelson, David, 1884–1952, author. | Murav, Harriet, 1955–
    translator, writer of introduction. | Senderovich, Sasha, translator,
    writer of introduction.
Title: Judgment : a novel / David Bergelson ; translated from the Yiddish
    by Harriet Murav and Sasha Senderovich.
Other titles: Midaas-hadin. English | Northwestern world classics.
Description: Evanston, Illinois : Northwestern University Press, 2017. |
    Series: Northwestern world classics | "Originally published as Mides-
    hadin, vol. 7, Geklibene verk (Vilna: B. Kletzkin, 1929)." | Includes
    bibliographical references.
Identifiers: LCCN 2017017681 | ISBN 9780810135918 (pbk. : alk. paper) |
    ISBN 9780810135925 (e-book)
Subjects: LCSH: Soviet Union—History—Revolution, 1917–1921—
    Jews—Fiction. | Jews—Russia—Fiction. | Soviet Union—History—
    Revolution, 1917–1921—Fiction.
Classification: LCC PJ5129.B45 M513 2017 | DDC 839.133—dc23
LC record available at https://lccn.loc.gov/2017017681

In memory of Joseph Sherman (1944–2009)

CONTENTS

David Bergelson's *Judgment*: A Critical Introduction   ix
    Sasha Senderovich and Harriet Murav

Judgment   1

    Translators' Notes   213

    A Note on Transliteration   219

    Acknowledgments   221

DAVID BERGELSON'S *JUDGMENT*:
A CRITICAL INTRODUCTION

Sasha Senderovich and Harriet Murav

"Rrrrree . . . vv . . . vv . . . vo . . . o . . . o . . . lluu . . . shshsh . . . un!!!"

This string of stuttering sounds comes from the mouth of a name-less character in David Bergelson's Yiddish-language novel *Judgment*.[1] The fragmented word—impeded, slow, and difficult to read—focuses attention on the 1917 Russian revolutions: the overthrow of Tsar Nicholas II and the end of the monarchy in February, and the Bolshevik takeover in October. The word breaks off, starts and stops, repeats, and pauses before it finally comes to an end. The ut-terance takes on a life of its own as an ominous, frightening incan-tation, while the revolutionary government, led by the Bolsheviks, turns to terror, violence, and destruction.

Opening the pages of *Judgment* means entering a confusing and violent world. It is 1920 in a border area between Ukraine and Po-land, and the Bolsheviks are trying to consolidate their tenuous hold on power on the eastern side of the frontier. Food is in short supply. The peasants are dissatisfied. There are counterrevolutionary upris-ings. Personal disputes and seething resentments boil over among individuals supposedly on the same side. In the fictitious town of Golikhovke, the Jewish inhabitants make their living by smuggling every kind of contraband; their non-Jewish neighbors from nearby villages cross the border back and forth as well. Rumors fly through the air, and no one knows for certain what side anyone is on, or what is going to happen next.

Almost immediately after Vladimir Lenin, the head of the state that arose after the October Revolution, pulled Russia out of World War I in 1918, the civil war began. This conflict pitted the Bolshe-viks (the Reds) against an array of political opponents, including the

Whites, who were loyal to the Tsar, and members of the Socialist Revolutionary Party. The Socialist Revolutionaries had supported the overthrow of the monarchy; they sat in Russia's Provisional Government between February and October 1917, but later split from the Bolsheviks. The hostilities unfolded across a vast territory reaching as far as parts of Siberia and the Caucasus.

Several national forces and foreign armies also fought against the Bolsheviks in the western borderlands of the former tsarist empire. The collapse of imperial Russia led to the independence of Poland and Ukraine; Poland fought a war against Russia in 1920.[2] Allied intervention and the presence of German troops complicated matters, especially in Ukraine. Declaring itself an independent republic in 1917, Ukraine was first recognized by the Russian government, but the newly formed Red Army took control in 1918, only to be overtaken by the Germans, then by the Whites. From 1917 until 1919 there were at least five different regimes in Kiev, before the Bolsheviks retook the city in 1919. In the unstable political and military terrain where Bergelson's Golikhovke is located, the outcome is not at all clear, and the town's residents, at odds with one another, hedge their bets.

The violence of the civil war—or, civil wars, as some historians refer to this period—was not directed only at military combatants.[3] The former Pale of Settlement, a territory outside the boundaries of which Russian Jews were permitted to settle only after 1917, was ground zero for the hostilities in the western borderlands of the collapsed empire. Instances of anti-Jewish violence—the pogroms—included rape, murder, maiming, and the destruction of property; victims numbered in the tens of thousands.[4] *Judgment* alludes to pogroms through subtle descriptions of characters possibly implicated in the violence and also through the recollections of some of Golikhovke's residents, fearful that they would suffer fresh violence.

Golikhovke is a shtetl: the Yiddish term means "small town" and refers to a type of market town where the population was largely but not exclusively Jewish. The vast majority of Jews in the Pale of Settlement lived in such towns before the revolution. Though geographic limitations on Jewish residence were abolished in 1917, the shtetl as the physical locus of Jewish residence in Eastern Europe persisted afterward.[5] In *Judgment* the shtetl of Golikhovke is engulfed in a painful transition from tsarist to Bolshevik rule.

Golikhovke's residents seek new sources of livelihood in a landscape where national boundaries—redrawn after the revolution and World War I—have disrupted trading routes of the imperial era. Situated next to the border with newly independent (and capitalist) Poland, Golikhovke is a center for smuggling. Consumer goods that are hard to obtain because of shortages associated with War Communism—the Bolshevik economic policy during the civil war—enter the country by way of the shtetl. At the same time, Golikhovke's well-off Jews rely on the smuggling networks to direct the outflow of capital subject to requisitioning and expropriation by the Bolsheviks. Non-Jews use the smuggling routes as well, adding to the shtetl's new and thriving shadow economy: Golikhovke's Jewish landlords stand to profit from hosting gentile passengers headed to Poland, just as the shtetl's coachmen can expect to earn money by ferrying them across the border and out of the Bolsheviks' reach.

The Socialist Revolutionaries (the SRs) use the smuggling routes in and out of the country to prepare for a local uprising against Bolshevik rule. Dr. Babitsky, an educated Russian Jew and former SR, resists active involvement after the revolution but passively sustains his previous connections by allowing the SRs to hide political leaflets in his house.[6] Historically, the SRs, who had perpetrated numerous acts of terror against the tsarist government since they began their activities in the early twentieth century, constituted the largest political party in 1917. They won a plurality of votes in Russia's first-ever democratic elections to the Constituent Assembly that autumn, only to see this newly formed parliament disbanded and single-party rule proclaimed by the Bolsheviks in January 1918. After the victory of the Reds in the civil war, in 1922, a group of SRs were defendants in the first show trial to be held in Soviet Russia. They were accused of plotting against the Bolsheviks with the aid of foreign powers, among other charges.[7] However, in 1920, when Bergelson's novel is set, the SRs still posed a threat to the Bolshevik regime.

Judgment unfolds in the midst of this disarray, its colorful cast of characters based on a range of historical types and political forces.

In Golikhovke, the smuggling trade is a major source of livelihood for the shtetl's Jews. Burly coachmen transport people and goods across the border. The former lumber mill worker Shmuel Voltsis, his wife, and most of their neighbors rent rooms to travelers who pass through on their way out of the country. The tailor has all but abandoned his trade for the more lucrative business of negotiating deals between the passengers and the local hosts and coachmen. Once in a while, those who intend no malice get swept up in the smuggling business, too: Pinke Vayl, a naive Jewish Red Army soldier loyal to the new regime, carries contraband across the border to help his family earn a little money.

A local group of Socialist Revolutionaries, led by Sofia Pokrovskaya, a priest's daughter from a nearby village, relies on the smuggling route as a communication channel with SR activists in exile on the other side of the border. She plots an uprising against the Bolsheviks in collaboration with unsavory characters in Poland, who are rumored to be responsible for deaths of Jews in recent pogroms. At the same time, Pokrovskaya's supporters in Golikhovke are mainly Jewish. They include Yuzi Spivak, who ferries political literature across the border; Yuzi's brother, the pharmacist Muli; the dentist Galaganer—a man so impatient to witness the end of the Bolshevik regime that he runs to the window to see whether the regime has fallen every time he numbs his patients during dental procedures; and the tall Pokras brothers in their gray army overcoats, among others. Dr. Babitsky, who no longer visits as many patients as he used to, has known Pokrovskaya since she was a child. The nameless character who stutters the word "revolution" works for the doctor as a servant; he could be the doctor's ward or his illegitimate son.

With a crucifix dangling prominently between her breasts, the novel's femme fatale shares her name, Anna Arkadievna, with the heroine of Leo Tolstoy's novel *Anna Karenina* but is referred to simply as "the blonde." She harnesses her seductive power to mislead border guards as well as the townsfolk. She sleeps with the Jewish smuggler and double agent Yokhelzon in order to learn the safest route across the border. She claims that her husband, a White general loyal to the imperial crown, is waiting for her on the other side. We never find out exactly what she carries in her two heavy cases.

All the smuggling and counterrevolutionary activity in Goli-khovke unfolds under the watchful eye of Filipov, newly appointed in this contested region as the representative of the Bolshevik state and the enforcer of its laws. Filipov and his staff are agents in the Special Section, a unit of the Bolshevik secret police (the Cheka) charged with prosecuting counterrevolutionary crimes, including espionage and treason. They are stationed not far from Golikhovke, in fictitiously named Kamino-Balke. There, they have taken over a monastery, turning it into a border outpost, prison, and interroga-tion center all in one. Comrade Sasha is an old-timer at Kamino-Balke: having reported the previous boss to the authorities for negligence, she devotedly assists Filipov and is possibly in love with him. Zubok, one of the agents, patrols the areas near the border together with the investigator Andreyev and Igumenko, a former sailor. None of these characters is Jewish; however, as the novel develops, several Jewish characters from Golikhovke come over to Filipov's side and offer assistance.

Everyone in Golikhovke and in the neighboring villages lives in the crosshairs of Kamino-Balke and in terror of the new boss who has taken over at the border outpost. Filipov's uncompromising approach to his role as the enforcer of Bolshevik law terrifies the residents of Golikhovke and those who pass through the town. The rumors of Filipov's unwavering sternness have led to widespread fears of Bolshevik Russia and the system of revolutionary justice it inflicts on its opponents.

✦

Born in 1884, David Bergelson was the youngest of nine children in the family of a wealthy timber merchant in the Ukrainian shtetl of Okhrimovo (now known as Sarny). He lost both parents at an early age and was raised largely by his older siblings, who deducted the cost of his living expenses from his share of the inheritance.[8] Edu-cated in traditional Jewish subjects, Bergelson received no formal secular schooling, except for a brief attempt to study dentistry in Kiev. He read widely, however, in Hebrew and Russian as well as Yiddish, and was well acquainted with new forms of artistic expression and the new ideas of his time; his circle of friends later included the Russian philosopher Lev Shestov and the Hebrew writers Chaim Nachman Bialik and Uri Gnessin.

Bergelson began writing while the three major authors of modern Yiddish literature who are generally considered its founding fathers—Sh. Y. Abramovitch, Sholem Aleichem, and Y. L. Peretz— were entering the final years of their careers. Aspiring Yiddish writers at the time usually sought audiences with Peretz in Warsaw, and Bergelson received one, after his first book came out. Sholem Aleichem's folksy, conversational style was alien to Bergelson's artistic intentions and too limiting for the characters he wanted to portray. Bergelson reinvented Yiddish for the new, uncertain world he lived in. At one point he said that his style seemed awkward because he was translating the Russian conversations his young characters would have had back into Yiddish, as if the language he wrote was not native to them.[9] It is important for us as translators that Bergelson understood his role as an author in terms of translation. Bergelson is frequently compared not to other Yiddish writers but to his immediate predecessors and contemporaries in other languages, such as Anton Chekhov and Knut Hamsun. Their works shared with his a search for a new way of expressing the interior worlds of literary characters alienated from the world and themselves.[10]

Bergelson's earliest attempts at fiction were in Russian and Hebrew. His first work in Yiddish, the novella *At the Depot* (*Arum vokzal*, 1909), was partially self-funded because publishers weren't willing to risk money on a book they saw as too unusual and challenging for Yiddish readers at the time.[11] The hero is a hapless grain broker who daydreams about the past; the setting—an old, decrepit train station—functions as another protagonist, also seeking, but not finding, a source of renewal. In this debut, the shtetl already belongs to the past as an object of the protagonist's memory. The decline of the shtetl would continue to occupy Bergelson throughout his career. In the novel *The End of Everything* (*Nokh alemen*, 1913) the heroine Mirl Hurwitz is unable to find her place in life; she feels as if "someone else has lived out [her] springtime" before she was even born.[12] Bergelson limits the dialogue in the novel, resorting to free indirect discourse in its place.[13] The boundary between the narrator and the protagonist's thoughts is almost entirely erased. Bergelson highlights both Mirl's overwhelming loneliness and the pervasive atmosphere of being stuck out of time in a place without hope. Bergelson's method of using the setting to impart the emotions and thoughts of his characters is key to his distinctive style. He uses it in *Judgment* as well.

In 1918, during Ukraine's brief period of independence and with the support of its government, Bergelson was among the founders of the Culture League (*Kultur-lige*). The Kiev-based association promoted Yiddish modernist culture in multiple media, including theater, visual art, and literature.[14] Bergelson also undertook the editorship of several short-lived Yiddish literary journals, including *Our Own* (*Eygns*), in which he published his second novel, *Descent* (*Opgang*, 1920). Written between 1913 and 1919, *Descent* is something of a metaphysical detective story. Set in the shtetl of Rakitne, the novel is dominated by the ghostly presence of a dead man, Meylekh, who is believed to have committed suicide but who appears more present and alive than some of the living characters in the story. Meylekh's friend Khayim-Moyshe is particularly affected. He returns to Rakitne, where he grew up, to investigate the circumstances of Meylekh's death. There, he develops an internal dialogue with his dead friend. The two argue over whether life is worth living and whether there is meaning in the world. While trying to understand his late friend, Khayim-Moyshe oscillates between his own hopes to find fulfillment in life and his desire to end it.[15]

Bergelson was married in 1917 to Tsipora Kutsenogaya; their son Lev was born a year later. In 1920, Bergelson escaped the violence of the civil war in Ukraine by settling in Moscow, but only temporarily. In 1921 he relocated once more, to Berlin. By this time Berlin had become a place of refuge for prominent writers and artists, including the Russian writers Vladimir Nabokov, Marina Tsvetaeva, and Viktor Shklovsky; the Yiddish writers Der Nister and Moyshe Kulbak; and several prominent Hebrew authors. The eminent Jewish historian Simon Dubnow made his home in Berlin as well. The Berlin years were greatly productive for Bergelson. In 1922, his collected works were published, in six volumes. He was the coeditor of the Yiddish-language modern art journal *The Pomegranate* (*Milgroym*).

In addition to *Judgment*, he wrote short fiction about the civil war, including "Civil War" ("Birger-krig"), "Currents" ("Tsugvintn"), and "Near a Burning Shtetl" ("Hinter a brenendikn shtetl"),[16] as well as a series of short stories about refugees and émigrés in Berlin.[17] While living in Germany, Bergelson wrote for the Yiddish newspaper *The Forward* (*Forverts*), later moving to the more leftist *Morning Freedom* (*Morgn-frayhayt*); both papers were based in New York. In 1926, when he first published a few chapters of *Judgment* in his own short-lived journal *In Harness* (*In shpan*), he switched his political stance toward a closer alliance with the new Soviet Union. He took a trip to the USSR in 1926 after announcing his intention to settle there, but did not.

After Hitler came to power in 1933, it was abundantly clear to Bergelson that he and his family could not remain in Berlin. Tsipora supported the family with her secretarial work at the Soviet Trade Commission. When she was transferred to Copenhagen in 1933, Bergelson and the couple's son Lev followed. In 1932 the first volume of his autobiographical novel *At the Dnieper* (*Baym Dnyepr*) came out in Moscow; the second volume, subtitled *Early Years* (*Yunge yorn*), followed in 1940. Comparable to *From the Fair*, an autobiographical novel by Sholem Aleichem, *At the Dnieper* offers Bergelson's most ethnographically detailed description of life in the shtetl. The second volume, set in Kiev, is usually criticized for offering a purely Soviet perspective on the years before the 1917 revolution. Still, it provides a rich account of the author's struggles with composing Yiddish prose, and describes how Bergelson constructed his own repository of personal and collective memory.

A year before bringing his family back to Soviet Russia, Bergelson visited Birobidzhan. Located in the Far East on the border with China, Birobidzhan was part of the overarching Soviet plan to make socialism the central goal in the cultural agendas of each of the country's numerous ethnic minorities.[18] The settlement of Birobidzhan, which was later named the Jewish Autonomous Region, also served security goals. A house was built especially for Bergelson, the famous Soviet Yiddish writer with an international reputation, in preparation for his promised relocation there. Bergelson wrote fiction and nonfiction about Birobidzhan, but upon his return to the Soviet Union in 1934, he preferred to settle in Moscow.

Once in the Soviet Union, Bergelson continued to write important works of Yiddish fiction and journalism, especially during World War II. He was a member of the Jewish Antifascist Committee (JAC) that was established in 1941 to help raise global support for the Soviet war effort against Nazi Germany. Bergelson was a regular contributor to JAC's Yiddish newspaper *Eynikayt* (*Unity*). "A Witness" ("An eydes"), his searing account of a man who testifies to the Nazi genocide, as well as other works of literary fiction in response to the Holocaust, have yet to receive the critical attention and acclaim they deserve. One of Bergelson's last works was his 1946 play in verse, *Prince Reuveni* (*Prints Ruveni*), set in the sixteenth century but linked thematically to the Holocaust. The play opens with a scene of Jewish passengers on a ship, fleeing the Spanish Inquisition. The captain of the ship selects which passengers are to be killed and which are to be sold into slavery. As the basis for the work, Bergelson used the historical figure of David Reuveni, a sixteenth-century Jewish imposter claiming access to a Jewish army in his brother's Jewish kingdom. The play went into rehearsal, but was canceled because of its purported nationalist undertones.[19]

During his final years in power, Joseph Stalin launched a campaign against Jews and other ethnic minorities. The campaign took various forms, including smear tactics and persecutions of "rootless cosmopolitans." In his victory toast to the Red Army on May 24, 1945, Stalin said that "the Russian people was the most preeminent of all the peoples that make up the Soviet Union," and from that time "cosmopolitan" as a term of opprobrium was practically synonymous with anything not Russian, including Western culture, technology, and science.[20] "Cosmopolitanism" was largely a code word for Jews—many of them among the country's political, professional, and political elites—whom Stalin suspected of dual allegiances, particularly after the establishment of the state of Israel in 1948.

A somewhat different accusation was used against Bergelson and the other members of the Jewish Antifascist Committee: "nationalism." The Soviet government began to investigate the committee in 1946. The charge the JAC had received from Stalin in 1941—to appeal to Jews the world over to support the Soviet Union in its war against Hitler—was used against it. Various aspects of the work the JAC had done, from emphasizing the fate of Jews in German-occupied territory to referring to Jewish history and promoting Yiddish culture, were labeled anti-Soviet Jewish nationalism. Solomon Mikhoels, the director of the Moscow State Yiddish Theater (GOSET), the chair of the JAC, and the face of Soviet Jewry to the world, was killed on Stalin's orders in 1948, his death staged as an automobile accident. Bergelson had been working closely with Mikhoels on the production of *Prince Reuveni*, and earlier, in the 1930s, Mikhoels had directed a play adapted from *Judgment*.[21] In 1949, Bergelson was arrested. After three years in jail, a forced confession, and a trial in which his confession was retracted, Bergelson was sentenced to death along with his JAC colleagues, including Perets Markish, David Hofshteyn, and other well-known Yiddish writers; only one defendant, the scientist Lina Shtern, did not receive the death sentence.

Several members of Bergelson's family were also arrested in the Soviet regime's common punitive practice of persecuting the relatives of its victims. At the time of Stalin's death in 1953, the writer's granddaughter Marina, a young child, was in jail.[22] She and her husband emigrated from the Soviet Union to Israel in the 1970s and now reside in the United States. Bergelson's son Lev, an accomplished scientist in the USSR, moved to Israel in the 1970s and lived there until his death in 2014.

Bergelson was executed on Stalin's orders on August 12, 1952—the writer's sixty-eighth birthday.[23] Although he could not have known that this was how his life was going to end when he began publishing *Judgment* two and a half decades earlier,[24] it is likely that Bergelson contemplated his own future in the "new, harsher world" of Bolshevik Russia—the world he imagined and described in his novel.

◆

The publication of Bergelson's *Judgment* in the late 1920s was an event of international significance in the Yiddish republic of letters;

the book's resonance continued to be felt later as well, when it was occasionally invoked as a ghostly presence. From Kiev and Warsaw to Minsk and Lodz at the time, and from Moscow and Jerusalem to New York, London, and Montreal in the years since, literary critics, translators, and scholars have debated the novel's contested place in Bergelson's oeuvre, in Yiddish literature, and in the Jewish culture and politics of the twentieth century. The narrative that took hold after Bergelson's death was shaped, to a great extent, by the Cold War. Bergelson's tragic end during the Stalin years was itself an opening salvo in that conflict. *Judgment*, in this narrative, demarcated the boundary between the "early" Bergelson—the master of modernist prose who brought stylistic innovation to Yiddish literature—and the "later," Soviet Bergelson, an author of works of lesser literary merit and a writer in service to the political regime that ultimately destroyed him. This English translation of *Judgment* is the novel's first publication in any language other than Yiddish. By making the work available to English-language readers, we hope not only to create opportunities for students of Jewish literature and culture to reevaluate Bergelson's oeuvre but also to introduce the public to an important work of literary modernism that takes on the Bolshevik revolution, one of the defining events of the twentieth century.

In 1962, the Polish-born and Montreal-based poet Rokhl Korn laid out her view of the periodization of Bergelson's career. Korn used the phrase "until here" to map out the writer's trajectory before and after *Judgment*. She mourned the writer who had used compassion in his earlier work, but who had become a "collaborator of Commissar Filipov," inflicting harsh judgments on his later protagonists.[25] Without either telling her readers that Filipov was a fictitious character or referring to *Judgment* directly, Korn explained this collaboration as the price Bergelson paid the Soviet regime for endorsing the revolution belatedly.

Later critics, editors, and translators of Bergelson into English—now the language of a revitalized interest in Yiddish culture in the era of and after *Fiddler on the Roof*—have maintained the essence of Korn's commentary. In the introduction to his 1977 translation of Bergelson's 1913 *Nokh alemen*, Bernard Martin noted that his essay was "not a proper place for a discussion or evaluation of the large body of literature produced by the later, 'Sovietized' Bergelson of the period extending from the second half of the decade of the 1920s until his death." Alluding to but not naming *Judgment*—Bergelson's most notable work from the second half of the 1920s—Martin added: "Suffice it to say that in it [later work] . . . the political ideologue, the revolutionary propagandist become ever more clearly discernible."[26] In so doing, he dismissed the writer's later work, which was as yet inaccessible to his target audience.

Irving Howe and Eliezer Greenberg's 1977 *Ashes Out of Hope* was a monumentally important volume that introduced Bergelson and other Soviet Yiddish writers to several generations of English-language readers. Howe and Greenberg also divided Bergelson's career into "before" and "after." They praised all his works for their combination of "modernist skepticism and a sardonic Yiddish irony," but noted, in the same breath, that it was "especially the earlier ones composed in conditions of relative freedom" that best embodied these attributes.[27] Noting that the later works "do not exude inner conviction, certainly not with the strength that [his] earlier fiction does," Howe and Greenberg explained that "it has seemed pointless to waste space by printing what Yiddish writers had to compose during the worst years of the Stalinist period—these should be familiar enough to anyone who has read equivalents in other languages."[28] Howe and Greenberg, who had earlier published a path-breaking volume of Yiddish short stories in English translation, reasoned that readers didn't have to acquaint themselves with Bergelson's later works because these were "things [that] it [was] better to leave in the past."[29]

But "the past," in the case of *Judgment*, was itself far from an unambiguous place: Bergelson's novel never really held the kind of uniform and clear-cut ideological meaning that later critics would ascribe to it. By the time *Judgment* was released in book form in 1929, three long years had passed since Bergelson had written about his embrace of Soviet-style socialism and announced his optimistic view of Yiddish culture in the USSR together with his plans to settle there. As nearly a decade passed before Bergelson actually returned, critics in the Soviet Union, like Marxist critics elsewhere, expressed their suspicions of *Judgment*—the reportedly unambiguously pro-Bolshevik novel that the writer had sent their way.

In 1929 the Soviet Yiddish critic Yashe Bronshteyn accused Bergelson of opportunistically jumping on the revolutionary bandwagon, even though he had not participated in revolutionary activity. According to the critic, Bergelson had sloppily mimicked Soviet literary fiction about the civil war.[30] By the time Bergelson began serializing *Judgment* in 1926, a template for Soviet revolutionary literature had already emerged. Filled with adventurous tales of a courageous and folksy military commander and his ideological education and grooming by a political commissar from the Communist Party, Dmitry Furmanov's novel *Chapaev* came out in 1924. In Alexander Fadeev's 1925 *The Rout*, the stern Jewish commissar Levinson, the novel's protagonist, led his Red Army troops against the Whites and their interventionist collaborators in the Far East. Stories from Isaac Babel's *Red Cavalry* had been in circulation since 1923 and had become an international sensation by the middle of the decade; they contained an extensive gallery of Bolshevik heroes admired by the narrator, a timid Jewish intellectual, for their masculine demeanor.[31] In these and other texts, Bergelson could have found suitable models for his characterization of Filipov as an agent of the revolution and, in Dr. Babitsky's formulation in the novel, "the ambassador of history."

Instead, Bronshteyn noted, Bergelson made Filipov too sickly to fit the contemporary literary mold. The novel's main character, though a giant of a man, suffers from a festering wound on his neck. He spends much of his time lying in bed, like the protagonists of Bergelson's shtetl novels who fail to get ahead. In this way, Bronshteyn noted, Filipov was uncomfortably similar to Mirl Hurwitz from *The End of Everything*. This portrait of history's ambassador hardly conforms to the emerging template of a Soviet hero. Wandering the premises of his domain like the unsettled characters in Bergelson's earlier prose, Filipov was, wrote Bronshteyn, inappropriately similar to Khayim-Moyshe of *Descent* despite being a Bolshevik from the working class and not an idle philosopher from the shtetl, to paraphrase the critic's pithy formulation.[32]

Bronshteyn chastised Bergelson for bringing his established literary techniques to the new topic of the revolution instead of adjusting his style to the revolution's unique artistic demands. By restricting his narrative about the civil war to the narrow area of Golikhovke and its environs, Bergelson, according to Bronshteyn, placed himself in the familiar territory of his earlier prose that focused on the smallness and proviniality of the declining shtetl. Filled with descriptions of moody landscapes and weather, Golikhovke seemed to Bronshteyn the sort of impressionist background that had become typical of Bergelson's prose. The critic saw it as a shtetl similar to Mirl Hurwitz's hometown—the staging ground not for dynamic new heroes that the revolution demanded but instead for typical Bergelsonian characters.[33]

Ultimately Bronshteyn, like other critics at the time, strongly suspected that *Judgment* was a story set amid theatrical props that looked like the revolution rather than a narrative of revolutionary struggle fitted to the evolving Soviet literary canon.[34] Noting, like other contemporary critics in the USSR and those sympathetic to the revolution elsewhere, the similarities rather than the differences between *Judgment* and Bergelson's celebrated earlier prose, Bronshteyn registered his anger with the writer over his having "bergelsonified" [*farbergelsonevet*] the revolution.[35]

However, for other critics in the Soviet Union and Marxist critics abroad, the apparent continuity between Bergelson's earlier novels and *Judgment* contained a silver lining. According to one critic, in *Judgment* Bergelson was, as an artist, destined to serve as a kind of undertaker of the Jewish bourgeoisie, whose slow demise he had already begun to observe in his earlier fiction. Bergelson, the critic suggested, had previously described the "dying breaths [*yetsies-neshome*]" of the once-wealthy landowner class represented by Mirl Hurwitz's father in *The End of Everything*. He had also described the rise of the nouveaux riches who clamored to replace the older generation in the shtetl's economic hierarchy. In turn, aware that the new world order ushered in by the Bolshevik revolution reduced those parvenus to mere smugglers, in *Judgment* Bergelson was cognizant of his artistic mission to depict their "death throes [*gsise-tsushtand*]."[36]

Taking Soviet critics at face value can be a tricky business because of the ideological commonplaces in so much of their writing.

But by the same token we should not pretend that subsequent critics in the West, especially during the Cold War, were themselves free of bias.[37] The question of Bergelson's politics was central to critics of *Judgment*, whether Soviet critics of the Stalin era or later anthologists and scholars.

For the first group, the Soviet critics, Bergelson's motivation for writing *Judgment* was, more or less, a matter of practical politics. They saw a writer who needed something to show as a kind of entry visa to the Soviet Union, a text that expressed his ideological commitment to the Bolshevik revolution. Bergelson may have succeeded in gaining entry, but, as many of these critics saw it, the goods that he carried past the border contained contraband. The critics, acting as border guards of sorts, were not going to let Bergelson fool them: they saw their task as exposing the writer's smuggling operation by outlining the extent to which his "new" wares were actually the same as the "old" ones he claimed he had left behind in the West.

For the second group of critics, those writing after World War II in the West, *Judgment* was not the trickily hidden contraband that Bergelson smuggled in but rather a kind of bribe paid to the doctrinaire border guards. For these critics, the price of Bergelson's admission to the USSR was the unambiguous endorsement of Marxist ideology and the new Bolshevik regime, accompanied by the requisite selling-out of his artistic integrity. The resulting blemish on the writer's reputation, in this view, could lend rhetorical power to a subsequent moral judgment on the writer's work and life. Writing about *Judgment*, Ruth R. Wisse concludes that though Bergelson significantly outlived some of the other Soviet Yiddish writers "by following the party line," he did so "not without damage to his later work and posthumous reputation"; this "later work," in turn, was not "free of [a] compromising stain."[38] In Wisse's formulation, the echoes of Korn's, Howe's, and Greenberg's dismissal or refusal to acknowledge as much as the existence of *Judgment* get amplified and become a posthumous moral condemnation of the writer himself.

In seeing Bergelson's novel either as contraband or bribe, critics overlook *Judgment*'s importance first and foremost as a work of literary fiction. We are not saying that the novel is free of politics. Rather, along with other scholars who have recently written on *Judgment*, we invite the reader to consider the novel within the broader set of literary paradigms generally accorded to works of fiction, including the writer's deployment of artistic methods to navigate particularly complex historical and ideological subjects.[39] The American Yiddish poet Jacob Glatstein recalls that Bergelson, during his lengthy stay in the United States in 1928, inquired about the prospects of having this novel published in English.[40] With this translation nine decades later, we hope *Judgment* will speak for itself, not as a litmus test for one or another set of political or ideological allegiances, but rather as a complex yet neglected artistic work of a major literary figure of the twentieth century.

✦

In "Three Centers," his seminal essay in the journal *In Harness*, Bergelson presented his programmatic vision for the future of Yiddish literature in the Soviet Union. He noted that the "new Jewish artist" would witness—and would have to find artistic means to describe—the terrible "destruction around him, unavoidable destruction crying to the heavens—the full severity of the law [*mides-hadin*]."[41] The devastation Bergelson had in mind was the product not only of the pogroms of the civil war but also of the Bolshevik legal system that governed the shtetl after the revolution. Bergelson's concern with Bolshevik law was not incidental. The new system accorded legal rights, material sustenance, shelter, health care, and other benefits only to members of the working class. As a result, large numbers of Jews—who, in the economic system of the Pale of Settlement, were primarily traders and brokers—fell into the category of the disenfranchised (the *lishentsy*).[42] In *Judgment*, economic conflict between the shtetl and the new Bolshevik government shapes the course of events. Filipov tells Golikhovke's Jews that if they don't find ways to make a living other than through smuggling, he will burn their shtetl to the ground. When one character expresses the fear that his townsfolk will simply starve, his sentiment reflects harsh conditions of the time and the punitive nature of the new legal system.

The initial chapters of Bergelson's novel about the arrival of the new regime in Golikhovke appeared in the same journal issue as "Three Centers." Echoing his artistic aspirations to depict the weight of Bolshevik law in postrevolution Russia, the writer chose the phrase from his programmatic essay—the Hebrew term *mides-hadin*—as his novel's title. The word *mides* means "the quality of," "the face of," or "the aspect of." *Din* means "judgment"—the kind associated with the holiday of Yom Kippur, also known in the Jewish tradition as *yom ha-din*, "the Day of Judgment"; indeed, Bergelson refers to the closing service of Yom Kippur near the end of his novel, making this allusion explicit. The entire phrase *mides-hadin* can be translated as "severe decree," "harsh justice," or, as we've already seen, "the full severity of the law." In our view, the single term "judgment"—our choice for the translation of the novel's title—already includes these qualities: judgment is never mild or soft.

In translating the title as *Judgment*, we also suggest connections between Bergelson's novel and the work of Franz Kafka. In 1925, just before Bergelson started publishing the initial chapters of *Judgment*, Kafka's novel *The Trial* came out posthumously in Berlin. In Kafka's novel the words "judgment" and "to judge" (*das Urteil*, *urteilen*)[43] are ubiquitous in discussions of the protagonist Joseph K's futile struggles with an arcane legal system. This system, in turn, came to represent the horrors of the modern state, which utterly lacked mercy, empathy, and compassion for the individual. In *Judgment*, Bergelson uses the same Germanic term as Kafka to refer to the discrete judgments (in Yiddish, *urteyln*) given to the prisoners at Kamino-Balke, thus emphasizing the Kafkaesque feel of the world in his novel.

Bergelson's novel suggests the many ways in which the opposite of judgment—compassion—is no longer a feature of the world. The story of the wealthy merchant Aaron Lemberger contains the clearest illustration of the legal system associated with the Bolshevik regime. Lemberger is accused of tax evasion and economic speculation, and Filipov, the representative of revolutionary justice, must sentence him accordingly. Filipov decides Lemberger's case on Friday, but it takes another full day, until the end of the Jewish Sabbath, before the accused learns of his punishment. The novel explores this window of time in which Judaism's concept of justice gets replaced by a verdict handed down by a revolutionary tribunal. An observant

Jew who is well versed in the Jewish tradition, Lemberger accepts the severity of the law as a just principle in determining punishment for transgressions against God. However, he fails to grasp the severity of the new Bolshevik order.

Judaism's system of law was codified over the centuries in the writings of the rabbis, legal authorities in late antiquity and the Middle Ages who formulated a vast corpus of Jewish law by interpreting and debating the meaning of biblical texts. In this legal tradition, *mides-hadin*—the measure of the law—is but one in a pair of attributes that need to be considered and weighed when determining a person's guilt or innocence. The other attribute is *mides ha-rakhamim*, the measure of mercy: Jewish law requires that the accused be afforded the benefit of the doubt, built on a compassionate assessment of potential mitigating circumstances. However, in the new world of Filipov's Bolshevik justice there is no place for *rakhamim*, the compassion that softens the dictates of *din*. By titling our translation of Bergelson's novel *Judgment*, we suggest a realm in which judgments are always severe and executed without mercy.

The two attributes of justice in the Jewish tradition originate in rabbinic commentaries on the creation story in the book of Genesis. In the Bible's original Hebrew, the creation story contains two different names for God, which are usually written in English as *Yahweh* and *Elohim*. The rabbis came to associate this doubling with the duality of God, whom they regarded as both stern and merciful in his assessment of his own creation. Jewish mystical tradition, which developed alongside the legalistic reasoning of rabbinic Judaism, offered a further interpretation of the relationship between sternness and what Portia, in Shakespeare's *Merchant of Venice*, refers to as the "quality of mercy."[44] Judgment, *din*, is one of the qualities or emanations of the divine revealed and released in the process of creation. It has two meanings that exist in tension. On the one hand, harsh and unrelenting, *din* is associated with evil, the demonic realm, and the condition of exile. On the other hand, *din*, in the sense of order, limit, and containment, prevents the force of God's creative power from overwhelming creation—it is a necessary force, so long as it is balanced by mercy. However, existence in a realm defined by *din* alone is, as Bergelson's *Judgment* suggests, a world of nightmarish, unrelenting punishment.

✦

Bergelson had never shied away from the themes of sexuality, betrayal, and violence. These themes emerge with particular force in *Judgment*, a novel written in Berlin—a city whose freewheeling street life, entertainment, experimental art, and commercial culture during the period of the Weimar Republic led the Nazis to deem it "decadent." The traumas of war, both World War I and the Russian civil war, emerge in Bergelson's fiction during this time. Wounded veterans, perpetrators of violence, and their victims populate his stories. The roaring, crowded modern city overwhelms them.

One of the most important new forms of art that Bergelson encountered in Berlin was German Expressionism, in which things, buildings, streets, and the natural world assume the intense emotions of human beings, sometimes turning violently against them. Bergelson had tried similar stylistic techniques in his earlier work, but they are especially effective in *Judgment*. The architecture of the prison interior is nightmarish, the prison gates thrust people in and out of their grasp, and trees make sounds of pain. People lose their individuality, and parts of bodies replace persons. An idiosyncratic ordering of physical space—up, down, right, and left—replaces the points of the compass, making the setting claustrophobic and hard to comprehend. Frequently, effects are severed from causes, and it is impossible to be certain as to who is doing or feeling what. The overall effect is deliberately disorienting: the world created by the revolution is "strange [*modne*]" as the narrator tells us, and Bergelson makes strangeness itself part of the experience of reading his novel.

Bergelson constructs the narrative out of a series of miniatures, in which the thoughts, emotions, and distinct speech habits of specific characters color the world and action conjured by the novel. Although many of the characters are not Jewish, this is a Yiddish-language text, asking the reader to imagine it as though Bergelson had translated what would have been Russian or Ukrainian conversations into the Yiddish literary idiom. The result is sometimes comical, sometimes jarring: "*az okh un vey*" says Filipov at one point when he is exasperated with his underlings—a Russian protagonist venting in a stereotypical Yiddish idiom, similar to "*oy vey*" or "woe is me."

In having bits of Russian, Ukrainian, and Hebrew appear in the Yiddish text, Bergelson aimed not only to reflect the multilingual world of the borderlands where the novel is set but also to rely on the qualities of the sounds in different languages to emphasize concrete characteristics of protagonists or actions. For example, Filipov—the man who holds the power of life and death over everyone—punctuates his every utterance with the Russian line, "*Chto vy, shutite*?" ("What, are you joking?" pronounced "shtovy shootiteh"). Whenever this phrase appears in the original, it is always in Russian, and is transcribed phonetically; we repeat both the original of the Russian phrase (spelled in Latin characters in this case) and the English translation whenever the phrase occurs in the text so as to retain the acoustic qualities of Bergelson's text. Filipov's voice, as the narrative tells us, is "harsh" and "hoarse," and the harsh and hissing sounds of the consonants in this phrase lend an acoustical reality to these qualities. Bergelson's use of acoustics produces a cacophony of conflicting sounds, emphasizing the disturbing nature of the world ruled by Filipov.

A fundamental shift has taken place in the world, and Bergelson's style reflects this change. Unusual syntax and narrative voice contribute to the larger overall effect of disorientation in *Judgment*. Transitional terms like "because," "as a consequence of," or "owing to"—the grammatical connective tissue of any narrative—are largely absent; the result is a jerky, disconnected story. For example, when the Red Army soldier Pinke Vayl carries a report back to Kamino-Balke from the distant villages at the border, where insurgents have been gathering, the scene goes as follows:

> The day—frozen, slippery, muddy, its eyes half-closed, about to sneeze.
> The road, tossing and turning 'til dawn, took five hours.

Here, as on other occasions in the novel, Bergelson transfers attributes of time to space and vice versa: it's the road that is icy, but Bergelson shifts this quality to the description of the interval of time, and so the day becomes "slippery." Verbs that would normally describe the motion of the human actor are omitted, replaced by adjectives and other modifiers that apply to the space and time in which the action is performed; instead of explaining that the human actor Pinke had caught a cold and was about to sneeze, the author portrays the day as on the verge of sneezing. The dash replacing the verb accentuates the staccato rhythm in the first sentence. The overall effect radically disorients the experience of reading *Judgment*, so that readers—like the characters in the world of this novel—don't know where they are, or how they got there. They don't recognize who is speaking to whom, or why events are taking place; they fail to predict what is going to happen next.[45]

Notwithstanding the deadly serious issues that it engages, the novel is quite funny. Part of the humor stems from the general confusion that reigns both in the novelistic world of *Judgment* and from misleading appearances of some of the characters. One of the characters carries himself as if the wind were blowing from all four sides, but it is perfectly still outside. Another character smells like smoked fish, but smoked fish hasn't been available since before the war. Filipov's posse of border guards are frequently found goofing off to pass the time: one of them uses a chair to show how to ride a horse, and another puts on a fake French accent when asking to see the papers of passengers he stops at the border. Occasionally, when recounting the conversations of Jewish protagonists who communicate with one another in Yiddish, Bergelson veers deeper into the realm of pure linguistic comedy. When Shmuel Voltsis is placed in the same convoy with the wife of the town's double agent, the swears and curses he unleashes on the woman are in a Yiddish so rich that she begs a Jewish soldier escorting them to intervene because he can understand and therefore should be able to stop the insults lobbed at her.

The staging of a play based on the novel at the Moscow State Yiddish Theater in 1933 emphasized its comic potential, especially where non-Jewish characters speak Yiddish. For example, the production gave particular attention to Aaron Lemberger's claim in the novel that, at the time of his arrest, he was passing through Golikhovke to attend a bar mitzvah. Comrade Sasha, a non-Jew speaking her lines in Yiddish, demands to know during the interrogation what a bar mitzvah is, and Lemberger, a pious Jew, can't explain it. He merely says, "A bar mitzvah is a . . . bar mitzvah!"[46] The script also relies on linguistic humor to soften the portrait of some of Golikhovke's Jews. For example, the quarrelsome couple Shmuel Voltsis and his wife are funnier in the play than in the novel. In one scene, they exchange monosyllables, culminating in sheer word play and nonsense.[47]

Nothing escapes Bergelson's deeply ironic sense of the world. The novel's ruminations on the nature of justice do touch upon religious law and mysticism, but they appear in sharp contrast with its savage mockery of Judaism and Christianity. Aaron Lemberger thinks of himself as a deeply pious man, yet he resorts to superstition while awaiting his judgment. He sends a prison guard to bring him a piece of challah to celebrate the Sabbath. If the bread arrives before evening—before the end of the Sabbath—Lemberger would take it as the omen that he would escape the death sentence. The bread arrives at nightfall, and Lemberger cannot ascertain whether the Sabbath is over or not: the certainty of his religious observance, compromised by superstition, fails him. The blonde is convinced that she can vanquish the Bolsheviks with the sheer force of her sexuality. Her rediscovered Christian piety is described using terms usually reserved for observant Jews. In one extremely ironic image, her eyes are said to be "as kosher as crucifixes." Like Lemberger, the blonde tries to divine her future from omens she conjures up herself: on one occasion she convinces herself that if she fasts long enough, she will surely make it across the border.

But Bergelson's irony extends to set phrases, mottoes, and symbols of the new communist order as well, coming close to exposing them as artificial, unstable, and thus similar to the religiously derived superstitions that the novel mocks. One of the characters feels as if his stomach is going to burst open from his eagerness to do something for the "happiness of mankind." The positive meaning of this ubiquitous revolutionary slogan is thus called into question. Toward the end of the novel, as the border outpost faces an attack from counterrevolutionary forces, concerns about the number of red Soviet banners available at Kamino-Balke arise among the troops and guards stationed there. Will having enough flags somehow mean that the Bolsheviks will be able to defeat the insurgents? The concern appears to be as much a superstitious divination as the blonde's prolonged fasting or Lemberger's wait for a piece of the Sabbath challah: signs acquire symbolic powers so strong that they appear to replace actions.

Like the red banners for those at Kamino-Balke, Filipov evolves into the revolution's symbol. He is its unique embodiment. In the imagination of those around him, Filipov acquires awesome powers and becomes synonymous with the revolutionary justice he is appointed to carry out. Filipov wins some of Golikhovke's Jews, including Socialist Revolutionaries, over to his side as the novel develops; among those newly converted to the Bolshevik cause, Yuzi Spivak is especially influenced by the sheer power of Filipov's physical presence. At the same time, Bergelson's novel questions whether the possibility for the revolution's success could be concentrated so strongly in the figure of a single person. When Yuzi Spivak becomes the person most directly tasked with continuing Filipov's work, Bergelson focuses the reader's attention on Yuzi's compromised ability to speak and be heard. The novel emphasizes Yuzi's shyness and his reluctance to give speeches to the Red Army soldiers who need inspiration to keep on fighting. Pinke Vayl chastises Yuzi for being "a silent type." When Yuzi finally speaks to the soldiers, readers never find out what he actually says, because the point of view is from one of the cells of the Kamino-Balke jail—too far to hear Yuzi's words.

Presumably Yuzi used his inaudible speech to extol the virtues of revolutionary justice. However, the fact that Bergelson does not convey to his readers what Yuzi said is striking, especially in comparison to other novels about the civil war published at the same time. Frustrated commentators noticed the absence of direct doctrinaire broadsides when Bergelson's novel was first published. One Soviet critic took particular offense at a scene in which Filipov himself inveighs against the smuggling practices of Golikhovke's coachmen, explaining the extent of judgment the disobedient would face, only to have his words missed entirely by one of the men, who is hard of hearing.[48] In a novel in which the peculiarities of rhythm and sound have such a significant effect on the story, the absence of words when they are expected and difficulties of enunciation and audibility are particularly noticeable.

Filipov inspires awe through the sheer force of his presence, but what he says cannot always be heard. Filipov's disciples don't cut such strong figures as he. Bergelson has given his "ambassador of history" a debilitating disease that affects his neck and throat, making it all the more difficult for Filipov to speak. Filipov's difficulties with speech pass on to those who take up the revolution's work after him, as his physical illness transforms into a kind of symbolic disability among those who follow in his footsteps.[49] There is an uncanny resemblance, moreover, between the challenges of articulating the objectives of the revolution by those appointed to lead it and the loudly haunting screams of the word "revolution" with which we began this essay. Bergelson's novel captures the revolution at a moment of uncertainty, when the hopes for equality yield to a starker, darker vision, and at a time of transition from the desire for a system of law guided in equal measure by severity and compassion to the realm of unflinching and relentless judgment.

Notes

1. Following its initial serialization in several periodicals in 1926 through 1927, Bergelson's *Judgment* was published in book form simultaneously in Vilna (then known as Wilno, Poland, and now as Vilnius, Lithuania) and in Kiev in the USSR (now Kyiv, Ukraine): Dovid Bergelson, *Mides-hadin*, vol. 7 of *Geklibene verk* (Vilna: B. Kletzkin, 1929); Dovid Bergelson, *Mides-hadin* (Kiev: Kultur-lige, 1929). For this translation we consulted the Kletzkin edition, which was the seventh volume of Bergelson's collected works.

2. Isaac Babel's *Red Cavalry* is the most famous literary treatment of the 1920 war between Poland and Bolshevik Russia and most certainly influenced Bergelson's own work about this period; *Red Cavalry* contains ruminations about Jews caught between the warring armies.

3. Jonathan D. Smele, *The "Russian" Civil Wars: 1916–1926* (Oxford: Oxford University Press, 2016).

4. For the discussion of pogroms in Ukraine during the civil war, see Henry Abramson, *A Prayer for the Government: Ukrainians and Jews in Revolutionary Times, 1917–1920* (Cambridge, Mass.: Harvard University

Press, 1999). Abramson suggests that Ukrainian nationalists, struggling for Ukraine's independence, tended to associate Jews with the Bolsheviks, and that this association led to anti-Jewish violence. On anti-Jewish violence and the monarchist ideology during the civil war, see Peter Kenez, "Pogroms and White Ideology in the Russian Civil War," in *Pogroms: Anti-Jewish Violence in Modern Russian History*, ed. John D. Klier and Shlomo Lambroza (Cambridge: Cambridge University Press, 1992), 293–313.

5. Jeffrey Veidlinger, *In the Shadow of the Shtetl: Small-Town Jewish Life in Soviet Ukraine* (Bloomington: Indiana University Press, 2013); Deborah Yalen, "On the Social-Economic Front: The Polemics of Shtetl Research during the Stalin Revolution," *Science in Context* 20, no. 2 (2007): 239–301.

6. There had been prominent Russian Jewish intellectuals among the Socialist Revolutionaries since the party's founding at the beginning of the twentieth century, including the writer S. An-sky; see Gabriella Safran, *Wandering Soul: The Dybbuk's Creator, S. An-sky* (Cambridge, Mass.: Harvard University Press, 2011), 95–148.

7. Scott Smith, *Captives of the Revolution: The Socialist Revolutionaries and the Bolshevik Dictatorship, 1918–1923* (Pittsburgh: University of Pittsburgh Press, 2011). On the trial of the SRs in 1922 and its role in establishing a script for future Soviet show trials, see Julie A. Cassiday, *The Enemy on Trial: Early Soviet Courts on Stage and Screen* (DeKalb: Northern Illinois University Press, 2000), 42–50.

8. The most complete biography in English is Joseph Sherman, "David Bergelson (1884–1952): A Biography," in *David Bergelson: From Modernism to Socialist Realism*, ed. Joseph Sherman and Gennady Estraikh (London: Legenda, 2007), 7–78.

9. Allison Schachter, *Diasporic Modernisms: Hebrew and Yiddish Literature in the Twentieth Century* (Oxford: Oxford University Press, 2011), 105.

10. Joseph Sherman, "Bergelson and Chekhov: Conversions and Departures," in *The Yiddish Presence in European Literature: Inspiration and Interaction*, ed. Joseph Sherman and Ritchie Robertson (London: Legenda, 2005), 117–33.

11. David Bergelson, "At the Depot," in *A Shtetl and Other Yiddish Novellas*, ed. and trans. Ruth R. Wisse (Detroit: Wayne State University Press, 1986), 84–139.

12. David Bergelson, *The End of Everything*, trans. Joseph Sherman (New Haven, Conn.: Yale University Press, 2009), 264.

13. Daniela Montovan, "Language and Style in *Nokh alemen* (1913): Bergelson's Debt to Flaubert," in *David Bergelson: From Modernism to Socialist Realism*, ed. Sherman and Estraikh, 89–112.

14. G. Kazovskii, *Khudozhniki Kul'tur-Ligi* (Jerusalem: Gesharim-Mosty kul'tury, 2003).

15. David Bergelson, *Descent*, trans. Joseph Sherman (New York: Modern Language Association, 1999).

16. David Bergelson, "Civil War," in *Ashes Out of Hope: Fiction by Soviet Yiddish Writers*, ed. Irving Howe and Eliezer Greenberg, trans. Seth Wolitz (New York: Schocken, 1977), 84–123.

17. David Bergelson, *The Shadows of Berlin: The Berlin Stories of Dovid Bergelson*, trans. Joachim Neugroschel (San Francisco: City Lights Books, 2005). On Bergelson's writing about Berlin, see Harriet Murav, "Technology, the City, and the Body: Bergelson and Shklovsky in Berlin," in *Migration and Mobility in the Modern Age: Refugees, Travelers, and Traffickers in Europe and Eurasia*, ed. Anika Walke, Jan Musekamp, and Nicole Svobodny (Bloomington: Indiana University Press, 2017), 260–75; Sasha Senderovich, "In Search of Readership: Bergelson among the Refugees," in *David Bergelson: From Modernism to Socialist Realism*, ed. Sherman and Estraikh, 150–66.

18. Robert Weinberg, *Stalin's Forgotten Zion: Birobidzhan and the Making of a Soviet Jewish Homeland: An Illustrated History, 1928–1996* (Berkeley: University of California Press, 1998). Masha Gessen focuses specifically on David Bergelson's biography in her book on Birobidzhan: Masha Gessen, *Where the Jews Aren't: The Sad and Absurd Story of Birobidzhan, Russia's Jewish Autonomous Region* (New York: Nextbook/Schocken, 2016).

19. Jeffrey Veidlinger, "'Du lebst, mayn folk': Bergelson's Play *Prints Ruveni* in Historical Context (1944–1947)," in *David Bergelson: From Modernism to Socialist Realism*, ed. Sherman and Estraikh, 269–84.

20. "Priem v Kremle v chest' komanduiushchikh voiskami Krasnoi Armii," *Izvestiia*, May 25, 1945, 1.

21. On the staging of the adaptation of Bergelson's novel as a play *The Measure of Strict Law* (*Mera strogosti*) at GOSET, see Jeffrey Veidlinger, *The Moscow State Yiddish Theater: Jewish Culture on the Soviet Stage* (Bloomington: Indiana University Press, 2000), 133–36.

22. Marina Bergelson-Raskin, "Radio v tiur'me ne bylo, i pro pokhorony my nichego ne znali," *05/03/53*, December 23, 2014; http://050353.ru/2014/12/23/bergelson-raskin/.

23. Joshua Rubenstein and Vladimir Naumov, *Stalin's Secret Pogrom: The Postwar Inquisition of the Jewish Anti-Fascist Committee* (New Haven, Conn.: Yale University Press, 2001).

24. Citing Michael Bernstein's concept of "backshadowing"—"a kind of retroactive foreshadowing in which the shared knowledge of the outcome

of a series of events by narrator and listener is used to judge the participants in those events as though they too should have known what was to come"—David Shneer notes that this rhetorical practice, prevalent among many critics of Soviet Yiddish culture, should be avoided. Shneer focuses, instead, on "the contingencies they encountered in the complex choices they were making in their time, the social and cultural context of the 1920s." David Shneer, *Yiddish and the Creation of Soviet Jewish Culture, 1918–1930* (Cambridge: Cambridge University Press, 2004), 3.

25. Rokhl Korn, "Dovid Bergelson: fun mides-harakhamim biz mideshadin," *Di goldene keyt* 43 (1962): 20. This article was part of a special issue of the Israeli Yiddish-language journal *The Golden Chain* dedicated to the tenth anniversary of the execution of members of the Jewish Antifascist Committee.

26. David Bergelson, *When All Is Said and Done,* trans. and introd. Bernard Martin (Athens, Ohio: Ohio University Press, 1977), xx. Both Bernard Martin's translation, titled *When All Is Said and Done,* and Joseph Sherman's translation, titled *The End of Everything,* refer to the same novel, *Nokh alemen.*

27. Irving Howe and Eliezer Greenberg, eds., *Ashes Out of Hope: Fiction by Soviet-Yiddish Writers* (New York: Schocken Books, 1977), 22.

28. Ibid., 25.

29. Irving Howe and Eliezer Greenberg, eds., *A Treasury of Yiddish Stories* (New York: Viking, 1954). In her paper "Kadia Molodowsky and Rokhl Korn: The Art of Correspondence," presented at the Association for Jewish Studies annual conference in 2015, Allison Schachter noted that Howe and Greenberg's 1954 anthology, though over six hundred pages in length, also did not include any work by female authors.

30. A. Mapovets, "Unter dem ployt fun yerushe," *Prolit* 6 (June 1929): 64–75. A. Mapovets was the pseudonym of the critic Yashe Bronshteyn.

31. On the positive character in Soviet literature of the 1920s, see Rufus W. Mathewson, *The Positive Hero in Russian Literature* (Stanford, Calif.: Stanford University Press, 1975), 179–210.

32. A. Mapovets, "Unter dem ployt fun yerushe," 69.

33. Ibid., 67.

34. Ibid., 69–71.

35. Ibid., 70.

36. H. Kazakevitch, "D. Bergelson. 'Midas hadin,'" *Di royte velt* 5–6 (May 1929): 197.

37. Citing examples of Yiddish scholarship in the United States during the Cold War, Mikhail Krutikov has pointed out the need to "question the

accepted truth that, due to the Stalinist regime, Soviet Jewry lived in intellectual and cultural isolation from the rest of the world" (Mikhail Krutikov, *From Kabbalah to Class Struggle: Expressionism, Marxism, and Yiddish Literature in the Life and Work of Meir Wiener* [Stanford, Calif.: Stanford University Press, 2010], 2).

38. Ruth R. Wisse, "The Jewish Informer as Extortionist and Idealist," in *Insiders and Outsiders: Dilemmas of East European Jewry*, ed. Richard L. Cohen, Jonathan Frankel, and Stephanie Hoffman (Portland, Ore.: Littman Library of Jewish Civilization 2010), 203.

39. Mikhail Krutikov, "Rediscovering the Shtetl as a New Reality: David Bergelson and Itsik Kipnis," in *The Shtetl: New Evaluations*, ed. Steven T. Katz (New York: New York University Press, 2007), 211–32; Mikhail Krutikov, "Narrating the Revolution: From 'Tsugvintn' (1922) to 'Mides-Hadin' (1929)," in *David Bergelson: From Modernism to Socialist Realism*, ed. Joseph Sherman and Gennady Estraikh (London: Legenda, 2007), 167–82; Harriet Murav, *Music from a Speeding Train: Soviet Yiddish and Russian-Jewish Literature of the Twentieth Century* (Stanford, Calif.: Stanford University Press, 2011), 62–64; Marc Caplan, "'A gast af a vayl zeyt af a mayl': Distance, Displacement, and Dislocation in Dovid Bergelson's *Mides ha-din* and Alfred Döblin's *Reise in Polen*," in *Languages of Modern Jewish Cultures: Comparative Perspectives*, ed. Anita Norich and Joshua J. Miller (Ann Arbor: University of Michigan Press, 2016), 252–74. We also gratefully acknowledge Catherine Madsen for sharing with us the late Joseph Sherman's proposal, from the mid-2000s, for his translation of Bergelson's *Mides-hadin* for the New Yiddish Library series; while Sherman's project never got off the ground, his proposal stands as a document of renewed interest in the novel.

40. Jacob Glatstein, "Der marsh tsu di goyem," *Inzikh* 14 (July 1935): 55–56. We are indebted to Saul Zaritt for bringing Glatstein's essay to our attention.

41. David Bergelson, "Three Centers (Characteristics)," in *David Bergelson: From Modernism to Socialist Realism*, ed. Joseph Sherman and Gennady Estraikh, trans. Joseph Sherman (London: Legenda, 2007), 353; Dovid Bergelson, "Dray tsentren," *In shpan* 1 (1926): 94.

42. Golfo Alexopoulos, *Stalin's Outcasts: Aliens, Citizens, and the Soviet State, 1926–1936* (Ithaca, N.Y.: Cornell University Press, 2003). On the disenfranchised (*lishentsy*) among shtetl Jews, see Gennady Estraikh, "The Soviet Shtetl in the 1920s," in *The Shtetl: Myth and Reality*, ed. Anthony Polonsky, Polin: *Studies in Polish Jewry* 17 (Oxford: Littman Library of Jewish Civilization, 2004), 199–202.

43. Additionally, in 1912, Kafka wrote the short story "The Judgment" (in German, "Das Urteil").

44. On *din* in the Jewish mystical tradition, see Elliot R. Wolfson, "Left Contained in the Right: A Study in Zoharic Hermeneutics," *AJS Review* 11, no. 1 (1986): 27–52.

45. The novel also contains several inconsistencies. For example, the child who travels with the blonde is said to be two years old at the beginning of the novel, but by the novel's end she is referred to as a girl who is three and a half years old.

46. Rehearsal of one of the scenes can be found in the following newsreel produced by the Moscow State Yiddish Theater: GOSET, "Gosudarstvennyi evreiskii teatr gotovit novuyu postanovku: *Mera strogosti*, avtor Bergelson," 1933; https://www.youtube.com/watch?v=V3TWU8xqFEI.

47. "Mera strogosti," RGALI, fond 2693, opis 1, ed. khr. 1.

48. A. Mapovets, "Unter dem ployt fun yerushe," 70.

49. Today's reader might find Bergelson's writing about disability objectionable, especially because the writer employs Filipov's and other characters' disabilities quite extensively.

Judgment

1

Zubok, one of the agents in Kamino-Balke's Special Section, was playing the accordion. The investigator Andreyev sat across from him, stretching out his slender legs encased in polished boots. He was a lady's man, tall and fair-skinned. He tapped his heels to the beat of Zubok's music gently, but the lamp on the table next to the hot iron stove kept flickering. Andreyev made loud hissing noises through his nose—sounding just like a gramophone. Imitating a gramophone was a particular skill of his.

The third man was the sailor Igumenko. He was little and restless: the whole time he kept running out to the dark, snow-covered courtyard to check whether the horses and saddles were still there and whether the night's storm had stopped. Now he sat quietly off to the side. Pretending that a bench was a horse, he demonstrated how to ride it. He took a puff from his short-stemmed pipe and gave a hint of a smile with only a crease on his left cheek. The crease had this to say:

"I've seen things like that before . . . You'll have to do better if you want to impress me."

In the middle of the room Marfusha was dancing. She was a homeless shiksa who cleaned the office. Every time they sent her out to a separate room to search and examine the women they arrested, she would return with burning cheeks, blinking back her shame, as if she had done something indecent and masculine to the women while they were in that room.

"No," she would answer, shrugging her shoulders apologetically, "I didn't find anything . . ."

Now she was dancing to the sounds of the accordion; she had been dancing for a long time without pausing to catch her breath, as if a dybbuk were dancing inside her.

The men in the room knew that Marfusha had a strange weakness: she would dance until she had no strength left, almost to the point of fainting. Zubok, the agent, was the one who detected this weakness: the sound of a melody would set her in motion—much like tickling someone under the arms makes them laugh.

Every now and again Zubok would play a few chords that signaled he was about to finish. Then with a couple of quick movements Marfusha would stop dancing. But a moment later he would continue, and Marfusha would once again spring to her feet to be carried across the room.

Suddenly something came over Marfusha. She froze. Her hair tousled, her bosom heaving, she remained standing in the middle of the room. Her wet, shiny lips began to tremble, and her glassy eyes looked across the room, fixing on the wall in sheer horror. She had the eyes of a madwoman.

The accordion stopped.

Andreyev bit his lower lip as if he had accidentally stepped on someone's foot, his eyes asking:

"What's the matter? . . . Again? . . ."

And three pairs of eyes followed Marfusha's frightened gaze and stared at the wall.

"Shhh!" Zubok whispered. "Shhh! Listen! Listen!"

A series of dull, hard thuds came from the wall. They sounded distant at first, as if they came from deep inside the earth. But the longer they continued, the more persistently they struck the wall and the more clearly everyone understood their origin. It was the boss, who had fallen ill; he was signaling from his room that it was ten o'clock—time for Zubok, Igumenko, and Andreyev to get on their horses and head out toward the border to patrol the snow-covered roads.

"He's not asleep," sighed Marfusha. "Oh, God . . ."

Her insane eyes were still fixed on the wall, as if it were a holy icon. Her moist lips quivered fearfully, almost begging:

"It's the third night in a row . . ."

But the sailor Igumenko drew his head down and stiffened his shoulders in anger.

"That carcass," he said, clenching his teeth, "what a pain."

And he turned away from the wall, annoyed.

The new boss was young, tall, and mean, with a bandage on his swollen neck, and with the harsh, hoarse voice of a person who just had a molar pulled out by its deep roots. If you tried to convince him of something, he would be silent and wouldn't even look at you, but as soon as you thought you had him persuaded, he would suddenly explode, and with great annoyance and irritation say, "*Chto vy? . . . Shutite?* What, are you joking?"

No one knew where he came from or how he used to make his living. From the beginning there were rumors that he had been a magnate who had his own mines and lived in a palace. Then the story about his former wealth was abruptly abandoned, although the connection to the mines was retained. He had been a worker in the mines all his life, people said, and the toxic gases under the surface of the earth had caused his illness and the infection on his bandaged neck. Comrade Sasha had brought him to Kamino-Balke to run things. She was young, as big as a man, widely respected, and held a high rank (she was the one who had had the previous boss fired for negligence). The air of silence that surrounded him and his heavy, immense figure weighed on everyone, stifling them, and the only hope was that after long years of work in the mines he had somehow become ill with a strange and serious disease and wouldn't last long.

When he removed the bandage, it turned out that the hard swelling on the side and back of his neck was not that big at all. But sometimes in the middle of the day, his face and eyes would turn yellow, as if someone had stuffed a dish full of saffron and fed it to him. And then he would lie in his room with the shades drawn and suffer excruciating pain. You wouldn't hear a thing from him on these occasions, and everyone would breathe freely, like under the old boss, when they were their own masters and could do as they liked.

It became clear, however, that even during the harshest spasms of pain he paid close attention to everything that was taking place at Kamino-Balke. To make sure everyone understood that he, Filipov, was in charge, he issued orders.

"Well?" Igumenko asked irritably. "Are we going or not?"

They had one last smoke and took a good look at each other.

As far as the new boss was concerned, one look said to the other: "A sick carcass."

"We're not going to make a single arrest at the border."

"A pox on his throat."

"Let him go patrol the border."

"Screw him."

Full of resentment, all three started to put on their coats, tie the ear flaps of their hats, and file out, one by one, into the stormy, cold weather.

Once they were outside, the sounds of dissatisfaction began to die down. The sailor Igumenko cursed on behalf of all of them:

"Son of a bitch! . . ."

✦

Kamino-Balke was a former monastery. It was located in an empty field, and its round courtyard, surrounded by trees, was covered in snow. In the middle of the courtyard there was a lamp on a post. It had been extinguished forever.

An eternal spirit—a wind—swirled around the post, rattling the remaining pieces of the lamp's broken glass.

Three horses stood at the post. They were saddled. They suffered from the night's storm, the cold reins slapping and stinging their flesh.

The snow flew around, dusting the horses; it came from the corner where a group of crooked church spires with broken crosses stood, gloomy and abandoned. No one crossed himself in their presence any more.

The snow formed plumes under the horses' bellies, it fell as if through a thousand sieves—only in the dark nighttime pallor, it was hard to know whether it was falling from above or below.

"A nasty, nasty snowstorm," called out the investigator Andreyev to his horse, even though he was still far away from it, "*raz, dva, tri!* one, two, three! *raz, dva, tri!*"

Like a man flinging himself into cold water, he leaped into the air, landing with his belly on the saddle of his thin, black horse; he dexterously gave himself a shake, found the stirrups, and knocked out a verse:

Over the earth a storm is prowling,
Bringing whirling, blinding snow . . .

"Well, what," he muttered. He was too lazy to turn around, and gestured instead with his hand in a fur-lined glove, pointing behind them. "Are we going or what?"

"That son of a bitch!"

This is what the sailor Igumenko had to do—march around his little horse a few times, like a Jew circling the synagogue on Simchas Torah, until he finally threw himself on top of it. The horse was somewhat addled.

"Screw it," Igumenko said after a pause. "What are we waiting for?"

He took a breath with difficulty. "Lead on, Andreyev."

"Where to?"

"All the way to the little wood."

"*Bien!*"

Now they rode out of the courtyard, three dots of the Hebrew vowel *segol*, and at the apex of the *segol* rode Andreyev.

Unable to resist finishing the verse, he cheerily added:

... Like a beast I hear it howling,
Like an infant wailing low ...

He was mild-mannered and the most relaxed of the three.

This was his character: easygoing, lazy, but also quick and restless—the legacy of his noble stock. Somewhere deep in his throat, there remained even now a few sounds of a young, pampered Junker.

With these sounds he astonished those around him; this would happen mostly at night, when they would hold up a whole row of horses and wagons at the border with a few shots from their Brownings. Whenever this happened, Zubok and Igumenko would curse mightily. Shrieking, yelling wildly at the shocked wagon drivers, they would create the impression that a whole regiment was cursing. If they happened to shake down the passengers, they did so not for themselves, and not for the law, but only for the joy of it—the bourgeoisie would have to empty their pockets.

Because of this Andreyev would work separately and entirely on his own. He would bow very politely to the women in their rich furs, sunk low in the wagon so that their wealth would not be seen. He would remove his hat and ask in a genteel manner:

"Does *Madame* have any money?"

And when he was given money, he did not count it and did not haggle. He would bow again nobly and say, "*Merci*," but in the manner of a real Frenchman, deep in his throat, "*Me-gsi.*"

As a rule it was very difficult to get a rise out of him. And even now in the stormy winter night, it hardly bothered him that the new, sick boss issued angry orders. However, for the other two, especially Igumenko, it struck home.

Igumenko was fuming. He unburdened his bitter heart to his little horse; earlier, while they were riding out of the courtyard, he had pulled all kinds of crazy stunts that he would have enjoyed playing on the new boss: he had punched the horse hard on the head, between its ears, and his feet unceasingly hammered out the rhythm of a certain curse on the horse's belly.

Finally the three of them rode out into the nighttime wind.

Ahead of them lay a flat, level field, lost and endless, covered in the snow, like a white desert. Here the storm flew in from the right and the left.

Large, invisible hands merrily picked up whole heaps of snow and just as merrily released them.

Andreyev realized that laziness was a beautiful thing even now, when the wind was hitting him right in the face, whistling its breath at him, and burying his galloping horse in snow up to its belly. He understood that it was best to hunker down and to keep his eyes shut, and to let the horse carry him wherever it wanted.

"I don't see a thing!" He let the wind carry his message to his companions, who had fallen behind. "All the roads are hidden."

"Lead on, keep going," a weak answer hastened him on from behind. "Keep to the left."

To the left there was less snow but the wind was stronger. There, the gallop of the three riders changed to a fast-paced limp.

Above them was the broken, jagged sky, as if made from silent mountains; from the smoky clouds a young, limping moon hurried the riders along. The moon waddled toward the edge of the snow-covered forest, where the riders took cover from the nighttime storm and wind.

And somewhere far across the field, by the glimmer of the same moon, the air dreamed of a sleigh's glide and the neighing of horses as they galloped.

The middle of the night was the time when entire bands of wagons would set out thievishly along the snow-covered paths opposite the forest. Travelers from the nearby town used them to get to the border. Night after night they wondered:

"How strange . . . No one is paying any attention . . . Free as a bird."

✦

And this is how Andreyev, Zubok, and Igumenko remembered one of those nights: a night of dreams and not much luck.

When they slept it off afterward, it was as if they had fallen sick. They couldn't tell:

"Did the night happen or not?"

All that remained of the night were bits and pieces that buzzed around their brains, dazzling their memories.

From the beginning:

The full, brass moon with the face of a cadaver was swimming and floating above them. It had no eyes but wanted to see.

A little later:

The edge of the woods in the middle of a cold night buried in snow. As soon as you got down from your horse, it bothered you.

This time the coachmen from Golikhovke took their passengers to the border using a more direct path than usual: they rode through the forest.

But later:

"Andreyev, you milksop!"

Igumenko, with fire in his eyes, told him off:

"What kind of an investigator are you, you . . . son of a bitch!"

Since they had agreed not to bring the new boss anybody they stopped at the border, this agreement had to hold.

Only Andreyev—provided that he wasn't drunk and too merry—was completely obstinate and stubborn as usual. When you talked to him, it was as if you were talking to a wall. Things got to him more than to Igumenko or Zubok. After smoking a cigarette, he pulled his head into his shoulders and let out the yawn of a man who used to be rich, a loud yawn—with a quiver. He still felt like catching a couple of coachmen together with their passengers at the border.

"You know what," he said, "may the devil take him, the new boss!"

Agent Zubok looked at him with haughty, arched eyebrows, as he always did while assessing lawbreakers. Only it didn't matter to Andreyev one bit. His eyes—the eyes of a half-slaughtered ram—looked oily after the yawn. They answered Igumenko:

"You are a swine, brother! It's time you learned this: an investigator from Kamino-Balke gets bored in the middle of the night, and when he remembers he used to be a Junker . . . he feels he has to do something."

He started promenading among the trees at the edge of the woods to make it look as if he had lost something. He disappeared and came back immediately with the news:

"Well, one thing is clear: there is certainly a path here between the trees—there are fresh tracks from a sled."

"A path? Where?"

"So, in a word . . ."

Much, much later:

A road appeared, a wily road—it had quite a nerve. It started out at the edge of the woods, narrow and hidden—no one had seen it before.

It was annoying that the thieving wagon drivers from Golikhovke had come up with the idea of getting to the border precisely here, right under Kamino-Balke's nose.

Igumenko was already in his saddle, pursuing the first of them along the road:

"Wait!" he hollered. "Damn you!"

That night they caught a wagon that strayed from the road, wandering along so lazily that it seemed to want to yield to the three riders and let them pass.

A strange, docile silence fell after the first holler to stop—as if the wagon were saying:

"So, here goes . . . Thank God it wasn't for nothing that I spent all this time stumbling around out here . . . The whole night I was certain it was going to turn out exactly like this."

Then the riders forced their way quite close to the little wagon and started looking at it and thinking it over:

A wretched wagon from the nearby shtetl of Golikhovke—a simple wagon with a thirteen-year-old boy for a coachman and, in it, a young woman in furs holding a sleeping two-year-old in her lap—a young woman who immediately confessed to everything.

They asked her:

"To the border?"

She answered very quietly, her lips just barely quivering:

"To the border."

Just then her head tilted upward and her eyes cast a look at the riders—strange eyes, each with another woman deep inside, and each of those women with a little crucifix hanging on her chest.

She was a Christian.

She whispered:

"No, my dears," she said, "you won't do anything bad to me . . . I know. You won't bring me to Kamino-Balke. I know your type and I like it."

✦

The following morning, after sleeping late, they were in a bad mood, as if they had committed a sin together. Souls covered in soot had to be aired out in the snowed-in courtyard at Kamino-Balke—after the prank they had played the night before at the expense of the new, sickly boss. To spite him, they didn't arrest the woman. She had a tail on her the whole night, she got followed around like a little goat pursued by a pack of dogs—and so she made it back from the border and returned to the small shtetl nearby.

And now to all three this was no more than a dream recalled from the night before, a dream like the woman's eyes—eyes with little crucifixes in their pupils: they stared with a beggar's charm and issued sinful promises.

They promised the best of luck.

"Just a little longer, my dears . . . Just a little bit longer . . ."

She kept leading them all over the forest the whole night through. And finally she ended up tricking them, easily slipping out of their hands in the gray morning light.

Now she clouded their memories once more. They recalled the two large cases she had with her in the wagon and her fine woman's body wrapped in expensive furs—they remembered these things with a pang of regret and resentment:

"What a bitch!"

"But when she comes packing again . . . the shit will fly."

2

Golikhovke:

A small shtetl, which spoiled the valley—an hour-long hard ride down from Kamino-Balke. It was here on a frosty morning that the young, unfamiliar woman returned from the border along with her blonde-haired child, a toddler around two years old.

Arriving back in the shtetl in the early morning was difficult, it was like getting undressed down to her slip and going out in the cold to show herself naked to the world.

The proximity of Kamino-Balke was the problem—not just the fact of Kamino-Balke alone, but also its new boss, the sick man.

Since his arrival, people had begun to travel to and from Golikhovke only at night.

Nighttime—that's when the smuggling took place. During the day Golikhovke did not go out, and when it did, it was on the quiet, in stocking feet.

During the day the window curtains slept.

The houses waiting for nightfall dozed off also.

The streets slept.

Far away in some corner every now and then bells would chime—from the old Catholic church. It was strange: the church was dead, absolutely dead, but then suddenly, its bells would chime.

By the time the church fell silent, the whole town would be dozing off, its expression saying:

"I don't see any wagons coming—I don't want to look."

The tired wagon hobbled and limped along on its way. The wagon's strength was gone. It barely managed to bring the woman back to the same house where she had been staying just yesterday. The first one to look out the window was the mistress of the house. She had time to do two things: clap her big hands and shriek to her husband, who was breaking a box apart in the kitchen:

"Oy, Shmuel, she's back!"

Only she was so afraid that she didn't do anything, except go outside.

It was always like that in Golikhovke: when you sent someone to the border and then saw him back again, you would be as frightened as if he'd come from the other world.

The mistress:

Tall, thin, young, with a voice that could raise the dead.

When she spoke quickly, no one understood her except her husband.

The husband:

Also tall, but not as thin. He said everything twice, clearly and slowly, once for himself and once for his wife, because he was a man who believed in being fair.

What he liked:

Walking around the house in his vest, preparing a basin of food for the cow according to his own recipe, all the while thinking about himself: "Shmuel Voltsis? The most refined man in Golikhovke. They all fleeced the passengers, but he didn't. It wasn't true that he did."

When he entered the house from the kitchen, his wife wasn't there any longer.

Looking through the window, he saw:

There she was, on the steps to the porch, shivering from the cold, her big hands covering her bare neck. She stood rocking back and forth before an unfamiliar woman.

"Oy," she said, rattling the window panes, "we knew it would turn out this way, me and my husband. Only we were afraid to tell you."

He had a good look: it was the woman from yesterday, the one who had told him severely, "Don't call me Pani."

Her eyes were odd. If she looked at you while you were saying something, you would start thinking, "Could I be lying?"

He saw how hard it was for her to get down from the wagon with her child, and thinking about his wife, said to himself, "It would be better to help her, you cow!"

"Nu, yes," he said, and with that, opened the door and grabbed the woman's cases.

"In Golikhovke when we look at someone, we can tell right away whether she's going to make it over the border or not."

The desire to go back into the kitchen overcame him; he wanted to find a seat on the sofa in front of the fire and just sit there.

The same thing had happened to him yesterday when the woman was staying in the house.

She had a strange beauty: a head of thick, blonde hair, smooth and gloriously shiny. She was a Christian and very severe—as if Christians, like Hasidic Jews with their rebbes, had dynasties among their clergy, and their daughters, pious and strict, held forth among their own disciples.

And besides that, when she had to pay, she paid, without trying to get a better deal.

Looking at the fire burning in the stove, he scratched himself.

"Nekhe!" he called to his wife to come to him in the kitchen.

He was annoyed.

He stood leaning against the fireplace as if it were a lectern, and said to the fire slowly, repeating himself twice, once for himself and once for his wife, "Can't you see, you cow; she's tired after a night like that. So what are you hammering away at her like that for, what? Stay in the kitchen, I'm telling you."

Then it was quiet.

Meanwhile, nearby in the dirty dining room, the two-year-old blonde girl was learning how to run in circles. Her light, soft shoes made slapping noises on the floorboards.

Every time the child ran into the kitchen, her mother called to her, "Come here!"

She sat there with her head propped on her hands, eyes closed, as though she had a terrible headache, her fingers buried deeply in her short, disheveled hair.

You could hear:

She took in a full chest of air and let it out, as if with each deep exhalation she wanted to pump out the entire night, the whole episode at the border.

Shmuel Voltsis said to his wife, "You fool, after what happened anyone would feel like that . . . like you had taken poison, but not enough."

He loved to speak in allegories.

He was still standing bent over the fire that burned in the stove. He was thinking about the woman, who apparently planned to try the border again.

"You'll see, she's going to take another dose of poison."

✦

The woman wrote a letter.

She asked Shmuel Voltsis to come to her room and looked him in the eye to see whether he would lie: "Do you know Babitsky?"

Shmuel Voltsis's face took on the expression of a man playing dead, to make it seem that he didn't know Babitsky was an old, decrepit doctor, whom people in Golikhovke had long since stopped consulting.

He lived behind the Catholic church in a run-down hovel, and grew nothing but pumpkins in his garden all summer long—yellow pumpkins. Dr. Babitsky himself was one of them, a yellow pumpkin with long gray hair. He ate no meat. As a young man he had been a Tolstoyan. Twenty years ago he had been put on trial for making a speech to the Shtundists; they were set free, but he was sentenced to twelve years. When he finished his sentence and returned home, he brought along with him from Siberia a deaf-mute young man.

People said: "Let it be a lesson! Of course, it's his child . . . and the mother was his servant."

By the time he got back, no one in Golikhovke would send for him any more. Only peasants from the surrounding villages would take him to their homes by wagon, sitting with him as if with their equal. In Golikhovke, for as long as anybody could remember, people had thought more highly of the physician's assistant, anyway. If they asked for Babitsky, it meant that the patient was on his last legs. In those cases Babitsky came quickly, and his visit itself was a sign that the sick person would die. On these occasions, Babitsky's yellow pumpkin face assumed the air of self-sacrifice. His vegetarian eyes would gleam, and if the patient were still conscious, and not in great pain, Dr. Babitsky would stay with him longer. Sometimes he would drive the family out of the sickroom. People said that Dr. Babitsky would tell the patient Bible stories, and everyone would feel bad, as if they had called a priest to the sickroom.

This was the person the woman had written her letter to.

Shmuel Voltsis kept the letter in his breast pocket for a few hours. He felt that taking even a single step with it was hard, as though he suddenly had a hernia—who knew what was in the letter?

"How did this woman know Dr. Babitsky, anyway?"

And besides, since there was no such thing as a kosher letter nowadays, what did Shmuel Voltsis have to stick his neck out for?

Slowly, very slowly, he put on his gray fur coat.

He thought, "The new boss at Kamino-Balke is an executioner. Better not to fall into his hands."

He pulled on an old pair of worn-out boots, because he wasn't charging anything for this trip. For this sort of thing you don't wear your new boots.

He set off in the early evening, because it was a lot easier then.

In Golikhovke the evening darkness fell earlier than everywhere else in the vicinity, even earlier than the villages.

"Khe-khe!"

Shmuel Voltsis's evening cough had this to say: "Here I go, Shmuel Voltsis, an intimate of these parts, I'm just going to have a little stroll outside."

"Khe-khe?" The cough asked again. "Does anyone know I've got something on me?"

As if with wooden clappers the frozen air echoed the first steps of his boots.

Now he was on his way.

The darkness trailed after him in stripes, climbing uphill along with him.

It first darkened the valley, the old mill with the little bridge, then the market, and the rooftops that scaled the mountain like the rungs of a ladder. At last the darkness swallowed the mountain and the old Catholic church.

There it hung, suspended, like a transparent wall, a faint sliver of light that was waiting as if for *havdole*, for the end of Shabbos.

Enveloped in darkness, Golikhovke lay waiting without any light and with bated breath . . . It was as if someone had scrambled to the very top of the church spire, where a sliver of the sky was still bright, and on behalf of Golikhovke had a very careful look: what was happening in the old monastery in Kamino-Balke?

At dawn a new group of people would arrive in the shtetl, a whole mob of smugglers, and also ordinary folk, who hated the revolution and wanted to escape it—places had to be readied for this crowd.

Around nine in the evening twenty or so wagons would take everyone who had slept there the night before.

It was the same story the previous day, but something happened.

This is what the woman, the stranger at Shmuel Voltsis's, recounted:

As the wagons, all in a row, were heading out of the shtetl, they approached the old empty shop, where a guard had been posted. Suddenly, a policeman ran out and started shooting at the wagons. The coachmen whipped up their horses, driving them on. But her coachman was still young, practically a child. He stopped and afterward didn't know the way. He was lost in the woods for a long time until three men appeared on horseback.

This is what the woman said.

Shmuel Voltsis said, "That the policeman fired shots is nothing. It doesn't mean anything."

The woman asked, "What do you mean, nothing?"

Shmuel Voltsis answered even more coldly, "He takes money for each wagon."

The woman asked, "So why shoot?"

Shmuel Voltsis answered even more coldly, "It's a smokescreen. He is afraid of Kamino-Balke."

The woman asked, "The new boss?"

Shmuel Voltsis answered neither coldly nor warmly, "Uh-huh, he's quite a killer."

This conversation had taken place during the day, before Shmuel Voltsis left with the letter.

Now, wearing his old, heavy boots, he made his way uphill, hiding in the dark, stopping every minute in front of narrow, dark courtyards to see whether any wagons were ready to go out. But there were none to be seen. Since yesterday rumors had circulated that someone in a sheepskin coat and hat down over his ears was hanging around Kamino-Balke.

"From far away," people said, "he looked like a peasant."

"He was wandering in the fields."

"He was inspecting the roads."

Shmuel Voltsis had the same suspicion as all the coachmen.

"Shh! Maybe it's the executioner himself, the new boss?"

Carrying the woman's letter in his breast pocket, he didn't have the slightest desire to run into the new boss. He walked very carefully and didn't let himself forget, not even for a moment, what his excuse was, what he would say to the world:

"What do I know? Me, Shmuel Voltsis . . . I am a simple man."

3

Dr. Babitsky went to sleep at twilight.

If he lay down in his clothes when it began to get dark outside, he could stay asleep deep into the night.

He acquired this habit after the revolution took the wrong turn, when he decided:

"What is this revolution? In a word, it's Kamino-Balke."

From that moment on, he began to snore when other people woke up; he slept through the revolution's evil waking hours, as if to spite it; he snored as a sign that between him and the revolution all bridges had been burned.

People in Golikhovke, however, interpreted this differently. They said:

"Look how destitute he's become!"

And they also said:

"You try being as poor as Dr. Babitsky, and see what it's like to take up philosophy by twilight!"

The fence around Dr. Babitsky's dilapidated hovel was broken here and there, and in some places had completely collapsed, so that you could get into the courtyard from wherever you wanted.

The gate, for its part, was intact; however, it was a gate that had a life of its own, and it was as little concerned with the courtyard that it enclosed as Dr. Babitsky was with the town that surrounded him. The gate didn't lead anywhere.

It was now completely dark in the house. Only one crooked window was lit up. This was the window in the kitchen, and Shmuel Voltsis headed for it in the dark.

When he took a look through the window, he saw Dr. Babitsky's deaf-mute, a fellow around twenty years old, with a flat face. It looked like peasant bread that was badly baked, in which someone had placed two black, small, and very narrow Asiatic eyes. In Golikhovke people marveled at them:

"Clever eyes, very penetrating."

In Golikhovke they said:

"Other people have children, but Dr. Babitsky has a faithful slave, who serves him and guards his house, like a dog."

The deaf-mute was standing at the hot stove, making buckwheat pancakes—apparently, before going to sleep, the doctor had told him to.

But look how big the pancakes were—each was the size of a plate. And look how many! They were piled in heaps on the kitchen table and the bench! They were falling on the floor, and the deaf-mute kept on making more and more.

If the doctor didn't get up and tell him—"Enough!"—the deaf-mute would flood the whole world with pancakes.

Shmuel Voltsis attempted a little tap on the window before he remembered that the deaf-mute couldn't hear anything. He scratched himself lazily, like a coachman whose wheel had broken in the middle of a journey, but who didn't see any human habitation close by:

"Well then, might as well cry out to Him who lives forever for all the good it's going to do."

Shmuel Voltsis had long ago drawn his own conclusions from experience: if you do something for someone for free, it's always more of a headache than if you do it for profit.

He tried the back door: it was open.

His hands groped blindly in the dark and found a ladder, a trough, and then another door.

His fingers ran across it, looking for the latch.

By the time he opened the door to the brightly lit kitchen, the deaf-mute had turned his back to the stove and stood facing the door. His mouth grimacing in anger, his narrow, black eyes lit with a wicked fire, he stood hunched over, like an animal ready to pounce on anyone who came in.

Shmuel Voltsis remained at the door in wonderment: had the deaf-mute sensed his presence? . . . It wasn't for nothing that people said the deaf-mute felt things that others didn't.

Shmuel Voltsis also bent over, he opened his mouth and smiled at the deaf-mute—not only did he smile, he smiled and winked, and smiled and winked again. One smile had this to say:

"You're big now, right? Probably want to find yourself a wife soon!"

A second smile meant:

"Making pancakes?"

A third:

"And where is the doctor? Asleep?"

However, the deaf-mute's mouth kept on grimacing, his eyes kept on burning with a wicked fire. Shmuel Voltsis consequently began to do what people do when they meet a deaf-mute. He puffed out his cheeks, made a dreadful face, pounded his hands on his chest. He pointed to his ears as if they had just heard a terrible noise; he flapped his elbows around, like someone driving away flies, and suddenly asked the deaf-mute a question using his hands:

"What's happening in the world? What's going on?"

Then the deaf-mute's expression changed. His eyes grew big, his face turned red, the veins in his neck bulged out.

His mouth opened very wide, as if he were going to throw up all his innards, his intestines, heart, and lungs. Honking and snorting noises erupted out of him, a honk and a snort, one after the other, from somewhere in his neck, deep, deep in his throat. The honks and snorts now intermingled, now wrestled with each other deep in his throat, under his palate, and only a well-trained and familiar ear could make out the word:

"Rrrrree ... vv ... vv ... vo ... o ... o ... lluu ... shshsh ... un!!!"

This was the word the doctor had taught the deaf-mute just three years earlier, in the first, festive weeks of the revolution.

By this time the doctor had long been dissatisfied with it; the word "revolution" grated in his ears, it was claptrap and dangerous besides.

The doctor scowled when he heard it and winked to the deaf-mute that he ought not to say it.

But taking the word away from the deaf-mute was a lot harder than giving it to him. Once the deaf-mute learned something, he learned it for good.

The deaf-mute took the word with him when the doctor sent him to the market to buy something from the shopkeepers.

After he screamed the word, both Shmuel Voltsis and the deaf-mute were satisfied. The deaf-mute considered anyone a friend who had made a terrible face, puffed out his cheeks, and asked with flapping elbows, "What's happening? What's going on?"

Only his honking and snorting had awakened the doctor, who was somewhere in the second or third room in the house.

Not someone's head, but a small, yellow pumpkin with long gray hair appeared in the half-open door of the kitchen. The pumpkin's lively black eyes slowly scanned the room to the right and left, and landed on Shmuel Voltsis. The eyes asked:

"What's wrong? What happened?"

And his hairy old hand squeamishly accepted the letter that was extended to him.

Then Shmuel Voltsis went home and felt light as air, as if he had gotten rid of a pound of lead that weighed him down together with the letter.

He strode along devil-may-care and gave a cough slowly and very loudly into the evening, enjoying the clatter his heavy boots made. The clatter let the darkness know that a person was walking along and wanted someone to appear and ask whether he had anything on him: it could be anyone, even the new boss from Kamino-Balke—now let the boss even search him, Shmuel Voltsis . . .

But no one approached him in the darkness.

Although it wasn't even that late, down below the evening remained dead; it was the time when people used to set out from Golikhovke in the direction of the border.

But in one narrow and very dark passageway, people were whispering to one another.

A bunch of coachmen's short fur coats shuffled past a squeaky back door, and behind them stood red-haired Bunem picking his nose. Shmuel Voltsis asked him:

"Going as usual, eh, Bunem?"

"Listen, they're scared of something tonight."

"What are they scared of, Bunem?"

"The one in the peasant cap, who hangs around Kamino-Balke . . . It's probably the new executioner, the boss himself."

"But they say he's sick, eh, Bunem?"

Bunem thoughtfully stopped picking his nose. He seemed to be answering someone else:

"Well, it . . . it's . . . if people are saying . . ."

◆

That evening the doctor did not come to see the woman who was staying in a room at Shmuel Voltsis's.

The next day she sent him another letter. Almost to tempt him, she got herself decked out, curled her hair, and began to wait impatiently.

Finally the doctor dropped in quite like he was just passing by.

This was around ten o'clock at night.

His old, black coat, heavy and worn out—which he never removed even in someone else's house—smelled of medicine and singed feathers.

His absentmindedness permeated the whole house. It was apparent right away that either he had not read the woman's letter or else he had not understood it. He quickly asked:

"Who's sick?"

He had stopped by on the go, just in and out. But the woman locked herself in with him in the room where her child was sleeping.

She had taken the lamp from the dining room. There she had begun to tell the doctor that she was the daughter or the sister of a friend of his from long ago, who was also a doctor and also a former Tolstoyan.

He answered her sourly, as if she were a patient who had just recited a list of symptoms:

"Yes, and? Hmmm, I see."

Meanwhile, Shmuel Voltsis and his wife were sitting on the sofa in the dark dining room. The stove had gone cold.

In her room the woman went on and on, but Shmuel Voltsis and his wife were tired from their day and couldn't keep their eyes open. As they drifted off, they dreamed that the woman was pumping Dr. Babitsky full of air—he grew bigger and bigger, like a balloon.

Every now and then the husband and wife on the sofa would wake up. Blurry-eyed they would catch sight of the narrow crack in the broken door to the room. The crack burned like a small, golden stripe. It looked back at them faithfully, as if it were a third member of the family.

This is what happened—the golden stripe would wink at them: "Wait, wait, now . . . Pay attention and listen."

But even when they listened attentively, Shmuel Voltsis and his wife couldn't catch a thing.

In their sleepy brains the woman's strange words got mixed up and lost all meaning, growing more senseless by the minute. A word would try to stand up on its own two feet, but then another word would arrive, and both collapsed in a heap.

The doctor kept silent as the woman spoke. It seemed she was scolding him:

"Are you a believer? You, who doesn't get involved? What kind of a believer are you? Everything you think comes from not believing. You don't believe that life is everything, you don't believe that death means the end. But I am certain: death is death. My life right now is all I get. I will never have anything else. And the revolution is my death. That's why I am running away from it. That's why I've come here to the border. I've put my life at risk, and my child's. I'm not going back home."

The doctor coughed. With that he apparently meant to say that he was sick of her, that he couldn't help her with anything.

But the woman didn't let him speak. She asked him only for one thing—to help her see Filipov, the new boss at Kamino-Balke.

The word "Filipov" repeated itself over and over again in her mouth.

"He may be a bastard," she said, "he may even be a murderer . . . but anyone can be seduced. A simple girl—the bride of a condemned revolutionary—made the former tsar change his mind. The only thing is, Filipov can't know that I came here to cross the border."

From this and many other similar things she said, it was clear that the woman wanted to remain here for a while, no matter what. She wanted to move to the doctor's house, she said she would take care of him.

Lots and lots of words reached the man and wife in the darkness. They looked at each other. The wife's eyes asked the husband's:

"Are you getting any of this?"

The man's eyes answered no and asked the wife in turn, "You?"

She motioned him over to a corner of the dark dining room. There she began to grind away:

"There's a hard one. A real Cossack! You don't want to fall into her clutches. She's got herself all done up, powdered her nose, put on lipstick . . . and no one's going to stand in her way . . . she's nobody's fool . . . knows how to take care of herself . . ."

But from this outpouring Shmuel Voltsis was none the wiser.

Only one thing was clear: the doctor wanted to get away from the woman, and was not going to bring her home with him, not for anything. What good was she doing here, in Shmuel Voltsis's house? She had two heavy cases with her. She guarded them closely, not letting anyone near them. God knew what was in them.

Finally Shmuel Voltsis took the lamp and lit the doctor's way as he left through the dark back entrance. He seemed to do this out of great respect.

As they neared the door, however, Shmuel Voltsis stopped the doctor and asked him about the woman: seeing as she was staying in his house, was he going to get into some kind of trouble because of it?

But the doctor just shrugged his shoulders:

"The times we live in," he said, "if you knew someone yesterday, that doesn't mean you know who he is today."

The doctor was a clever one. He kept silent for a minute and added, "And who says, who says I didn't know her yesterday?"

And with that the doctor's expression made it seem that the tip of his nose wanted to add to the witticism he had just made, but held back. He was not the type of person to get involved. And the joke was not only aimed at the piece of work that was spreading such good cheer in Shmuel Voltsis's house, but at everything that had been going on around him for the past few years.

Suddenly he asked his host, "What's your name?"

"Shmuel."

"Oh yeah, Shmuel . . . the times we live in, eh?"

And the doctor closed the door behind him and went out, his nose ready to utter the next witticism: "the times."

The wind chased him uphill. Waves of roiling wind gnawed at the darkened houses, houses that had fallen asleep.

And both were tired and sleepy in the middle of the night—the doctor and the wind.

The wind tugged at the doctor's frayed coat, and the tip of the doctor's nose smiled as if it were having a joke at the world's expense—on the outside, he seemed to everyone a man on the sidelines, someone who didn't get involved. The doctor, however, noticed everything that was going on everyday and everywhere, even here, near Kamino-Balke.

"Strange things . . . and this woman . . . a piece of work . . ."

The doctor now understood the meaning of his own joke: the woman was a temptation that Satan had sent to the new boss at Kamino-Balke. She had said:

"It would be enough for Filipov just to meet me . . ."

Feh! These people were going to be tested, as if they were saints. And who was this Filipov? Nobody knew, even though he'd been at Kamino-Balke for over two weeks. They said he was sick and wouldn't take care of himself.

Well, fine, then. Dr. Babitsky was convinced that Filipov was either a saint or a sucker.

Everything to do with Filipov was murky, that's what it was. Murky, like the darkness surrounding the sleeping houses in the middle of the night at the edge of town. That was Filipov for you.

In the deep darkness naked branches clattered. A hoarse cry of pain broke from the disheveled trees. The events hidden in the nooks and crannies of the countryside seemed to be rifling through their leaves. It sounded as if the rustling was causing someone pain.

If they were to come, these events, they would engulf the entire area, like a fire, and would spare only his house, the doctor's house with its dilapidated fence and broken gate, because he was a man on the sidelines. He hadn't even told anyone the fact of his neutrality. He kept silent. People just didn't know how to live in times like these.

The doctor wrapped himself even more tightly in his old, worn-out coat.

As he hunched over, a warm feeling of coziness descended over him, the warmth that comes from knowing how to live in times like these.

The wind that had chased him uphill renewed in him a feeling of friendship, a strange friendship between an old, decrepit doctor and a young rake—the wind that tousled his gray hair.

Looking over his house—which would remain untouched even by the storm of the great events that would come crashing down—he thought about the new boss at Kamino-Balke, the boss whom he feared:

"That's what it is . . . In the past men like Filipov didn't exist, which means he's playing a role, that's it . . . A comedian, that's what he is."

And he was afraid to let the smile fall from the tip of his nose, as if together with the smile he might lose his balance in life.

4

To the right of Golikhovke, a young forest noisily awoke from the wind that swept through it and over the fields. Past the forest on the other side of the hill, Yanovo huddled like a petrified herd. This was a large village of sly little white houses whose courtyards, black with dung, were enclosed by stone fences. It stretched along both banks of the narrow, frozen river.

Stone fences suited the inhabitants of Yanovo, for all of them were as stubborn as their stone fences: stone upon stone. Once upon a time, the residents of Yanovo would regularly come to blows with their neighbors over the fertile plots of land down by the river, each vying to have his property reach the shore. But that was all in the past—no one fought there any longer.

As Dr. Babitsky tried to make his way to Yanovo along the empty road behind the little forest, the village was groggy, all that was visible of it were flecks of white sinking into the falling darkness. A certain mood, felt more clearly than ever before, was in the air—the sense that Yanovo was lying in wait at the river, united by a pernicious conspiracy, and in the middle of this conspiracy stood Sofia Pokrovskaya, the daughter of Yanovo's lame priest.

Sofia Pokrovskaya was short and quick; her face was swarthy with a hint of a moustache that made her mouth seem even blacker; her cheeks, because of their proximity to her mouth, looked unwashed.

Now, at nightfall, it seemed that the bells of the church in Yanovo's most remote corner were not ringing because Sofia Pokrovskaya had commanded them to be silent—maybe the church bells didn't chime because she had willed it. Sofia Pokrovskaya was Dr. Babitsky's closest and only friend for miles around. He was now going, on foot, to visit her in Yanovo.

As he set out from Golikhovke, he walked quickly, and even though he didn't turn around once, he felt in his hunched shoulders that someone's gaze was wandering around Yanovo—that Kamino-Balke had Yanovo in its sights.

It wasn't the first time the doctor had traveled on foot to Yanovo to visit Sofia Pokrovskaya. This time, however, he was propelled by a particular worry. He had left first thing in the morning when the frost—fresh in its whiteness—still covered locked doors, when nostrils and mouths exhaled visibly into the air, when a small kerosene lamp could still be burning somewhere, as if at a sickbed. It was then, first thing in the morning, when the dentist Galaganer stopped the doctor in the market. He looked no more than thirty-eight years old, but he might as well have been a hundred if his grumpiness were taken into account. Whenever he opened his mouth, he looked as if he were ready to pick a fight about whether he was right, his eyes twitching after every word he spoke. Every time he put a piece of gauze in a patient's mouth, he would run to the window to check whether the current regime had been abolished.

In the market, Galaganer was haggling with a peasant over the high price of a load of firewood. Speaking to Dr. Babitsky, who happened to be passing by, he pointed at the peasant:

"So there you have it—go deal with these price gougers!"

"What, what?" The doctor stopped and twisted his mouth, like someone who understood little in everyday matters.

"Overnight they doubled the prices, you see?" said Galaganer, staring at the peasant's face with a look that could kill. "A new boss at Kamino-Balke! They are afraid of him, but why should we have to pay more because they are afraid?"

"Yes, yes . . . a new boss," replied the doctor, looking like a man who wanted to continue on his way without getting involved.

"They say he used to own some coal mines," continued Galaganer, "and lived in a palace with serfs and servants."

"Ah . . . ah . . . hmm."

And the doctor pretended he had never heard that the dentist was a Socialist Revolutionary, that he was an SR from early on—and that now he was drawn to the circle of people who saw themselves as Sofia Pokrovskaya's disciples and participated in the "work" she was doing here in the region.

Galaganer walked alongside the doctor for a short while and apologized to him for the package of "literature" that Sofia Pokrovskaya had left under the bed at his—that is, the doctor's—place:

"She asked me to tell you she will be coming any day now to pick it up."

"Hmmm ... Hmmm ..." the doctor answered coldly.

When he got home, however, the doctor stole a glance at the dusty, illegal package that was up to no good under his bed and thought to himself: "After all, the former owner of a mine ... he used to live in his own palace ... Who knows if it's true or not—in any case, it's better not to cross such a person." And the dusty package under his bed robbed the doctor of his rest: the doctor could not lie down to go to sleep, but was forced to spend the entire night thinking instead.

That was why he was now headed to Sofia Pokrovskaya's in Yanovo. He had long felt comfortable in her company; he remembered her from the time she was a still a child.

✦

Sofia Pokrovskaya as a child:

At the age of twelve or so, she was a girl with crooked shoulders, an epileptic. When she walked quickly, her belly protruded and she waddled like a pregnant woman.

Sofia Pokrovskaya's lame father was the village priest. Like all priests, he was a fat man with a dark complexion and a heavy tongue that was constantly licking his lips. His hands were dirty as if covered with soot, his voice always repeating, "Lord have mercy on me."

He owned a prosperous estate: well-fed horses, squealing pigs, and tall, bent-over boys with flaxen heads and eyes burning with devotion—sons. Each son lost his mind the same year he finished his seminary training, each time in the hottest, quiet summer months when it was the season of threshing and reaping the harvest, and they didn't go to the market. On hot, long days peasants, dressed in white linen clothes, as if for Lent, would gather white ears of corn in the field from dawn until nightfall, while dogs and children roamed unobserved in the nearby villages. Meanwhile, in Golikhovke, women knitting socks would yawn madly, scratch under their headscarves as they wondered to themselves:

"Look—another day has passed. And a long day at that!"

On this kind of day, in the heat of the motionless afternoon, the Yanovo priest's long, iron wagon would slowly squeak its way through Golikhovke. And in the cart, atop newly threshed straw, would lie a tall lad stretched out, with hands and feet bound—yet another one of the priest's sons who had gone insane. He would be driven in the direction of the train station, and then the train would take him somewhere else farther still—to the big city where the priest had relatives and where there was also an insane asylum. It happened this way one summer—and then also the second summer, and, subsequently, the third.

Once the priest's twelve-year-old daughter sat in the corner of the wagon as it screeched its way through Golikhovke. A girl with crooked shoulders, she sat at the head of her tall, insane brother. This was Sofia Pokrovskaya. The priest was sending her along with her brother who was tied up—to their relatives in the big city where there was a seminary and an insane asylum. It was in that city that she was raised and received her education.

By the time she finally returned to Yanovo, the war was over, and a few years had passed since the revolution. Dr. Babitsky found in her a good friend—someone who agreed with him that, as he'd say, life "got rerouted onto a strange crooked path." She would keep him informed of the "happenings" she organized in the region—and in such a way, too, that nobody else ever knew that he was aware of any of it.

He had come to her a couple of days earlier with news about the "temptress"—the blonde—whom the devil himself had sent to Filipov, the new boss at Kamino-Balke. Dr. Babitsky told Sofia Pokrovskaya:

"A real piece of work, that one, eh? You should have heard her: 'Introduce me to Filipov,' she says. 'I can help you get things done.'"

And he had added:

"You tell me: who gets to lord it over us these days?"

Now he was heading to Yanovo to pay Sofia Pokrovskaya another visit. He thought to himself that when he arrived, he would find a cozily heated house and a lamp burning on a small table covered with a tablecloth—like tables in poor Jewish households on Shabbos. He would sit with her in this domestic comfort, and using his nails, he'd peel the skin from the hot potatoes that she'd put on the table to welcome him. He'd remind her about the package that she had left under the bed at his place:

"The times we live in!" he'd say to her with a chuckle. "Even for knowing something they grab you and whip you just the same as if you'd done something . . ."

Sofia Pokrovskaya would answer him with the angry grimace of an SR who had sacrificed herself so as to live her life exactly this way:

"*Nu da, vot imenno*. Yes, exactly, that's how it goes."

Today, however, the doctor wasn't fated to experience this satisfaction—as if someone even older had warned him: "Stay home, old man . . . Take care of your old bones . . ."

✦

When Dr. Babitsky arrived in Yanovo at dusk, he somehow sensed that it was too quiet in the village. It could have been because Yanovo realized that the new boss at Kamino-Balke was different from all the previous ones. On his account, Yanovo—just like Golikhovke—received its dose of fear.

The houses on both sides of the street looked as if they had just sprung up and didn't belong there. It was very quiet around the houses but the doctor's ear dreamed of weak voices lingering in the air.

The barking of dogs from faraway parts of the village became audible, as if it had come from faraway worlds. It seemed that in that distant corner of the village something was happening in all the barking; later, quiet returned.

There was no one to open the door to the dimly lit entryway of Sofia Pokrovskaya's house when Dr. Babitsky knocked. He sensed immediately that Sofia Pokrovskaya wasn't home right that moment, even though one couldn't say with certainty that she wasn't to be found at all—a light was visible through the curtains covering the windows, but the light was simultaneously calming and alarming.

The doctor entered. As always, the house was warmly heated, and the lamp was burning on a small table covered with a tablecloth—like the tables in poor Jewish households on Shabbos. But Sofia

Pokrovskaya wasn't there, and the walls looked like the inside of a guesthouse where the proprietor changes from day to day, each leaving behind a distinct smell.

Sonorous snoring was the first thing the doctor heard at the early evening hour. After looking around, he saw the two Pokras brothers sleeping on the long benches between the stove and the table. They were both tall men with pimples on their healthy, rough faces. As always, they smelled of leather and were dressed in gray cavalry overcoats, even though no one could recall with certainty whether either of the brothers had been in the military.

They were both Socialist Revolutionaries, disciples of Sofia Pokrovskaya. And maybe because Sofia Pokrovskaya wasn't there, they were tasked with keeping an eye on her house and with waiting for something alarming that might happen that day. They were snoring so loudly now, in this early evening hour, that it was easy to believe they had spent the entire previous day and night running errands all over town for Sofia Pokrovskaya.

The doctor knew that the inhabitants of the region's faraway villages took them for Christians, so he took a good look at their sleeping faces: foreheads knitted in wrinkles, raised eyebrows, and smiling lips. In Golikhovke he used to know their late father, Yehiel Pokras, a burly Jew. He was a man with blue veins visible on his face and his fleshy nose, the nose of a respected village elder. The nose created an impression of homey generosity each time it was loudly blown. It also reminded you of his shop. In his shop, Yehiel would offer a heartfelt wish of good luck to customers buying a length of fabric.

In those days Yehiel Pokras had a house full of children. They studied and learned to be crafty and good-natured nose-blowers like their father. After Yehiel's death, his children scattered across the whole wide world; only two of the brothers—the ones now snoring in their cavalry overcoats here on the benches at Sofia Pokrovskaya's—returned. They didn't say anything, but every snore served as a reminder that they had sacrificed themselves for the "work" Sofia Pokrovskaya was carrying out in the region and that, like her, they wanted to save the peasants nearby, to save life itself all over the country . . .

The doctor sat down on the bench in the middle of the room to rest from his long, pointless journey. Conjuring up the image of Yehiel Pokras, he once more assessed the two sleeping men, a smile on his lips:

"So, in conclusion: what? ... The wheels go round and round ..."

The doctor felt a weakness—like after a steam bath; a pleasant numbness spread through his limbs. He could doze off any minute, his eyebrows raised in wonderment and a smile fixed on his face. His stomach felt lighter and lighter, his vision clouded, and his eyelids drooped. But the doctor knew that he had better not fall asleep. Suddenly, one of the snoring men stirred, his eyes still shut, and sat up on the bench. He quickly jerked his head first to the right and then to the left, as if he had clearly heard someone calling his name without knowing the direction of the call.

Immediately, the doctor sensed that for him—a man who didn't want to get involved—it was better not to strike up a conversation and that, in fact, it was better to let his eyes droop as if they were oiled, so the young man on the bench would think he was sleeping. His shoulders still tense, he was careful to remain still—but in this half-awake state he could feel and nearly see everything that was unfolding around him. Here was one of the Pokras brothers looking at him dully with his sleepy eyes, unsure where the doctor had come from. And then the young man headed in the direction of the door, coughing forcefully as if he wanted to spit out all his bad dreams—but maybe also intentionally, so as to wake the doctor. But it was more convenient for the doctor to remain half or even three-quarters asleep ...

The young man opened the door to the entryway and, from there, the door to the courtyard. A blast of cold, dry air streamed into the room: the village evening under a bright moon was palpable inside.

It was quiet, but then suddenly dogs started barking in a faraway corner of the village; the barking seemed to come from distant worlds. Now it was clear: there, in the corner of the village, amid all the barking, something really was afoot—a commotion of one sort or another could be heard, and it was heading toward the house from that direction. All this anxiety was mixed with calming voices—voices one might hear after a fire had been put out. The voices were getting closer and closer. Suddenly, the second brother woke up, his body jerking in the direction of the voices.

Only for the doctor, as a man who wanted to remain uninvolved, it was better not to get mixed up in any disturbances and not to hear the voices. The doctor cut the last string of consciousness that connected him to the surrounding hubbub, let his head drop onto his chest, and allowed the remaining quarter of himself that was still awake to fall asleep.

Before long, he was dreaming of voices and people:

"Right near the village . . ."

"How do you like that? . . ."

"*Merzavtsy* . . . Bastards . . ."

"Hooligans . . ."

✦

Yuzi Spivak bent over the lamp burning on the covered table. He was a short, swarthy man with eyes black like inkwells and an even darker moustache. It seemed that he was examining a splinter under his nail. Having only recently recovered from typhus, he was still wearing his thick, black flannel shirt, which made him look like a tailor's apprentice: someone who had been hired to help with the sewing but who didn't feel that this position required him to speak—or smile.

Yuzi Spivak was the SR sent on the most difficult missions by Sofia Pokrovskaya and her disciples. Every week he would steal across the border: it was with his help that the group kept up the connection with the SRs on "the other side." He would shuttle news there, and carry instructions and "literature" back. Yuzi was stubborn—as stiff-necked as you could be. Like two peas in a pod, he and his brother Muli looked very much alike. Muli was the young pharmacist in Golikhovke's newly nationalized pharmacy.

Sofia Pokrovskaya and the Pokras brothers stood at the table next to Yuzi. Still dozing, the doctor could sense that all of them had run into the house from outside—but, perhaps, he was mistaken, given that he had just barely opened his eyes. His ears rang with their voices—joyous voices celebrating a victory over their enemies.

"*Merzavtsy* . . . Bastards . . ."

"Hooligans . . ."

"How many of them were there?"

"Three . . . On horseback."

"Just three—there wasn't a fourth one. But it seemed like there might be a fourth one—a shadow of an oak growing in the copse."

"The moon was out behind the woods."

"And you could see everything from behind the fence."

"And the dogs kept barking and barking."

A sobering shiver traveled up the doctor's spine—and everything was immediately clear and plain as day. The three riders were three visitors from Kamino-Balke—the sailor, the agent, and the investigator—who had managed to get very close to Yanovo that night. Never before had they dared to get so close: apparently, because their new boss had sent them this time. Sofia and Yuzi had looked from behind the fence of the last peasant yard near the edge of town, where a wagon was being readied for Yuzi Spivak's nighttime ride across the border. They watched as the three horsemen circled the field bathed in moonlight.

And the dogs barked and barked . . .

The doctor, regretful, wondered why on earth today of all days he—a man who didn't want to get involved—ended up coming to Yanovo.

As he got up and put on his overcoat, getting ready to set out on his return journey, Sofia Pokrvoskaya glanced in his direction. She regarded him with empathy, as if he were her old father who had come for a visit at the wrong time. She asked him to wait—and then continued getting Yuzi Spivak ready for the road. Standing beside the lamp, she licked and sealed a large envelope and a package.

A wagon rolled into the courtyard. The clanking of its wheels on the uneven, frozen road gave the impression that the wagon had something to fear, even though it didn't want to be afraid. The doctor, too, felt that he had something to fear, even though he didn't want to be afraid.

The doctor watched Spivak getting dressed. It was a strange sight: Yuzi was taking his time slipping on a simple peasant coat. He lazily thrust his arms into the sleeves. He seemed to have had enough of this and had no particular desire to travel this time.

Everyone went into the courtyard. Yuzi got into the wagon. Sofia Pokrovskaya was walking around it, her belly protruding like a
pregnant woman's. Both Pokras brothers and the peasant tasked
with driving the wagon stood there, when suddenly someone asked:

"Wait, where is the doctor?"

"He should get into the wagon, too."

"Yuzi will drop him off at Golikhovke . . ."

The mere suggestion scared the doctor: he was paralyzed just
thinking about it . . . But to convince himself once and for all that
he was truly not involved, he climbed into the wagon. In the doctor's mind, the biggest proof that he didn't know Yuzi or anything
about Yuzi's plans was the fact that he was riding in the same wagon
with him. In other words, he wasn't someone who knew others but
one whom everyone else around here certainly knew—and because
people knew who he was, whenever he'd be seen walking on foot,
an offer of a ride would inevitably follow. The only problem was: all
this sounded too logical to be believable . . .

As the shaking wagon began to move, the doctor felt as if he
was the center of attention and that the short Yuzi Spivak, who was
probably going to get himself killed at the border later that night,
was no more than his sidekick. The tip of his nose smiled again, as
if it had just told a joke—and the punch line of the joke had something to do with the fact that listening to logical explanations was
not something usually done at Kamino-Balke . . .

"That's Kamino-Balke for you . . . One of its distinguishing
traits . . ."

The doctor kept thinking to himself:

"Just imagine: if the three riders from Kamino-Balke were to appear now, completely out of nowhere, in the moonlight behind the
woods . . . The first thing they would do is open fire, eh? Go explain
to them afterward that shooting wasn't a logical thing to do! A rotten story, no other way of putting it . . . As soon as you stick your
nose outside, you get mixed up in all kinds of stories . . . It would
have been better to stay home . . ."

The doctor was suddenly filled with yearning for his house at the
edge of town behind the church—as if for a beloved whom he had
abandoned for no reason at all, and hadn't treasured until that mo-

ment. Late in the evening, after Yuzi Spivak dropped him off, he paused for a moment before approaching his house and considered it lovingly. At first glance, it was a rickety house with peeling plaster, not much different from all the other houses. If trouble came, the fire would envelop the entire region, including this house with its crooked fence, its gate still standing . . .

The doctor quietly went inside. From then on he almost completely stopped venturing out.

✦

Several days later Sofia Pokrovskaya arrived at the doctor's. She was out of breath, as if she had run from a big fire on the other side of faraway empty fields. It was early in the morning, and the doctor was still in bed.

Her hands trembling, she quickly removed her package from under the doctor's bed. Wrapping it in a colorful shawl, she smoothed it down with her hands while tying it into a bundle, so that it would look like laundry. At the same time, she rapidly issued a stream of curses at Kamino-Balke's new boss:

"Are they really saying he's a magnate? An owner of coal mines? They also used to say: a former typesetter or a machinist at a printing press. 'A dangerous communist,' even! And now they're saying: a simple coal miner. All that was said before was pure rumor—probably an intentional rumor, too, just to confuse everyone. But here's the real problem: at the border, a couple of days ago, he arrested a clockmaker carrying a bunch of fake passports, and the clockmaker spilled the beans—he told him absolutely everything. Once he smuggled passports for us, too—and earlier this evening Filipov arrested Yuzi Spivak at the border . . . He had him arrested when Yuzi was trying to cross. This time the leaflets Yuzi was carrying were well hidden—why would they hold him if they hadn't found anything?"

She stormed out of the doctor's house. She was on her way to Kamino-Balke, to pour out her wrath on the new boss and get Yuzi released: that day, people saw her in the market, getting into a wagon and riding off in that direction. Muli—Yuzi Spivak's younger brother, in a white lab coat and visibly shocked—stood on the steps of the pharmacy (recently nationalized), his body turned toward the market, as if he had forgotten to say something to Sofia Pokrovskaya before she left.

In the evening, people found out: Sofia Pokrovskaya was in jail. The new boss told her that the investigation into Yuzi's case would continue, and if he were found guilty, the guilt would fall on everyone who had interceded on his behalf.

Several days later Sofia Pokrovskaya was released from Kamino-Balke. Back home in Yanovo, she lay sick in bed.

Yuzi Spivak, however, was still in jail, locked up, and no one was allowed in to see him. Yuzi's brother Muli received a note from him—a short note consisting of four words. No one understood it.

Several times a day, the dentist Galaganer would barge into Muli's pharmacy and, blinking nervously after every angry word, would say:

"Who is he referring to as 'honest' in the note, eh? . . . Who? Can you tell me, eh? . . ."

Yuzi's note was forwarded to Sofia Pokrovskaya, sick in bed in Yanovo. Sofia, in turn, sent it on to the dentist Galaganer, with a comment:

"This is pure horror!"

It was impossible to discern exactly what she meant: whether she was referring only to Yuzi's situation or to the situation Yuzi addressed in his note.

That evening everyone streamed to Yokhelzon's back door. An undercover agent, he had traveled to Kamino-Balke early that same morning and had just returned. Yokhelzon's wife, who used to make women's hats, wrapped herself in a silk Turkish shawl and stood guard, not letting anybody in. Nevertheless, everybody eventually found out what had happened to Yokhelzon at Kamino-Balke earlier that day.

Although he was in pain, the new boss had to get up from bed to sign Yokhelzon's permit to cross the border. This happened when people were beginning to turn the lights on in the office. Filipov said to Yokhelzon:

"You, brother, are a suspect now. They say that besides smuggling out communist literature, you also bring back contraband. Living large, aren't you? What do you say, brother?"

The visitors stood in a circle at Yokhelzon's back door, and everyone said what had now become clear:

"It's him, the new boss, who is the one wandering around at night near Kamino-Balke."

"He is as big as a giant."

"He wears a long peasant coat and a worn-out sheepskin hat."

"They say he's clean-shaven."

"No, his face is very prickly."

"When he rides out of Kamino-Balke, the sailor, the agent, and the investigator always follow him."

"They say: 'Everyone at Kamino-Balke wishes him dead.'"

"They also say: 'He is deathly ill. Spends his days in bed. He's a goner.'"

5

For two nights in a row the new boss, on his own, guarded the roads to the left of Kamino-Balke. On the second night he stopped all six wagons that had set out from Golikhovke. Everyone was arrested.

Later they realized what had happened:

He had caught them unexpectedly in the forest close to the border. It happened late at night, just as the tired horses, sensing that that they had come to the end of the forest, were starting to whinny with relief and joy, as if they had received the good news that they were about to arrive at the other side.

He fired off a couple of shots, making the sign of the cross with his bullets. At the same time he shouted a few unclear words. To everyone waiting in the wagons it was terrifyingly, instantly clear that this was "him"—the new boss.

After the arrests Golikhovke froze, like the wintry distances padded in white that stretched all the way to the border.

The houses were buried deeper in the snow. Like wrestlers in the ring too exhausted to throw their opponents, they remained hunched over in their corners.

All this took place early in the morning after the second night.

From early morning on the raging frost hammered out new strength.

From the height of the rust-colored sky, the weak sunrise flashed a zigzag of golden light along the road downhill to Golikhovke.

The windows of the houses looked out blindly. The chimneys on the rooftops forgot how to release smoke.

Every now and then the clattering of wooden clogs could be heard in the frosty fog. This was the sound the wives of the arrested coachmen made running to each other's back doors. All they had planned earlier was lost in the fog.

The woman rooming at Shmuel Voltsis's slowly opened the window and stuck out her freshly combed and smoothed head.

It was quiet in the frosty fog. No one complained. Something hardened, severe could be felt in the speech and movement of the coachmen's wives, as if they had sent their husbands off to war.

Some of these women running to each other's houses were wives whose husbands had not been arrested and were still at home. Even Shmuel Voltsis's tall, thin wife was there—chin-wagging along with everyone else.

"Shmuel!" she would yell. "Wait a minute, Shmuel!"

In her short, calico housecoat she dashed out into the cold, and ran with her hands folded across her chest, as if bombs were falling in the town. She caught a few words from one of the coachmen's wives who was running back and forth from one back door to another. Her voice—a voice that could wake the dead—raked the air. The woman watching from the house remained motionless the whole time. She tried listening closely to the voices outside, but it didn't help: she couldn't understand a word of Yiddish. She scolded her child to keep quiet, but it didn't help.

Only a few separate words hurled themselves through the air: "Shmuel, just listen!"

Shmuel Voltsis planted himself across from his wife, head sunk into his shoulders, teeth clenched, and shook both fists at her:

"You cow! . . . What are you sh-sh-sh-rieking about?"

In spite of the misfortune that had befallen the town, he wasn't in a talking mood. He stayed in his house and cleaned the ash from the stove. This was his regular habit: whenever the world was in upheaval, he set himself some demanding task in the house.

He entered the room where the unfamiliar woman was staying. He didn't give her a single glance. He kneeled down, eyes squeezed almost shut, face set to look like someone who had a job to finish, and began peering into the nooks and crannies of the stove and scraping out the cold ashes into a bucket.

His lodger asked, "Did anyone try bribing him?"

Shmuel Voltsis didn't take notice of her.

He said abruptly, "Bribing who?"

"The new boss."

Shmuel Voltsis remained cold, like the ash he was scraping into the bucket. He answered just to get out of dealing with her. "So people know who he is?"

The woman didn't give in. "What's the plan?"

Shmuel Voltsis was fed up. He took hold of both buckets full of ashes and went outside to empty them. He trudged over to a small huddle of people standing next to the coachmen's wives, and heard what they were saying:

"They arrested women also, women from the six wagons; they're at Kamino-Balke."

"Rich people, too. From far away."

"And also Aaron Lemberger from the big tannery."

Shmuel Voltsis felt he now knew why he had kept silent the whole morning and why he was in such a foul mood.

He butted into the conversation, saying, "How idiotic can you get? You cows . . . Aaron Lemberger should . . . The rich should take care of their own business. It's nothing to them. They have money."

Suddenly someone from across the way ran up and interrupted the conversation with a nasal twang. "They're here in Golikhovke—straight from Kamino-Balke."

Then the signal, "Inside, quick!"

Shmuel Voltsis later remembered that as he was running back home, he had sneezed—a sign that the approaching danger would spare him. He entered the front hall, quickly bolted the door, and listened carefully: it was quiet. Quiet as if creation was about to start all over again.

Shmuel Voltsis bent down, his eye at the hole where the bolt was, and had a good look: across the way two visitors from Kamino-Balke appeared on the newly deserted street, the sailor Igumenko and the homeless shiksa Marfusha, who cleaned the offices. Both were chewing sunflower seeds. Their mouths spit out the shells and their eyes looked very earnest and agitated, especially Igumenko's—like the eyes of a clever deaf man that have too much to say.

Suddenly, Shmuel Voltsis's tall wife sprang up next to him in the dark entryway.

She asked, "Who is that? Huh? . . . Shmuel?"

Shmuel Voltsis kept his eyes peeled on Igumenko through the hole in the door.

"That's him, the guy from Kamino-Balke."

"Who?"

"The one . . . In a word, when they have to shoot someone, he's the one to do the job, they say, and the only one."

"What does he want? Eh, Shmuel?"

"C-c-c-cow . . . that's what I'm trying to see!"

Later everyone found out:

Marfusha had come to Dr. Babitsky for treatment. She had a note with her from Kamino-Balke, which read: "Examine Citizen Marfusha Yantshuk and treat her eye problem. Issued by Kamino-Balke, Special Section. Signed: Filipov."

✦

Marfusha entered Dr. Babitsky's house without a word and handed him the note without a word. Her glassy eyes looked up at the ceiling and blinked, as if she were blind. Her fleshy face was impassive, hardened by cold and wind, and was covered with bright red flecks.

The doctor allowed himself to linger awhile in the kitchen, and very lazily began to soap and scrub his hands. He always made a face when he examined a patient, and this time was no different. At such moments he would pronounce as if for the first time:

"Feh! How repulsive . . . It's disgusting what you have to do as a doctor."

Finally he told the girl to sit down and started to examine her eyes. But Marfusha's eyes were glassy and refused to let anyone near them.

The doctor wanted to find out whether Marfusha had heard what she had been told, whether she knew whom she worked for, and whether she had any understanding of what was going on at Kamino-Balke.

He asked, "Well, what about Filipov? . . . The new boss, that is— has he recovered?"

Marfusha didn't seem to be paying attention.

The doctor pressed his thumb harder on her eyelid.

"Filipov," he repeated. "I heard he's still sick . . . So, is he?"

It was as if the girl hadn't heard him and hadn't felt the pain of the doctor's thumb pressing on her. On her neck, under the skin, a bone moved, as if her throat were constricted.

"*Serchaiut,*" she said in Russian, "they're angry." The words came out of her mouth suddenly, with a sigh.

The doctor didn't understand.

"I mean, is he sick, really? I heard he doesn't sleep at night. Is that right?"

Something stiffened in the girl, her glassy eyes still fixed on the ceiling.

"*Stonet noch'iu, stonet.* He groans and groans at night."

Once again, the doctor didn't understand.

"*Tak, tak.* Uh-huh," he said to himself.

He squinted at her and considered her again. "She's not too bright . . . That's clear."

Then he started washing his hands again, and the lively black eyes in his yellow pumpkin face watched the woman snatch the prescription from the table, hurriedly tie the black shawl around her head, and rush off, as if she had accomplished what she was supposed to at the doctor's house.

Her note remained on the table: "Examine Citizen Marfusha Yantshuk and treat her eye problem. Issued by Kamino-Balke, Special Section. Signed: Filipov."

In order to remove all traces of Kamino-Balke, the doctor gingerly picked up the note, using only two fingers to avoid any contact that wasn't absolutely necessary. Looking around, he searched for the right place to put it and threw it into the stove.

But traces remained anyway.

The stillness in the doctor's house was different, it was a stillness that remembered the sounds left behind; it remembered: "*Stonet noch'iu, stonet.* He groans and groans at night."

In order to banish these lingering words from the stillness, the doctor turned his thoughts to the shiksa. She was not quite right in the head, a little slow, and Filipov, the new sickly boss—was an executioner, obviously, a true executioner: he didn't seek medical help for himself, and instead sent this girl to the doctor for treatment. This was a person who was his own worst enemy, how would he treat people who fell into his clutches?

And just at this moment, the doctor's uneasiness returned with renewed force. It came from outside, from Shmuel Voltsis's house at the bottom of the hill, where the blonde and her child were hiding.

The doctor thought:

What had that woman gotten herself into? What had she entangled him in? What did she want with him and that letter? He was supposed to bring her to Filipov, that's what she wanted . . . as if that was no big deal . . .

✦

In the afternoon, Yokhelzon the undercover agent went for a walk.

His young, beautiful wife remained at home. She would sit there for weeks, as if after a drinking bout—she was gypsy dark with big gold hoops in her ears, with a pair of eyes that always looked exhausted, worn out from her own beauty.

She would wrap herself in the silk Turkish shawls that Yokhelzon had brought from the other side of the border, too indolent to speak.

People said:

In Odessa she had been a milliner; Yokhelzon had taken her straight from the shop.

Voices from both sides of the street chased Yokhelzon down.

"Yokhelzon!"

"Please."

"Just a minute, Yokhelzon!"

Yokhelzon walked quickly.

The snow squeaked merrily under his brushed, well-wrought boots, as if under the boots of a bridegroom serving somewhere in the army, who had leave to come visit his bride.

A brand-new military uniform—that seemed to have come straight from the tailor—tightly encased his small figure. His eyes (which inspected everything, people said) had already taken in the horror of death—they winked joyfully, so that the horror would not show afterward.

His cheeks were red as if fresh from the barber's blade; they were powdered like a woman's.

He glanced at two women who were approaching him from both sides of the street—these were women whose husbands had been arrested.

The blonde noticed all this through the window of Shmuel Voltsis's house. She quickly shoved her child at Shmuel Voltsis's wife—into her lap—and ran outside.

When she got there, the two women were still standing next to Yokhelzon; they were buttering him up and flirting with him. They smiled at him, and he smiled at them. The women blocked his path and, pretending they were all old friends, mocked him:

"Listen, Yokhelzon, when will the devil take you? When will you fear God?"

"Of course, it depends only on you, Yokhelzon."

"You're on friendly terms with everyone at Kamino-Balke."

"You should get a boil as big as all the help you're not giving me."

Yokhelzon kept on smiling. He sized up the stranger from head to toe—the blonde, who was approaching him from the direction of Shmuel Voltsis's house.

"Well now, what about you?" he asked her. "What might you want?"

He looked surprised, like a man who had not known until now that he had another young, beautiful bride in town.

✦

His acquaintance with the blonde from Voltsis's house began at that instant—Yokhelzon set off on a stroll with her.

After that he visited her in her room. She wanted to know about the hidden path that bypassed Kamino-Balke and led to the border. Somebody from Kamino-Balke could be guarding this path. But if you gave them a sign that Yokhelzon had sent you, they let you pass.

Yokhelzon smiled and said, "No, not now, you have to wait a bit." And he laughed at himself. He was so easygoing that anyone could get anything out of him.

He saw the two big cases in the woman's room.

"Uh oh," he said. "A capitalist! I know, all you capitalists want to run away from us."

By the time Shmuel Voltsis's wife stopped sweeping the house and peeped into the room through the crack in the door, they were sitting down. Both of them were smoking; they would look each other in the eye, take each other's hand, let their gaze sink and then look up again.

Yokhelzon was telling the blonde that he was among the very first communists, and that therefore no one frightened him. On the contrary. Everyone was afraid of him . . .

"Well, yes," the woman tossed her head back, tracing the arc of smoke from her cigarette, "and me too, I'm a communist like you and everyone. That is, not officially. Why shouldn't I be? People should be happy. Once I even worked for them, look: my documents say I was a secretary . . ."

And she told him there was some unpleasantness having to do with her position; they were arrested, she and one of her girlfriends, their boss also . . . a "mama's boy," with red cheeks and a beaver collar, a Jew. Because of him, they released everyone—this is how "protection" worked. She fled from her boss . . . afterward she made the trip here, to the border . . . her husband was there.

Yokhelzon asked, "Where?"

"Over there," the blonde answered, "on the other side."

And she suddenly gave an abrupt wave of her hand with the cigarette in the direction of the border. Her gesture was so quick that you couldn't tell whether the husband on the other side really existed.

And after that there was no more conversation . . .

Shmuel Voltsis's wife couldn't keep standing there looking through the crack in the door, because a misfortune was taking place there—for Yokhelzon's wife.

✦

In the evening there was a gathering in Shmuel Voltsis's kitchen around the little lamp; all talk was of the blonde:

"Does anyone know who she is?"

"In a word, in those two cases of hers, she's carrying all her 'good deeds.'"

Shmuel Voltsis was there in the kitchen with his wife and also a rather grimy, drowsy young man, an accountant at the same sawmill where Shmuel Voltsis had recently been sacrificing his health for nothing.

Shmuel Voltsis complained, "Who, me? Do you take me for a fool? I should keep working at a sawmill? I should remain a pauper while everyone else gets to rake in the money from travelers passing through town?"

One of his neighbors was sitting there, too—a musician, an anxious man with a yellowish beard, closely trimmed, with blue-tinted glasses and a smell of smoked fish, although there was no smoked fish to be had since before the war.

He talked about the bad times. "The worst thing is," he said, "that they—the Bolsheviks—summon you to their holidays to make you play their marches . . . just like that . . . and do you think they pay? I'd throw their money right back at their faces, anyway."

He talked about the six wagons that the new boss had stopped on his own, about this Jewish Red Army soldier, who turned up in one of these wagons, how Filipov came to see the soldier in his jail cell and called him by name. Filipov asked, "How did this happen to you?" He gave him some paper and said, "Here, write everything down."

Suddenly the conversation was interrupted.

The doctor in his heavy, old coat snuck in through the back door.

He crept along the side with rapid little steps, without looking at anyone. His face was all irritation:

"I've already done my time . . . twelve years in Siberia . . . and I'm still a coward, eh? It's a disgrace . . ."

He scowled as he entered the woman's room. He hated asking anyone for the smallest favor, even the favor of being left alone. The woman looked at him in shock. Her eyes were innocent, as kosher as two crucifixes.

Then she smiled at him, but only with her eyebrows. Her powdered nose began to flirt with the doctor. It was charming. It charmed the air they breathed. And soon after that, concerned about which of the chairs in the room would fit him most comfortably, she considered the size of the doctor's behind.

Sitting down across from him, she quickly lit a cigarette. Her eyelids smiled.

"In any case," she said, "I shouldn't come see you any more. The dreadful new boss at Kamino-Balke shouldn't bother you. I've dealt with people far more terrible than he, and as for your advice to return home, many thanks to you, doctor, thank you very much. I'm not leaving here, not under any circumstances. Because a journey of a mere four or five hours gets you to a place where the revolution is over, do you understand, doctor? There, on the other side, it snows every morning, just like here. Only it's a different kind of snow, whiter and freer, a snow from the other side of the revolution. By the time I return here from the other side, spring will be in full bloom there. Somewhere in a city at the seashore music will be playing—just music, without speeches. I'll meet a poor man there and give him alms. Here, on this side, as I was leaving, I gave a poor woman some money, but she threw it back at me. She cursed me. There are two types of beggars, doctor. There are mean, unworthy beggars: give one of them alms, and he'll curse you—so that you end up just like him. And then there are pious, kind beggars, who bless you. They were created so that you would have joy when you give them charity. Yes, yes, doctor, don't laugh . . . They are the same holy ones who were with Jesus."

The doctor was sitting across from the woman, hunched up and seemingly asleep, because it was exactly the hour of the evening when he would lie down fully clothed and sleep until late. Finally, he got up.

He forgot to say goodbye on his way out—just as he always forgot such pleasantries when he was called to see a patient. He remembered this only in the dark entryway where Shmuel Voltsis had led him with a burning lamp in his hands. He kept him hidden there for a while. Shmuel Voltsis asked him again about the woman.

This time Shmuel Voltsis returned to his wife with an answer. What the doctor said about the woman was: "Filth . . . filth . . ."

6

The area next to the border: a cavernous hole.

Once busy roads had rushed to it, crisscrossing at that spot. Now the snow raged there as if to lay waste and destroy everything around.

A few days had passed since Filipov, on his own, stopped the wagons and arrested everyone—since then the wind had not ceased blowing.

In the middle of a field lay traces of straw that the wind had buried under snow. The straw had fallen from bundles that someone had gathered and lay in bits on the ground. It was quiet—the kind of quiet that comes after a protracted uproar.

The residents of Golikhovke were shoveling the snow.

The words they exchanged hung suspended in the air:

"What's that?"

"They are not going, right? What I mean is . . ."

"They are going."

"Not."

"Are."

The houses in Golikhovke were full to bursting with smugglers trying to escape misfortune. The houses were swollen like the piles of snow in front of their windows. Wanting to seem extremely respectable, the smugglers looked extremely suspicious.

They came in the middle of the night but did not go any further. Where they came from and why was a secret—they all had their own secrets.

Golikhovke's two toughest coachmen—Bunem the Red and Hatskel Shpak—went from one back door to another. They looked like sleepy fiddlers after a night of performing at a wedding—and took their advance payments almost unwillingly.

Smiling lazily, like people who know something before anyone else does, they boasted that if both of them had driven that other time—the night that everyone in the six wagons was arrested—they would have known what to do with the new boss:

"It would have been easy. One or two whacks on the head with an ax. That would have been it. We'd be rid of him."

Everyone eyed Bunem and Hatskel with suspicion. No one believed them, and everybody feared them. Still, the smugglers paid up—Golikhovke's landlords themselves had summoned these two to take money from their lodgers. At the conclusion of each visit, the landlords would see Hatskel and Bunem out to get their share of the spoils.

The smugglers—looking very proper yet very suspicious—seethed with the resentment befitting highly respectable people. They whispered to one another:

"They're fleecing us . . . it's highway robbery."

"And look who's doing it."

"Jews!?"

"Jews fleecing Jews!"

✦

And then it was daytime—a day that was as deceptive as Bunem the Red and Hatskel Shpak—it seemed as dark as night. A few snowflakes fluttered in the air, wavering to the left and to the right, as if they were going to stop. But then they suddenly started up again, all at once, tiny snowflakes falling very quickly.

Once again a storm lashed Kamino-Balke and its gloomy environs. A bedraggled horse, fitted with a saddle, and with a long, mangy tail, a bent, tired head, and eyes yearning to close in sleep—emerged from the storm and drew closer and closer to Golikhovke.

A huge, mighty figure of a man was riding the nag. He sat tall in the saddle; everything he did was measured and coldblooded, like the storm. He could be recognized only by the bandage on his neck, his peasant coat, and sheepskin hat pulled over his ears.

Slowly, as if to spite the swiftly falling snow that stung him and his horse, the great giant of a man rode up to what had formerly been a shop. It had become a police station. The man tried out his voice—it was sour, hoarse, and mean.

A policeman ran out of the station, frightened out of his wits. He stopped abruptly, like a soldier obeying a command, and then disappeared quickly downhill.

All the streets had been emptied by the time the policeman arrived in town with his order.

This is what happened:

The fear emanating from the towering figure arrived in town a few seconds before the policeman did. All the inhabitants knew:

"Filipov is in town."

"He rode in on his horse—himself."

"He wants to discuss something."

"He is waiting for us at the police station."

"He sent for all the coachmen."

"And the innkeepers, too."

"Why only the innkeepers?"

Around the back of the houses there were quarrels between coachmen and their wives, each ranting and raving:

"Drag out the rabbi too. It's clear he keeps guests. There are lodgers at his house, too."

"Everyone has to go with us. Everyone. Around here every house has paying guests."

The sky darkened.

Outside the empty shop that had become a police station, coachmen's sheepskin jackets and the fine, sensitive faces of ordinary Jews huddled together. Frizzy beards, crooked faces, bent shoulders, and backs twisted from shrewdness—these were the homeowners. It was hard for them to straighten out, just as it was difficult to corral lazy horses unused to enclosure. Their unhappy wives were there, too.

They felt like men with gray beards who had to present themselves for military service again in old age.

They looked at the station door in anguish.

The boss, however, did not come out.

✦

Filipov sat at a little crooked table in his coat and sheepskin hat, his back to the door, and faced the window. He kept on frowning.

Slowly, grimacing in pain, he unwrapped the bandage from his neck and throat.

He said to the policeman irritably, "Let them in one by one."

The policeman walked toward the door to let them in, but Filipov didn't look in his direction.

Instead he picked up a small mirror from the policeman's desk and, looking into its scratched surface, gingerly poked at the hard, swollen bumps on his neck.

Scowling at the mirror, without even turning around, he asked the first coachman who came in—it was Bunem the Red—how old he was.

Bunem's bloodshot eyes looked at his own clumsy, bent coachman's fingers splayed out in a ragged row, as if he were consulting them: suddenly he was afraid of saying how old he was.

"Thirty . . . eight," he said. He wondered at the words coming out of his mouth so hesitantly and felt that he would soon regret speaking.

"Um, me too, give or take," said Filipov.

Bunem felt suddenly that the boss didn't have anything on him. The boss was the same age.

Bunem felt more confident. But suddenly the boss turned his head toward him. His eyes flooded with yellow.

"If you keep on taking people to the border," he said slowly in a clipped tone, "I'll shoot you."

He turned to face Bunem and had a good look at him:

"I swear . . . now go, you can go."

And he resumed looking at himself in the mirror and poking his swollen neck.

"*Vot ono, vot ono* . . . that's it," he exhaled hoarsely, "*pomirat' pora* . . . I'm finished."

By the time Hatskel Shpak was let into the former shop, Filipov had begun to rewind the compress around his neck and tie it. He didn't bother to look at Hatskel.

"The revolution," he said, "is a sack. We keep on patching it up, but you here at the border are like mice, nibbling away. You are eating out a hole at the edge of the sack and everything's going to spill out . . . What do you think—that we're joking with you?"

Then he got up, pulled his hat down over his ears, and went outside. Suddenly he seemed young and vigorous.

He didn't take notice of anyone, as if he hadn't been the one to order all these people to line up and wait for him. He quickly mounted his horse, as if he were about to race back to Kamino-Balke without pausing to catch his breath.

But before he left, he unexpectedly turned to the people in front of him and began addressing them.

At that moment an old innkeeper, who was hiding behind the coachmen's shoulders, let out a groan. He had weak, runny eyes, sallow skin, was hard of hearing, and didn't understand much. He grabbed someone's sleeve and started asking, "What's he saying, huh?"

The old man got his answer: "He says he has the authority."

The old man scowled. "What is that, then?"

"From the revolution . . . he says he has the authority from the revolution to reduce everyone standing here to ashes, and all of Golikhovke, too."

"For what? Huh?"

"Because people are smuggling every damn thing across the border."

The old man's runny eyes kept on squinting.

"What's he saying now?"

"He's saying not to get in the revolution's way. He wants us to come up with a more respectable livelihood. He says we should tell all the strangers in town to get out of here and go back home."

And all the people waiting outside the station went home as if they had come from a funeral.

Quickly and silently they started to disperse among the first houses that lined the road toward the bottom of the hill. They shut the doors behind them with finality, as if for forever, as if they would never leave again.

At Shmuel Voltsis's, people warmed themselves at the stove and talked about the blonde living there with her child.

"Well? Why didn't she go to him while he was at the station? What kept her? Why didn't she go over there so he would fall in love with her?"

All the streets were empty, even though there was a good hour left until dark.

Only the Pokras brothers in their gray military overcoats were riled up, and they raced from Galaganer the dentist to Yuzi's brother at the pharmacy that had been nationalized. At first they walked slowly, then they sped up, first alone, then with Galaganer. They were very preoccupied, as if they were preparing for something on the way, and each one hurried the other.

People looked at them from their houses as they went by— with derisive sympathy, almost with pity. It appeared that they were offended that Filipov hadn't given them as much as a thought, that he had forgotten to order them to show up with everybody else.

Later the inhabitants of Golikhovke found out:

"Filipov had caught a cold."

"That very night."

"He had taken to his bed."

✦

A few days later the wagon from Kamino-Balke's Special Section rushed to Golikhovke. People feared this wagon like a hearse. Sometime in the afternoon, it suddenly sprang down from the mountain. It spread fear along the entire length of the market as it flew by. It quickly turned left toward the blind alley behind the Catholic church and then came to rest at Dr. Babitsky's desolate house, right outside the window. It waited there for a long time.

The two big horses, their coats flecked with white, looked tired out. They had the eyes of strangers, eyes that didn't come from Golikhovke. Each eye said, "A curse on these damned smugglers and their contraband."

Aside from the wagon driver—a grimy soldier with a rifle on his back—there was also the sailor Igumenko from Kamino-Balke. Igumenko, who was short, stood there leaning against the covered wagon. He hunched his broad shoulders and didn't show the slightest interest in Dr. Babitsky, for whose sake the wagon had been sent. He sucked on his short pipe sullenly and didn't look anywhere.

"Taking aim," he directed a few disjointed words at the soldier who was sitting in the wagon right behind his shoulders, "you have to take aim with certainty. You're right that it depends on the rifle: some rifles require you to take aim a half a finger higher, others, a half a finger lower. That's it, you idiot. Andreyev is a milksop; he's never tried. Everything that he told you is crap and nothing else."

Igumenko was waiting patiently with downcast eyes; from across the way the doctor's deaf-mute ward was staring at him with an open mouth. He was standing next to the door, freezing, as if he were a dirty piece of the cold, gloomy street, and he peered at Igumenko with terrified, wide-open eyes.

The deaf-mute kept running into the house and pulling on the doctor's sleeve. He would bend over, bite his lower lip very hard with his front teeth, so that the nostrils of his flat nose flared. His eyes winked at the doctor, telling him about the sailor outside; his feet gave a spring, and with his finger, he showed how you slit someone's throat.

With a bitter expression on his face the doctor asked him to stop. He indicated with his hand, "I know already . . . I know . . . Get out."

His old cheeks quivered in agitation, like a cow chewing its cud.

His head shook.

His long hair had never gotten in the way as much as now; it blocked his ears.

He stuck his face through the window a few times to try to find out who in Kamino-Balke was sick. They told him coldly, "The boss . . . Filipov."

"Is he sick in bed?"

"Yes, sick in bed."

Only a minute later the doctor would forget.

Either because he was distracted or because he was frightened, he didn't show any sign of finishing lunch and thrust his head out one more time.

"Who ordered you to come here . . . to get me, that is? Who said to bring me?"

"Comrade Sasha."

The doctor's eyes sparkled with curiosity. Then it was true what everyone was saying yesterday. Comrade Sasha was back at Kamino-

Balke. She was the one who got the old boss fired for negligence. She was devoted to Filipov—she looked after his health.

And Filipov himself was in bed, that's what people were saying—he was in bed suffering from great pain, and wouldn't let anybody in.

It seemed to the doctor that Filipov was sick with a strange illness that nobody had ever heard of. This was an illness that could infect only a man like Filipov. When he ordered someone's death, when he gave the command, "Shoot!"—there was no wisdom that could dissuade him, because it wasn't Filipov who was giving the orders. It was History.

The doctor finally emerged from his house, drowning in his huge sheepskin coat; he had a scarf wrapped around his neck.

Braced by the cold and the wind, he returned to his senses. His nose crinkled as if it was about to utter a little joke: "And who has fallen ill, hmm? . . . The ambassador of History!"

But taking a trip with the two people who had come for him was not overly pleasant. And besides, the deaf-mute was right at his heels.

The deaf-mute had thrown on his coat, which was ripped and too small for him, and pulled his ragged hat over his ears. Scowling, in a deep voice he barked at the doctor, Igumenko, and the wagon driver to wait.

The wagon was just about to go. The doctor was in front, Igumenko and the grimy soldier near the horses, their shoulders to the doctor.

The whip cracked. The deaf-mute, however, had decided not to entrust anyone with his old man. He managed to jump in and ended up sitting near Igumenko with his feet still sticking out of the wagon.

The wagon stopped.

"What's he doing here?" the soldier grunted.

"Get out!" This is what Igumenko's look said to the deaf-mute. He started to wink at the deaf man good-humoredly, encouraging him to get down.

"Tell him to get down," Igumenko's look said to the doctor, "the wagon is overloaded."

The doctor didn't seem to hear him. The deaf-mute didn't stir. The wagon wavered for a minute and was off.

The noisy wheels swallowed Igumenko's gripes. His shoulders shuddered in annoyance, as if to get rid of something stuck to them. The soldier holding the reins cursed.

Unexpectedly, one of them gave the deaf-mute a little push. With a clever shove of a strong elbow, the man was thrown out of the wagon.

The doctor barely managed to note the spot where the deaf man had ended up on all fours.

"Stop! Stop a minute!" he waved both hands, "Hey, hey, stop, stop!"

But no one even looked at him.

The wagon only picked up speed and shook even harder along the bumpy stones of the road. Because no one answered him, the doctor's words echoed strangely, as if he were not a living being, but merely a clump, a bundle, stolen from his house by the men in the wagon, who got away as quickly as possible, spurring the horse on and on.

"Not very nice," he shook his head, "not nice at all."

The two pairs of shoulders right in front of him, however, remained hard and cold. They didn't want anyone else in the wagon. The heads on these shoulders bent toward each other, spewing out words that had nothing to do with the doctor, and the doctor suddenly felt that they considered him a much lower sort of human being than he considered himself. These shoulders—of the men sitting in front of him—considered him their prisoner, and they were like the bars of his cell. They were the strong ones, they had come from *there* . . . from Kamino-Balke, and knew the real reason they were taking him there: maybe someone had slandered or denounced him.

In any case, this was a strange journey, too hurried—like a trip straight to hell.

A few times the doctor asked them to go a little more slowly, so that he wouldn't be shaken so hard, but neither of them even gave him so much as a look. No one heard his words, and the doctor's spirits consequently sank even lower.

Forlorn, he looked around: the wagon was swiftly carrying him along a path in the middle of a field.

There was no trace of any living person.

No one to cry out to.

Even if there had been someone, screaming would have been pointless, even foolish, it would not have helped at all.

All was lost, everything had turned out badly: he was riding in some strange wagon—he was the unwilling passenger of a conveyance that belonged to the revolution.

Without even noticing it himself, the doctor—in his mind—began going over the last forty years of his dissolute life in Golikhovke, searching for the sins for which he would now be punished at Kamino-Balke.

But he couldn't remember anything important, aside from the petty gossip he used to trot out for Sofia Pokrovskaya—in his present state he couldn't manage anything else.

He could not bring order to these forty years of his undisciplined life. They seemed incoherent and vague, like so many unpaid debts that had never been recorded in the ledgers.

Everything that had taken place in his life now seemed to him foul, cold, and frozen, like the world around him. His life was like the dirty snow that lay on the fields, dotted here and there with heaps of trash, like the crows, which flew over them, and the entire cavernous emptiness near the border. This place, this no man's land that was consuming his senseless life, plunged into the dull winter twilight—taking him with it.

Going round in circles in the dusty cracks and ruts of his life made the doctor deeply uneasy, as if he had accompanied his own funeral procession and was considering the impression it made.

He hunched over even more, sinking deeper and deeper into his big sheepskin coat; little by little he let his head fall to his breast, and dozed off.

When he woke up the twilight was closer and darker. From across the way, between the many hills scattered here and there, one higher than the other, the dead spires of Kamino-Balke's abandoned churches emerged—churches from the monastery that had been destroyed.

From a distance the sleepy doctor thought they resembled a toy, made either from cardboard or copper. The cloudy sky cut a deep, rusty gash into a corner of the horizon. It had been a few years since the bells stopped ringing. The walls of the monastery were cracked and dilapidated, like the walls of ruins—and yet everything seemed to be infinite, it seemed that this was no end, but instead, a beginning.

The first fires that had been lit appeared there, ascending high in the sky, and they too were no simple, ordinary fires; they were the cold fires of judgment, fires over which "he"—Filipov, a worker from the mines—presided. They were the fires of some strange, new, harsher world.

7

It was almost completely dark when the wagon carrying the doctor approached the entrance of Kamino-Balke.

Freezing women—allowed in once a week to see their husbands—were standing there preparing for their return trip to Golikhovke, where they would spend the night.

A peephole shaped like a heart was cut into the gate.

Inside the peephole—the wrinkled tip of a nose and the icy lips of a bundled-up soldier emitting steam into the air:

"Who do you have there?"

"The doctor."

"Enter."

The gate opened from inside.

This was toward nighttime, when the cold let up a bit. The wagon drove in.

The first thing that confused the doctor in this whitish twilight hour was the sharp cawing of black crows—blacker than the falling night. A whole flock of crows fluttered about in the air before settling, still in formation, along the rows of naked trees that stood on both sides of a long alley.

The crows were shrieking. They seemed larger and angrier than all other crows, but perhaps it was simply the twilight itself that was to blame—or maybe it was the evening that made them seem this way.

Abandoned buildings peered out from all the dark corners. They were whitewashed, with mournful, rusted crosses on top of old-fashioned, sharp-angled roofs, their cornices and steps looking like crosses, too. And it seemed that these buildings had once been inhabited by monks who crossed themselves.

There was a warm smell that seemed to flow from a kitchen in which sauerkraut had been fermenting for days on end.

The wagon carrying the doctor passed a small observation post topped with a flag and entered a second courtyard, much larger and quieter than the first.

Here, small buildings—all of them the same size—had narrow, abandoned hallways. In the evening darkness, one window was brightly lit from a large, wide-open oven burning hot right in front of it. The smell of freshly baked bread tickled the nose: the doctor's empty stomach hurt, and he was suddenly so overtaken with the desire to eat that everything he saw felt natural and ordinary because of the smell of freshly baked bread.

Several women prisoners stood next to the well on the left, guarded by a Red Army soldier with a weapon in his hands; they did not look familiar. They helped each other wash their hands and faces, scrubbing the sticky dough from under their fingernails. The slow pace of their movements suggested it would take them a long time to get used to life here in Kamino-Balke, a life without profiteering and contraband. Their faces were a deep shade of red—and that, combined with their light clothing, led to the conclusion that it was very warm inside the prison buildings.

Here the doctor climbed out of the wagon and hatched out of his furs.

The women stopped washing for a moment to observe the doctor being taken past them—he was then led to a building of medium height across the way. A red flag hung from its roof.

The women had apparently decided that the doctor had been arrested—he was a "newcomer"—and silence descended on the courtyard.

Climbing the steps to the building, his eyes fixed on the red flag hanging from the roof, the doctor heard one of the women pitying him and another one sighing with strange sympathy for him, as if for one of their own, guilty of profiteering:

"*Oy, vey iz mir, vey!* They open the gates wide only to let people in, not out."

At this point, the doctor realized that he lacked some feeling that would enable him to act superior before these women. Quickly, he understood what this feeling was:

"Mercy . . ."

And now, because he did not wish to admit that he felt mercy for himself, he instead made himself think that it was mercy for those women, for the red flag, for the sick boss for whose sake he had been brought here. As soon as this thought crossed his mind, he felt that even though he usually preferred not to get involved, he was a decent man. Exceedingly decent—and the proof was his mercy . . .

Sensing that the women at the well were still following him with their eyes, the doctor glanced in their direction. He didn't want to part with the feeling that he was an exceedingly decent man:

"For instance, who?" he pondered. "Who would help them here?"

However, he felt his own confusion, the usual twilight sleepiness, and anxiety about everything that had happened that day. He remembered the shove the deaf-mute had gotten from Igumenko's elbow—the elbow of a stubborn man who would never again let anybody take an additional passenger with him. The doctor remembered the place where the deaf-mute had been abandoned in the field, and then answered his own question:

"Help? . . . I certainly wouldn't."

He was now satisfied with the realization that he was nothing but a small man, and coming to terms with his own insignificance released him from the burden of helping anyone else.

✦

It was like an absurd nightmare from which you want to awaken but can't. The doctor paced back and forth along a dark corridor. At its end crooked steps led up to a narrow gallery just below a glazed roof.

The corridor veered to the right and, after a few steps, dropped off below into the darkness. It seemed that the distant, dark stairwell had no terminus: from below, the prisoners began to emerge hurriedly, bringing a drafty dampness with them.

They scattered and walked quickly. As if wearing coarse socks, they trudged ahead, looking happy because of the long, straw-filled sacks on their shoulders—sacks of straw to sleep on.

They kicked up a cloud of dust, as if on purpose, whenever anyone burst into mocking laughter—not all of them believed they were being punished for their transgressions; many had committed these sins only recently. They wanted to stop and look at the doctor, who was being led past them.

"Don't stop! Keep moving!" a voice spurred them on from behind.

But the doctor didn't know who was being given orders: the prisoners carrying the straw mattresses, or him.

Through the large, wide window on the left, the darkness swept in from outside for the last time; from the right, the murmur of speaking mouths could be heard. Enclosed by wooden boards, the entrance to the general holding cell came into view. The cell was filled beyond capacity: it was here that the prisoners were taking their sacks of straw.

A small lamp had just been lit but was immediately covered in soot. Several faces peered out from behind it, looking across the sparse wooden boards nailed together near the entrance. They stopped whispering to each other and turned to the doctor with a look that could kill. Someone's eye looked familiar to the doctor—but, again, the voice pushed on from behind:

"Don't stop! Keep moving!"

And once again the doctor couldn't tell whether the command was directed at him or the prisoners in the corridor.

He exhaled only later, when, after climbing three or four steps, he entered a different room. This room was large and empty: its walls had recently been whitewashed, and the yellowish red color of the freshly painted floor stung his eyes.

There, with a lamp in her hand, Comrade Sasha greeted the doctor. She was tall and masculine. In her white robe, she looked like a dentist or a midwife.

"Come here!" she called out to the doctor with her eyebrows and gave him a warm look as if he were an old acquaintance or a colleague. "Come here, to the corner, doctor."

From up close, she showed him her masculine face brimming with energy.

"Listen," she said as she stood in front of the doctor with a burning lamp in her hand, "I managed to convince him to send for you. I must tell you: he is very stubborn when it comes to seeing doctors. And he didn't want . . ."

She listened at the open door of the adjacent room, from which a calm, dark gray light shone—she listened not just with her ear, but with the entire side of her body:

". . . he didn't want this at all. He is precious to us. You should know—you've probably heard this before—don't ask him for anything. Remember not to."

Once again she looked toward the room.

"Now he seems to be asleep, after two nights of terrible pain . . ."

Suddenly, the sound of a bed squeaking could be heard from the room.

She stood still, biting her lip, eyes lowered in fear. A tired, sour, and sleepy voice could be heard from the other room:

"Who's there, eh? Sasha?"

"It's me, Comrade Filipov . . ."

"And who else?"

Comrade Sasha lowered her burning eyes further:

"It's me and the doctor."

"Huh . . . the doctor?"

A pause.

And again—a screeching noise from the bed, and then a voice that sounded sour and half-asleep:

"The doctor? Well . . . Well, now you've done it . . ."

8

"Tick-tock, tick-tock."

There was a cheap alarm clock in a dark corner of Filipov's room.

Its ticking was like cold drops dripping in the stillness. And the stillness was as hard as stone.

Filipov, the sick man, was lying on his back on a wide bed in the middle of the room.

It seemed that the clock was counting out his last minutes—except that it had been counting for so long that no one knew how long it would continue.

Stepping softly, the doctor entered the room and bashfully stole a look at the patient from under his brow.

"A simple peasant, huh? . . . He really is a simple worker."

Filipov's appearance:

Like some village lout, who had been beaten within an inch of his life and then collapsed, and didn't even give a damn. But if he got up from bed for a final reckoning, everything around him would go up in smoke.

Puzzled, the doctor's expression changed. No longer examining Filipov, he wrinkled his brow.

"So that's him . . . But what is he? That whole story of the former magnate is a lie. Fables get concocted by the dozen about the likes of him."

Filipov dozed off. One arm was lying next to him limply, as if it wasn't his; the other was bent at the elbow and thrown over his head, blocking his eyes and forehead.

His eyes and brow were not revealed, even when Comrade Sasha brought the night table closer to the bed and the lamp shone directly at his face from under its green shade.

Comrade Sasha stepped out quickly on her tiptoes.

The tick-tock of the alarm clock restored the doctor's calm—the calm that came over him whenever he examined a sick peasant. With cold fingertips he felt the pulse on the arm that seemed discarded and limp. The arm seemed to feel nothing. The doctor moved his chair closer, put one end of a stethoscope to his ear and the opposite end on the patient's chest, and listened attentively while he looked at the expression on his face.

"He looks dissatisfied . . . People fear him as they fear an inquisitor, but his heart—is ordinary, like everyone else's."

Very carefully he started to touch Filipov's throat and the swollen bumps under his unshaven, scratchy cheeks. He felt at ease.

"So these are the diseases these people get?"

Suddenly, as if afraid of being bitten, the doctor snatched his hand away and, quivering, placed it back on his knee.

"Sasha!"

With this, Filipov took his arm away from his temples and sent Sasha away on an errand. His big eyes looked sleepily at the doctor, and it seemed that they were burning up with fever.

The alarm clock tick-tocked from its dark corner.

It was a clock like any other—cheap, made of copper—its ticking was like cold drops dripping in the stillness, and the stillness was hard, like stone, like this man, whose face was covered in dissatisfaction and whose heart was ordinary, a heart like everyone else's.

✦

Filipov was sitting up in bed with his back hunched over, legs bent, covered by a quilt—sitting was uncomfortable for him. Head bowed, he dozed off every now and then. While he was falling asleep, a few drowsy words came out of his mouth. They sounded rusty and swallowed their own meaning.

It seemed to the doctor that Filipov meant to say, "You're palpating me, tapping me . . . everyone has tapped me out."

And then, "Nonetheless, you won't manage to tap into the core."

And because these words were not entirely clear, they terrified the doctor no less than the fever in Filipov's sleepy eyes. The doctor was on guard with all his senses; he tensed up. He tried to smile, and he wanted the smile to say, "I'm listening, listening . . . you like to joke, Comrade Filipov."

His fingers resumed their palpation of the soft and hard spots on Filipov's throat and neck.

But he felt as if he were actually examining not only Filipov, but also the entire revolution that was simmering and boiling in all the big cities, and had thrust Filipov up from its depths.

Then Comrade Sasha came back from wherever she was. Her gait was uncertain, and her guilty face even more troubled.

She whispered a few words into Filipov's ear, and he instantly returned to his normal self. "So that's it," he spat out, his voice stubborn and irritable, and he lay back down. "You've gone and done it."

And the doctor's tapping fingers remained hanging in the air, dancing their foolish dance. In order not to feel so uncomfortable and lost, he searched within himself for a witticism: "There's no peace in the world anywhere, hmm, even here between these two, who run Kamino-Balke."

Soon, however, it was obvious that the tension in the room had to do with him, the doctor.

This was the problem: the prisoners in the cells had discovered the doctor was there. In the general holding cell a few inmates claimed to be sick, while one woman was either truly hysterical, or pretended to be, so that the doctor would be brought to her.

Comrade Sasha started to say that none of the prisoners was sick.

Filipov interrupted her: "It's all the same. I said we didn't need any doctor. You brought him, so be so good as to take him to the cells."

And the doctor suddenly forgot both his hidden witticism, and the smile, which he had tried to bring to his face.

Upset, he listened to the last thing Filipov had said.

He looked worriedly to the right and to the left.

When Comrade Sasha, obeying Filipov's order, brought him through the hallway to the prisoners in the cells, he was all in a tizzy and didn't want to go, he didn't want to get involved, he didn't want to listen to the prisoners asking for favors . . . But he had no choice, because he was obliged to do the revolution's bidding, without having agreed to it. Whether he wanted to or not, he had to follow the revolution, and moreover, he would examine the sick in the cells, coldly and indifferently, as coldly as the revolution—with all its Filipovs—examined them. People like Filipov were forced to do its bidding, and so was he, the doctor. It didn't matter that they—the

Filipovs—knew why they were so obligated, and he didn't . . . he didn't want to know any more.

Agitated, he followed Comrade Sasha down the long corridor back to the general holding cell. He was upset as he entered and was greatly surprised to see that it wasn't just three or four sick people who were waiting for him. All the prisoners—tired, tense—were looking at him with a thousand excited eyes. Some were standing around him, others were sitting in groups on their bundles and packages on the floor in the corners of the room; they were all silently asking, "Help us, help!"

And they meant, "You have to do things for us."

Again at the entrance someone's eye fell on the doctor, someone who knew him. Ashamed and sad, this gaze begged the doctor: "I'm a former patient of yours, doctor, don't you recognize me?"

But aside from this one, multitudes of eyes looked at the doctor, pleading—and they all seemed familiar.

Under the weight of these stares the doctor's body swayed as if he were going to fall; lost and uncertain, he started to move toward one spot; his hands seemed to ask: "Where to go? Whom should I approach?"

From deep within himself, someone—a second messenger from the revolution, as it were—mocked his reticence: "Ha! Not getting mixed up, right?"

He was shown where to go: "Come over here. Here."

A quiet woman with young blue eyes was sitting on one of the benches across from the doctor in the holding cell. A warm shawl, wrapped like a cross, covered her full bosom; after her hysterical fit, she was sitting quietly, as if at any moment her name would be called and she would be told that she was free. But perhaps she had been sitting like that the whole time since her arrest—perhaps she had even sat like that for three weeks or more. She looked at the doctor, eyes red from crying, and smiled painfully, "A fine mess we're in!"

Bending his head to her breast with his stethoscope, the distracted doctor strained to remember who she was.

Listening to the woman's heart, the doctor determined it was healthy; there was nothing wrong with her at all. As he straightened up, removing his stethoscope from her chest, he could only remember that across from him, high up, the hanging lamp was smoking a lot, and black flecks of soot lay on all the cornices, up to the very ceiling.

New faces crowded in around him. Several familiar Golikhovke coachmen blocked his view of the sitting woman with their shoulders.

From deep inside the cell someone was calling the doctor's name at the top of his voice, when the woman, hidden from the doctor's view by the coachmen's shoulders, collapsed with a wild shriek.

The crowd started pushing and shoving. Someone wriggled out of it, almost tripping; the obsequious voice of an elderly Jewish woman shouted loudly enough for the doctor to hear: "Ask him, the doctor, fall to his feet, beg him to help . . . He can help!"

At the same time the woman sitting behind the partition of people squealed and barked hysterically, and the doctor started walking backward to the entrance of the cell. He placed his hands over the mouth of a prisoner who wanted to kiss him.

"Why?" and he grimaced, as if from pain in his temples, his lips quivering. "You mustn't, you mustn't."

Then he was summoned to Filipov's room; Comrade Sasha didn't follow him back there this time.

The doctor didn't know why he was being summoned, just as he hadn't known why previously he had been sent to the prisoners in the holding cell.

Filipov was sitting up in bed, hugging his knees with his hairy elbows. His head was bowed, and his eyes, which didn't look anywhere, were closed. Nonetheless, it seemed that he was not asleep. He was frozen in this pose out of sheer stubbornness. It was quiet for a while. Without opening his eyes, he asked the doctor whether he had lived in the area for a long time. Suddenly the feverish whites of his eyes yearning for sleep gave the doctor a look.

"Anyway," he said, "don't come crawling back here again, old man. Even when Comrade Sasha sends for you. You have a bad influence on everyone . . . And there's nothing you can do for me; I have a serious illness. X-ray therapy would help; there are also pills, but they are unavailable now. Go, you can tell Comrade Sasha to send you home."

When the doctor and Comrade Sasha left the room, Filipov remained sitting up in bed for a long time.

It was cold in the courtyard, where the doctor put on his heavy coat and waited for the wagon.

A starry sky looked down at the cold night. A Red Army soldier stood at the gate; he was to open it for the wagon leaving Kamino-Balke. He yawned and stretched lazily, as if the doctor's departure depended on him alone—even though he had not the slightest interest in him.

9

Yuzi, a Socialist Revolutionary, faced execution at Kamino-Balke. He was kept in a separate cell at the end of a corridor. Cold as a basement, the cell had thick, green walls—a monk had once lived in it, but all the monks had disappeared.

The walls looked at Yuzi indifferently, not the least surprised that they should be holding him and not someone else. Yuzi learned a lesson from these walls and regarded himself without regret or surprise. It was no wonder that out of so many places, out of a whole world of places—he was fated to live out his last days in this very cell, where a monk, whom he didn't know and who had disappeared, had prayed and mortified himself. Yuzi was full of indifference.

The indifference began in a gray dawn at the border, when he was arrested and Socialist Revolutionary documents were discovered sewn into the sleeves and lining of his coat.

Yuzi was silent and dark. His eyes were as black as ink, and together with his black moustache, which was even blacker than his eyes, they gave his face a dull, greenish hue, as if he were frightened of something. At the time of his arrest, he had looked from under his brow at the faces of the people searching his pockets; for one minute, he thought their thoughts and thought about himself and reminded himself what was in those documents, and then he banished from his mind and heart everything that he had previously thought and felt—he decided he was going to be shot.

As soon as he reached this decision, he didn't want any of the suffering that would come from going back on it. It was as if he had already died once. He was afraid of letting this thought go, because if he permitted himself false hope even for an instant, he would have to be shot a second time.

Listless and half-asleep, he sat quietly in his cell. Because he didn't know exactly when death would come, his heart froze from the very first minute. He sat waiting for the sound of steps in the corridor—they would be the sign that "he" was coming.

Yet nonetheless, hard days and hard nights crept by in his cell, and death still did not come. He was in great torment.

It seemed that the officials in charge had deliberately forgotten him. They didn't summon him for interrogation; they didn't shout his name during roll call; during the exercise hour they regarded him with indifference; they looked him straight in the face as if they didn't see him.

Yuzi didn't understand what kind of trick this was or where it came from: Filipov or his deputies. What did they want to accomplish?

And the very fact that he didn't understand was a sign—he thought—that death must come and that he was half-dead anyway. He was so far from living beings that he stopped understanding what they intended by this or that action.

Without realizing it, he started to use the same tactics with others that they had used with him. He stopped going outside during the exercise period. He stopped noticing that he had stopped being noticed and was no longer even seen.

Regardless, he still remained as stubborn as ever.

Only he didn't know that he was doing this and what he was doing it for. He was certain of his death, just like a man who falls madly in love with a woman, or conceives an equally strong hatred of her, and is certain of only one thing: that it could not be otherwise. He could not help loving her or wanting to get rid of her—all the minutes of his life taken separately and as a whole had led to this point. Anyway, the hell with it, the hell with it all, what difference did it make? The main thing was to figure out what you had to do before death.

He cast away his twenty-eight-year-old life with its steadfast revolutionary consciousness, exactly as a soldier who had served out his term would set aside the habits of military life and change into civilian clothes.

Instead of the hardened revolutionary Yuzi, who had until his arrest served his cause and with his arrest ended everything—a new Yuzi took his place in the cell. He was nothing but a rag, a person who must die, because dying was his fate.

Sitting in his cell with his eyes closed, he forced himself not to have a single thought in his head.

This is what he imagined:

Everything was over; he, Yuzi, had already been shot; he was no longer alive.

It was easier for him this way.

From that time on he stopped recognizing the world around him and didn't want to acknowledge it any more; from that time on he was neither awake nor asleep. He dozed away his time in a lethargy on the border between life and death.

Little by little, with every passing hour, he sank more deeply into his torpor, and gradually the daylight around him changed, it looked like sunset, as if somewhere, far from the barred window of his cell, one and the same sun was taking days to set; never had it set so far and for so long as now.

Then, during the long sunset, the strange thought came to him that his death had begun with his life, and not only his own life, but also with the lives of the generations before him. During the long sunset it felt odd to think that here in this area there once had lived a tall, broad-shouldered person named Mosi—a pious and devout Jew, with a cold smile hidden by his beard and moustache, which had gone from blonde to milky gray. This Jew made his living from endless lawsuits against a nobleman. He was a hothead in everything he did: he prayed passionately, he liked the bathhouse to be as hot as possible—his naked body would turn a bright red from the heat, with visible marks from the whisk broom on his back, the folds of fat on his stomach, and the two naked grandsons right at his feet. The grandsons were from his daughter, who was as big as he was, but far more talkative.

With the tip of his cold smile hidden by his beard, he would say about his daughter, "She knows Hebrew."

His daughter's husband—on the short side, clever, a perpetual little boy—read Torah with a velvet voice and knew Hebrew grammar and accounting, which he learned just in case. He died very young and took his velvet Torah voice and his just-in-case knowledge of grammar and accounting to the grave with him.

Yuzi's grandfather died very old, and the unsettled lawsuit against the nobleman, the cold smile at this world, and his love for fiery prayer and for the world to come—went with him.

The tall, talkative daughter, who knew Hebrew, dragged herself from city to city with her two little boys, and surprised people who didn't know her with her liturgical quotations, and also her energy, which enabled her to study midwifery at the age of forty-eight.

She died, and her talkative mouth, full of Hebrew sayings, and the energy to learn midwifery when she was middle-aged—went with her.

By that time her apartment in the big city had become a place where all kinds of revolutionary young men and women gathered illegally, and her two boys had finished their studies in a *Realschule*, first the older, and after him, the younger. Muli, the younger one, was the pharmacist in Golikhovke's nationalized pharmacy, and the older one was he, Yuzi, the prisoner who had been a Socialist Revolutionary, who dozed off in his prison cell with the constant feeling that somewhere far, far away the sun kept setting. As he slept, he feared waking up, because he had already tossed his life aside and had prepared himself for death. If, however, he woke up, he would have to prepare for death all over again . . .

While he sat, eyes closed and motionless, entangled in memories of his grandfather, mother, and father, whose lives had determined and paved the way for his own imminent death, he actually did fall asleep, at dusk, when the sun—somewhere far from his barred window—was in reality taking a long time to set.

He dreamed of the same thick, green walls behind which he now found himself in actuality, and in his dream, the Pokras brothers, Sofia Pokrovskaya, his brother Muli, and the entire group of SRs to whom he was ideologically committed during his lifetime—were there with him in the cell. They were saying something to him, the indifferent one, they quarreled about something, they were hurrying to go someplace and do something, and he was astonished that everything they said and everything they were preparing to do was foolish and pointless, because after he had bound himself to them, he had already done everything possible for their cause. He was surprised they didn't know this themselves.

Still dreaming, he waited apathetically for them to leave, and when they finally did, he had one thing left to do—in his dream—run and shut the door behind them. Everything depended on his success or failure at this, but he didn't manage to get to the door, because at that very moment steps were heard coming from the corridor—the steps that he had waited for with his heart in his throat the whole time. The door opened. And when he, Yuzi, woke up, he saw before him agent Zubok and the investigator Andreyev. Both of them bent over to search the corner where he sat; they were looking for someone, as if they were surprised that he was alone in the cell.

"Come!" Zubok said to him, when Andreyev lifted the lantern from the floor.

Yuzi then awakened not only from his dream, but also from his torpor and from the feeling that he was dead. He greatly regretted this, especially the thought that he would have to prepare himself for death all over again.

Zubok and Andreyev were only taking him to another cell.

A prisoner named Pinke Vayl was sitting in the pale evening darkness of the new cell. He looked troubled as he tried to assess Yuzi and the entire unknown world from which Yuzi had come to end up with him. All of a sudden, and quickly, almost in one breath, he said:

"Eh . . . After three weeks of being here, every new person seems familiar, like someone from home. Eh! . . . Like a cousin. Every new person to me is a bit of a relative. I'm from Kiev. And where do you come from?"

After he found out that Yuzi was a local, he fell silent. He seemed to have lost all interest in Yuzi.

✦

In the gray light of dawn, Yuzi heard a voice.

"You didn't sleep?"

"Huh?"

"The whole night?"

"I'm used to it."

"Well, if that's it . . ."

"And yesterday I thought you were from Kiev. I thought I once saw you in Kiev. But maybe it was Zhitomir? You haven't been to Zhitomir?"

Yuzi wanted to lift his head, but didn't, because his neighbor kept on peppering him with questions. Keeping his head down, he looked at his neighbor from under his brow, and not so much at the man as at his mouth, a mouth that could so easily and quickly open and shut and release from between its teeth a whole crowd of questions.

What he saw was a nineteen-year-old boyish figure, which felt comfortable in its big Red Army uniform, a childish, sunburned face with a sparse moustache, with a mouth and eyes that were girlishly charming, and which asked you to be a relative, if only a distant one.

This figure was found at one end of the floor, on top of some bedding. There was something heavy in the way it sat, all alone, as if the person sitting there was paralyzed.

"I'm finished," Pinke said. "Done for. I know perfectly well that they'll never make a man out of me. A soldier is coming for me, coming to shoot me. But you should know how it began. Do you understand or not? In a nutshell, it began with a punch in the belly . . ."

Yuzi didn't understand what began with a punch in the belly: the fact that Pinke would never become a man, or the fact that they were going to shoot him. He searched deep in himself for the slightest feeling for this boy and, to his surprise, found none. He dug deeper and again found nothing. After the torpor he had experienced in the past few days, he was empty through and through.

Like someone who had already been shot, he didn't have the slightest compassion for Pinke, who was about to be shot.

His only wish was that his new neighbor would talk less. Pinke, however, after three weeks of imprisonment, was full of chatter, brimming over with his young, gawky life, and only wished that his new neighbor would be less silent.

✦

Pinke Vayl had a lot of picture postcards of the city of his birth and showed them to Yuzi. Pinke took great joy and delight in the fact of this city's existence:

"Kiev," he said. "Do you see? A beautiful, beautiful city! Its shores are lined with green trees. One half of the city is high, high up, and the other is down in the valley, and if you stand at the city's high point, you can hear its great noise from below: brrr! brrr . . . It was as if you were at a big river at Passover time and you could hear the frogs croaking. We lived in the lower part, see? Here, on this street."

There was one big photograph among the many tinted postcards, a family portrait of Pinke's father, mother, and him, when he was little, twelve years old, wearing the hat of a gymnasium student, although no one had ever thought of sending him to a gymnasium.

The photograph looked as if it came from olden times, which made it seem that everyone in it was long dead.

On the right:

Pinke's father, the one from whom "everything had begun," because he had once hit Pinke with his fist in the belly—hit him hard—like that, with all his strength. He was sitting in a soft armchair. He was a big, fleshy Jew with glassy eyes that stared into the distance. His full, open lips smiled from under his closely shaven moustache; they were like the lips of a Jew at a wedding who was owed a seat at the head of the table, but because of a mistake had been put at the far end, among the beggars.

Pinke's mother stood behind his chair; her face looked younger and more energetic. From the way she rested her hand on her husband's shoulder, it was clear that she acknowledged the claim that his lips made; they were doing the right thing, those lips, with their smile.

Pinke clearly hated both of them.

He said, "Do you see or not? A fine family, huh. This family was nothing but trouble."

He had run away from them two years earlier, because his mother was always picking on him, constantly nagging, and because his father had once punched and hit him in the belly with his fists, like that . . . with fists like hammers. He wanted to get as far away from them as possible, and he thought the Red Army was the furthest he could get away, even though its barracks were right on the same street as his family.

He served in the Red Army for two years, fighting on different fronts and against different groups, and had become a communist. He didn't know whether his family was looking for him or not. But around three months ago he had been wounded on the left arm, here, a little higher than the elbow. It didn't hurt that much, and in the first few days the wound was precious to him, as if the girl he loved had bitten him.

It didn't hurt that much. Every morning when he got up, the first thing he did was remind himself of the wound, which belonged to him, Pinke, the communist, and he would feel happy. And because he felt so happy, he sent a postcard home from the infirmary train. It didn't occur to him that they would answer. But it turned out that his mother had pawned a fur coat and set off to find him.

After three weeks she found him in a hospital in Moscow. When she saw him in his uniform, she started to cry. "Look at him in his fine clothes! Look at his patched boots! Trotsky should go around in those boots!"

And she told him that they had become poor, they didn't have the store—the kitchenware store—they didn't have servants any more, and lived in one room and used the heating stove for cooking.

His father remained an invalid after his typhus; he had become hard of hearing and was on the verge of death.

"You should visit your father," she said to Pinke, "he wants to see you before he dies." And she burst into tears again.

After that Pinke was discharged from the hospital, and sent home on medical leave, although he had not forgotten that his father had beaten him on the belly with his fists.

It turned out that his father was not as sick as his mother said, even though he was in bed and had truly become deaf after his typhus.

While Pinke was home, all the relatives descended on him; day and night they chattered away about his former "comrades." Practically all his friends had become commissars and were decked out with riding crops and revolvers and weren't like Pinke—no matter— they wouldn't abandon a sick mother and father.

In order to come find him, everything had been sold or pawned, and now there remained one hope—he, Pinke, would help . . . They knew someone who would pay a lot of money to have a small case brought back from the border.

Every day this person sent someone to find out: "Where is your Pinke?"

Everyone said it would be easy. "Who would search a wounded Red Army soldier?"

And because they pressed him hard at home, he went to the border to get the case—to be free of them. He didn't even want to know what was in the case. He still didn't know. It was only after he had been arrested at the border and told he would be shot that he first understood what his own parents had done to him, Pinke, the communist.

And now . . .

Now Pinke was writing it all down on a piece of paper, with a pencil and in a nervous, quick hand—he was writing to ask a favor from the boss.

Only he didn't know how to end the request and gave it to Yuzi to read so he could ask for his expertise.

"And now I am asking you, Comrade Chief Officer . . ." he had written.

Because he didn't know how to end the request, which was supposed to persuade them to let him live, he finished abruptly, according to his own understanding of how a true communist would conclude: "Now, for this reason, I am asking to be shot as soon as possible."

Pinke was satisfied that his request ended in the most forceful terms. He was pleased that his petition had the ending suitable for a true communist.

But after he turned in his petition, he gradually began to believe that he was a true communist, and that he really did want to be shot as quickly as possible and that was the reason he wrote his request.

"The worst thing," he told Yuzi, "will be when they bring me to Kiev under arrest. What do you think? That I won't be sent to Kiev? I have friends there. I don't want to be taken to Kiev . . . I already spoke to the boss, he got angry, not only at me, at other prisoners, too. He said, '*Chto vy, shutite?* What, are you joking?'"

Nonetheless, Pinke was sure that the boss treated him better than other prisoners, because he, Pinke, was a Red Army soldier. He even let Pinke's mother come visit him in the middle of the week, when they didn't allow any visitors. But Pinke didn't want his mother to come. He didn't want to leave the cell to see her, he said to her, "Why do you come here? Go home, who needs you?"

Pinke waited with impatience for the answer to his petition. But the answer came much more quickly than he expected. He was summoned to the office: the boss was sitting there with his back to him, holding the petition in his hands.

"What do you want?" he asked Pinke.

Pinke suddenly felt very strongly that he was a true communist. He stood as straight as he could, like a soldier before the most important senior officer, and barked out, "I'm requesting to be shot."

Then the boss answered him very coldly, calmly looking him over again.

"*Khorosho,* very good," he said, "We'll see."

Pinke told Yuzi all about this afterward.

Yuzi listened just for the sake of politeness. He looked Pinke in the face, with wonderment that after the suffering he had endured the last few days, he, Yuzi, was full of emptiness. He felt the emptiness inwardly and didn't have the slightest compassion for Pinke, and although he tried to dig deeper into himself, he didn't find any compassion there, either. Earlier, before the experience of the last few days, he would have surely said that it was the system that was guilty—the system that made Red Army soldiers out of people like Pinke and then later arrested them at the border, like criminals. Only now none of this bothered him. He was full of emptiness, full of indifference.

After this the officials in charge returned to their usual procedure, which was incomprehensible to him—they didn't summon him for interrogation.

And again he didn't know what they wanted to accomplish and who ordered it: Filipov or his deputies.

And again he behaved as if he didn't notice it.

As if on its own accord, a silent struggle began between him and his jailers. And every day, all by itself, the question arose as to which of the two stubborn men would give in first: Yuzi, who sat moribund in the cell with Pinke Vayl, or Filipov, who instructed his deputies to forget Yuzi, although it wasn't certain that Filipov had, in fact, ordered this.

Every evening Yuzi went to sleep with the feeling that besides the emptiness, which came from his torpor and which filled him, there was something else, heavy and oppressive, and it came from the office and from Filipov.

Night after night in his restless, light sleep, he felt the oppression, but didn't know what it was.

And in the time between sleep and wakefulness he was frightened; he was afraid not so much of Filipov as of the incomprehensible justice that Filipov embodied—a cold, iron justice, on which he, Yuzi, and the second half of his death depended.

Only afterward it became clear to him that something else had begun to sink into his inner devastation, the suffering that he had endured and that remained with him—something that until now was alien to him, but was connected to the cold, iron justice that Filipov had. Filipov's cold, iron justice would decide whether to shoot him. It was possible that Filipov would decide not to. It was more likely that he would decide yes, to shoot him. It didn't matter, however, because the decision belonged to the cold, iron justice.

Then he began to notice that the same thing happened to a lot of the prisoners let out every day for exercise, as he was. All their hopes and fears were concentrated on Filipov's justice; their lives depended on it. As long as he did not carry out the death sentence, they worshipped him. All of them, like Yuzi, were terribly interested in knowing what this cold, iron justice was, and who the person embodying it was—who exactly was Filipov?

10

At night, following the doctor's visit, Filipov's pain intensified. He was in a foul mood. Furious with Comrade Sasha for calling the doctor, he stayed in bed with his eyes closed, eyebrows raised in irritation. He didn't say a single word.

In the morning, when Comrade Sasha entered the room, she found that he had gotten dressed, seemingly out of stubbornness, just to spite his increased pain. He sat on the edge of the bed with his eyes closed.

"It's high time, my darling, that you got married," he told her. "Then you could have some children to take care of. We have a revolution here—this is no place to play with dolls."

Comrade Sasha emerged from his room with red blotches on her face and the scattered look of someone who was supposed to take care of something extremely important but had forgotten what it was.

Soon quarreling could be heard from the office. Comrade Sasha was yelling at investigator Andreyev, who had gotten up late. She was scolding him for carrying out far too few interrogations and for not filing proper reports for the ones he did.

New prisoners were waiting their turn in a small corridor nearby. They were listening to Comrade Sasha's voice. And since she yelled loudly and at length, it was apparent that the revolution in the country was still going strong and would last a long time, steadfast and firm. Investing hope in Filipov's illness was not the right thing, either: there were clearly others to replace him.

✦

In the afternoon, Filipov—in a long peasant coat and a cap tugged right over his eyes—walked across both courtyards. This was on Friday, just before the tribunal that included him, Comrade Sasha, and investigator Andreyev was to be convened.

Dirty hours stretched slowly before someone's sentencing—just like the dirty snow trampled in the courtyards.

To the left, behind the dilapidated fence, a few prisoners could be seen in the exercise area. Someone's nose breathed in some of the frosty air that smelled like freshly baked challah and a Yiddish-speaking voice said loudly:

"I swear: it smells just like Friday . . . it smells of roasting meat."

Filipov reached the entrance, angry with the group of women—mothers and wives of the prisoners—who had been banging on the gate since morning asking to be allowed inside.

"No need for you to be standing here freezing," he said. "Once a week is enough. Myself, I haven't seen my mother in eighteen years, and I haven't died from it yet."

There, he bumped into a boyish soldier with the wrinkled face of a slim eunuch and small legs that got tangled up in the long flaps of his big cavalry overcoat. This was a messenger from a distant border outpost who had arrived a couple of days earlier with complaints about the torn boots everyone had to wear and the bad food that Kamino-Balke sent them.

Filipov glanced first at the doors of the stables nearby and, after that, at the soldier's boots—old, gray, patched-up boots, their tips full of wet mud.

"Well, what do we have here, comrade?" he asked the soldier. "I see that you still haven't gone back to your post. A pity . . . a pity . . ."

The soldier first glanced at Filipov and, after that, at the piece of bread in his hands. Suddenly, he stopped chewing.

"How can we go on like this?" he said. "You send us only bread and herring . . ."

By this point he had forgotten to complain about the boots.

Filipov looked at the soldier's boots—his old boots with their puckered-up and patient tips.

"Bread and herring," he repeated quietly. "Well, yes, I myself . . . I myself also eat bread and herring."

Suddenly, he called out to one of his own soldiers hanging around the stables.

"Take this comrade to the kitchen and the warehouse," he said. "Show him what we eat here."

He stopped listening to what the soldier from the border outpost kept complaining about and, instead, headed for the office. Angrily, he muttered something that the others were supposed to interpret as:

"All of you are eager to strangle me, tear me to pieces—you disobey me out of spite, you make demands, you ask for mercy."

A middle-aged Jewish woman in a long, velvet overcoat was walking across from him along the tree-lined alleyway that led from the office. A dark shawl sat crookedly on her shoulders, as if she'd forgotten it. When it fell, she didn't even look at the soldier who picked it up from the snow and threw it over her shoulders. This was Pinke Vayl's mother—the only person whom Filipov allowed in to see her son every time she visited.

Tousled, graying hair spilled out from under her headscarf. Upset, her eyes scanned the entire length of the alley, looking for someone, while she sighed and groaned like a woman returning from visiting graves at the cemetery. Finally, she noticed Filipov and approached him, speaking in a trembling and frightened voice:

"Comrade Filipov! Comrade boss! I beg you . . ."

"Well, what do we have here? . . ." Filipov took a long look at her. "Who are you pleading with?"

"With you," said the woman, wringing her hands. "With you, comrade boss, with you, comrade Filipov!"

Filipov glanced at her as if she were a wild animal.

"But Filipov," he whispered secretively into her ear, "Filipov, if you'd like to know, is just my pseudonym. My real name is Anastasyev. But Anastasyev has nothing to do with any of this business here, he is a completely extraneous man, do you understand? Anastasyev can't help you at all."

With this, he continued on toward the office, located in the middle building. However, the Jewish woman wouldn't stop following him, her frightened voice continuing to quaver. Filipov stopped at the entrance and pointed at the red flag hanging above. The Jewish woman thought he said:

"This is who is in charge around here!"

Suddenly she heard Filipov get angry:

"What do you think? You think this is a joke? I am a sick man—why have all of you ganged up on me?"

Slowly, he entered the office, which had been cleaned just a short while before. Darkness had fallen, so the light was on inside, and Comrade Sasha and Andreyev were waiting for him.

"So, what do we have here?" he asked. "Are you ready for the tribunal? Which files are we reviewing first?"

The first order of business was the case of Aaron-Yisroel Yosifovich Lemberger, the owner of the only tannery in the region. His age: sixty-four. His crime:

> Following the decree requiring all factory owners to indicate the quantity of finished goods they had, he reported only thirty percent. He shipped the remaining seventy percent to the other side, for which he received payment in foreign currency. He therefore speculated on the seventy percent of the goods with the purpose of personal enrichment—now, of all times, during this period of etc. etc.

Filipov closed his eyes to feel the pain less and pay more attention to what Comrade Sasha was reading. Now he was that other Filipov who had just shown the Jewish woman the red flag outside. He was cold and indifferent toward himself exactly the same way that he was cold and indifferent toward the destiny of the being referred to as "Aaron-Yisroel Yosifovich Lemberger," who was preoccupied with personal enrichment now of all times, during this period of etc. etc . . . He remembered the cold, dirty snow outside, and the red flag.

The entire time he strained his memory to recall some very important issue—but what this important issue was he could not remember at all. Only later, when he again encountered the Red Army soldier who had arrived with grievances from a faraway border post, did he remember the very important issue:

The soldier had come with a warning: "They'll all abandon their posts and go home, they'll all run away."

✦

That same night Pinke Vayl awakened Yuzi:

"Comrade Spivak! Hey! Comrade Spivak!"

In the corridor between the cells footsteps became audible—nocturnal steps, familiar as if from long ago. They were mixed with something else, and the something else was even darker than the steps themselves.

The clamoring of heels and the clanging of keys kept interrupting an angry voice in the hallway—it sounded as if the door of a nearby cell had been opened by mistake and then quickly shut again. Someone swore angrily and loudly, as if at the entire world and this very night.

"Comrade Spivak!" Pinke tugged at Yuzi softly. "Can you hear? The tribunal has already met . . . It's Friday . . . It was also Friday after their session when they brought you to my cell . . ."

Yuzi sat up even before he was fully awake and before he felt the terrible sleepiness that filled him, overwhelming his inner emptiness. He didn't know what Pinke wanted and whom he feared when he kept saying: "They're coming . . . Someone's walking in the direction of our cell."

Now, when the deep night infused him with its strong potion of slumber, it would have been easy to follow those steps and not notice you were following them, to be killed and not realize that you were being killed.

When he finally woke up, the door of the cell was open. First he saw a lantern near his face and only after that four or five men—somehow too many men.

"Which one of you is Spivak?"

He didn't answer and wished that he could fall back asleep, but Pinke was standing right next to him, creating the appearance that he was helping him get dressed. As if in wonderment, Yuzi fixed his eyes on Pinke's face. He didn't understand why it was that he had met him here in this cell and why it had happened precisely then, eight days before he was supposed to die, and why it was precisely him that he had encountered—why this Pinke with the girlish charm around his mouth and eyes pleading for a tiny bit of warmth from everyone he talked to.

"It's nothing," Pinke started telling him almost joyfully. "They didn't even summon you to meet with the investigator. I've asked them. 'We are taking him,' they told me, 'to the general holding cell.'"

Yuzi felt a pang around his heart—a powerful nocturnal longing, which he felt the entire time he was being led along the damp corridor. He was led outside, where it was cold, seemingly to allow him to freshen up; then, up the steps, into a new passageway and from there, into one of the two general holding cells.

11

In the middle, square-shaped cell a small wall lamp made of tin smoked the way this sort of lamp would usually smoke on any winter evening.

The prisoners were lying on the floor, some of them fully prostrated and some not, all of them pressed against each other without realizing it. The first one to move when Yuzi entered the cell was a young man lying far from the door, next to the hot stove. Half-asleep, he sat up and rubbed his eyes but didn't notice Yuzi. He stooped over and quickly began to wake his neighbor, lying next to him on the floor:

"Reb Aaron . . . Wake up, Reb Aaron!"

The young man's neighbor—a gray-haired, solid Jew in striped pants and a black kapote—didn't move. His firm, round chest heaved much more strongly and regularly than those of the other prisoners: it seemed that all the snoring and wheezing that filled the air in the room had issued from him alone.

"Reb Aaron!" the young man said, trying to wake him. "What a pain! I have something to tell you. Reb Aaron!"

The old Jew's chest briefly stopped moving. His eyes closed, he turned his thick and carefully combed white beard toward the young man, as if to say:

"So, you want to rip it out? Go ahead."

Suddenly, he scratched under his beard, covered his face with the skirt of his black coat to block the light, and fell back asleep. From under the raised skirt of his coat, the part of his body that filled his striped pants to bursting became uncovered—the thick part of a person who may have been over sixty but was stronger than many young people.

"So, that's how it goes," the young man sighed, "to wake him up you have to be an expert." He glanced at Yuzi, who was sitting across the room on top of a small chest.

"What a strange person," he said to Yuzi. "Even dying is easier for him than for others."

The young man looked more deeply into Yuzi's unfamiliar face, turned to the right, then to the left, then suddenly set off crawling in Yuzi's direction.

"Listen." He hid behind Yuzi's back. "You shouldn't say anything . . . There is an informer here . . . that one, the clockmaker." He pointed at a tall man in the middle of the floor. "They say that he got sent here by Mister . . . by Comrade Investigator himself."

Yuzi didn't really understand, and the young man crawled back to his corner.

The tall man who had been pointed out to Yuzi was sleeping in the middle of the cell—or, perhaps, he was pretending to be asleep. He lay on his side, turned unnaturally, all in a heap, his sleeping eyes half-open, his cheek glued to the bare floor. He looked like an epileptic right after an attack.

His arms were hairy and thin; his fingers, long and shiny, as if he had just been digging through the innards of a roast chicken— and, having finished, he licked the fat from his fingers, but didn't wipe them off, and was left with the greasy dirt drying under his fingernails. His elongated face, with unshaven cheeks and lips, looked similar—shiny from grease that hadn't been wiped off.

But it was also possible that this was all a mirage. The light from the small, soot-covered lamp on the wall could have been responsible for this. The lamp was much too weak to illuminate the stinking room. For some reason it seemed that the stench was coming not from the burning lamp but from the tall man. Suddenly, as if seized with fright, he sat up, inserted his thin, shiny finger into his long nose, and looked at Yuzi sitting across from him.

"What?" he asked, barely awake. "Has the tribunal met already?"

Yuzi didn't answer, so the young man remained there, blinking his birdlike eyes and peering into Yuzi's face. But then right away he got up. His expression turned to anger, his face puffed out, and, forgetting where he was, he got up and started walking around the room.

His long, shoeless feet stepped over the bodies, arms, and heads of the sleeping prisoners. His long arms in white sleeves hung motionless like the arms of a golem. His mouth whispered, tensely, to itself:

"Well, there you have it . . ."

"Enough already . . ."

"Agreed, agreed . . ."

He stopped briefly with his back toward Yuzi and started counting on his fingers:

"The tribunal met last night . . . This would mean that today, this morning . . . or this afternoon . . . or tonight . . . they'll shoot me."

Suddenly he turned to Yuzi, sat down near him, and whispered in his ear:

"Listen," he said, "perhaps you already know. I am a clockmaker— that is to say, I *was* one. For two months I ran passports across the border. Counterfeit Polish passports. Eighteen—that's how many got confiscated. Mister Boss himself caught me. They say that it's better when he is the one making the arrest. The tribunal met yesterday, right? What do you think? They'll have me shot . . ."

Slowly Yuzi closed his eyes so as not to see the glistening grease on the tall man's face. Yuzi, too, used a fake Polish passport whenever he stole across the border. It was entirely possible that his Socialist Revolutionary cell bought his passport from this very clockmaker. It didn't matter, whichever way he looked at it—the dirty prison stench that emanated from this person came from him, Yuzi, too. Only all this seemed to have happened long ago—the emptiness inside him was the same regardless of whether any of this had happened or not; his emptiness only wanted one thing—to fall asleep . . . to sleep and to remember:

If a righteous hand were to purify the world, it would certainly sweep away all the dirt from this room together with him, drowsy Yuzi.

And then he fell asleep.

When he opened his eyes one more time, a gray morning light was visible.

With a sleepy face the gray-haired Jew in the black kapote and striped pants was standing in front of the hot stove. Breathing angrily through his nostrils, he removed the collar from his neck:

"Do you see?" he said, "It's wet. It should be wrung out . . . They took me in the clothes I was wearing, straight from a bar mitzvah."

He started combing his beard; the expression on his face suggested that he was prepared to unearth a piece of straw or a feather. He got carried away in his own thoughts, then appealed to everyone in the room and to no one in particular:

"In any case . . . do you really think I didn't foresee all this?"

He sat down on top of a sack containing someone else's belongings, exhaling as if he meant to say:

"I saw it . . . I saw it coming."

Once more he got carried away in his own thoughts, then he started calling the guard—the Red Army soldier with the rifle in his hands who occasionally appeared in the doorway:

"Listen here, listen here!" He pointed in the soldier's direction. "Comrade! I already inquired yesterday . . ."

"Reb Aaron," the young man called out to him from the other room, "there is a bit of water here—enough for you to wash up."

The young man was standing next to two girls stretched out on the floor—two Christian street girls. They pulled an old shawl over both their heads and started shaking with laughter. The kettle that the young man was offering to Reb Aaron belonged to the two of them.

Reb Aaron wasn't in a rush to accept the offer. Worried, he kept on sitting on a sack containing someone else's belongings, and eyed the kettle suspiciously.

"Who did you take this kettle from?" he asked. "From those whores, eh?"

He thought it over:

"Listen! Comrade! Comrade!" he called out to the soldier, who again appeared in the doorway for a minute.

Then, as if he had forgotten where he was, Reb Aaron started pouring water over his fingers right onto the floor near him—three times over the tips of his fingers, one hand at a time. As he poured the water, he moved his lips in a whisper.

"I beg you," the tall clockmaker grimaced at Reb Aaron. "Please lend me your tallis. What kind of a Jew are you? I want to pray just once more before they shoot me . . ."

Suddenly, moved by his own words and by his wish to pray once more before his execution, he grimaced even more and sobbed loudly, though without tears. Reb Aaron shook his shoulders as if to say he couldn't figure out what the clockmaker wanted from him.

"No need to get all worked up." He stopped whispering. "Have you asked me, and have I refused you? Here's my tallis, take it."

Once more, he threw the word "comrade" in the direction of the soldier who stood at the door of the cell with his rifle.

The young man, who used to work for Reb Aaron, approached Yuzi.

"Today is Shabbos," and gave him a wink in the direction of Reb Aaron. "I've learned his ways quite well by now. I used to work for him. Since yesterday he's been bugging the soldier for a piece of challah. He found the right time for it! A piece of white challah he wants!"

But suddenly he noticed how absolutely still Yuzi had been sitting the entire time on top of the chest by the door—and grew frightened. Others in the cell started looking at Yuzi—looking, whispering, and asking what he was looking at.

◆

Around eleven o'clock they came from the office to call the roll.

Rumors started circulating in the cell. Everyone was counted according to the list from the office, without exception. But it still wasn't clear:

"Who did they mean?"

Later they came back, with the same list in hand. Looking into everyone's staring eyes, they called out a name:

"Jan Kalina!"

They yelled loudly:

"Who is Kalina?"

Jan Kalina was a peasant. He had a dark complexion, a strong protruding chin, and a big red spot around his left eye. You could almost make out his reflection in his large, sparkling new shoes and fancy clothes. This was what a smug kulak would wear. He had probably changed into this outfit not long before his arrest. He was sitting in the far corner of the cell next to a sleeping priest who was trying to keep his head propped up by placing his elbows on the little table in front of him. The peasant slowly got up from his seat, as if he knew in advance that he would come to regret it. Before he was fully upright, he sat back down again.

Something dull and unfamiliar looked out from deep below his eyes—but it wasn't his eyes. The red spot around his left eye seemed to be burning.

In the cell, people said about him:

"Involved in slaughter—three times . . . A follower of Petliura . . . The birthmark around his left eye gave him away—that's why he got arrested."

Jan Kalina got a long, cold stare before his name was checked on the list; a breath of fresh air lingered in the cell after the official left, taking with him the soldier who had been guarding the door.

The prisoners in the cell found out: "They put two new ones in his place." Someone asked naively: "Why new guards?"

No one had an answer.

Reb Aaron started chanting his Shabbos prayers quietly. Suddenly the prisoners felt that the morning had dragged on far too long. They felt someone else's presence—in addition to Filipov and his deputies, someone sterner and more severe than all other earthly bosses. He, this other presence, was in Kamino-Balke even though nobody could see him or even imagine him. In their great fear they had forgotten to be God-fearing.

Since no one in the cell knew definitely for whom death had come, everyone thought, "For me." Except that a moment later the very same prisoner who had just thought, "For me," would change his mind: "Maybe, instead, it's for him, eh? For that one—well, definitely for him." That was why the prisoners looked sternly at one another and, more than at anyone else in particular, at Yuzi—while he, Yuzi, wasn't looking at anyone and was just sitting at the door without so much as moving an inch, looking half-dead.

Then, suddenly, a sob shattered the stillness that reigned in the cell. It was one of the street girls who had previously been sleeping on the floor, covered by an old shawl. This took place when it was already two in the afternoon. Everyone felt sorry for her, as if the tribunal that met the day before was on her account, and this was the reason she was crying now. Everyone felt lighter for a moment, the prisoners suddenly seemed thankful to her for crying.

But, soon enough, every prisoner remembered about himself, realizing that the girl was just sobbing in the usual way about something small and not terribly consequential.

One by one, the prisoners who had earlier approached the sobbing girl returned to their places—just the young man, who had been busy with Reb Aaron, remained near her. He stood with his back toward the girls and, speaking indirectly and in Yiddish so they wouldn't understand, told someone about them:

"For espionage . . . The soldier mentioned yesterday that these two are Poles . . . And they said, 'We got arrested because, when we were drunk, we paraded around town . . . showing off our naked boobs.'"

The young man's cheeks turned red, but he couldn't laugh. He rubbed his burning cheeks nervously as if trying to squeeze his face into a smile.

"You should have a look at those boobs of theirs," he said, "all cracked, covered with boils—on account of a certain illness . . ."

That same moment, though, his expression changed—as if he hadn't said what he just said. Instead, he started talking about his own arrest and about Reb Aaron, his former employer:

"Me?" he wondered aloud. "What have I got to be afraid of? I just worked for him. What of it? I only did his bidding."

At the exit door of the cell the gray-haired Jew whom others called Reb Aaron started fidgeting. He was waiting for the soldier who had guarded the cell to return. His bulbous nose looked like Tolstoy's—his nose was pale, although the back of his neck was red, the tough-looking nape of a strong old Jew. He sat down close to Yuzi and thought to himself:

"Filipov," he sighed. "So, what? Let it be Filipov! As far as I'm concerned, he's no more than a messenger."

He hugged his knees with both hands.

"There is a passage in the Mishnah," he said. "'Four paces away from the place where he is to be stoned, remove the criminal's clothing.' That's what it says. Know-nothings, that's what you are—what we're seeing here is exactly as it is written . . ."

Slowly stroking his beard with one hand, he looked at Yuzi.

"In the tractate called Sanhedrin," he said. "In the section known as 'the execution of judgment'—that's where it's all written down. You see? Young man . . ."

He looked at Yuzi even more intently:

"What, you haven't studied this?" he inquired. "Not even once?"

Slowly, Yuzi shut his eyes.

Inside the cell, the light grew dimmer.

✦

By the time the little smoking lamp was lit again, it was dusk.

Yesterday's guard—the Red Army soldier—rushed into the cell. His face was red-hot and his burning eyes were darting about the room with worry. Like a busy man of his word, he took out the promised piece of white challah from under his coat. He breathed heavily as if the only thing he had done the entire day was carrying around that small piece of challah.

"Come here!" he summoned the young man to his side with a quick wink. "It wasn't easy. I had to run four miles. One of yours, a Jewish woman over there in the village, told me: 'I don't have any challah.'" The soldier winked mischievously. "And then I told her: 'It's for one of your kind I'm asking—for one of yours, some challah as a remedy.'"

He bolted toward the door, not paying any attention to the young man who followed him to ask a question.

"Let him leave! Just let him leave!" Reb Aaron called out to the young man.

He took the small piece of white bread into his hands as if he were blind, his eyes straying across it.

That small Shabbos challah was the kind of medicine that was brought to someone who was dangerously ill as a measure of last resort. The challah contained a secret—only it knew whether it was going to help or not. Reb Aaron was holding it awkwardly in his bent fingers.

"I decided it would be a sign," he said coldly, while looking at the challah. "When I asked for the challah, I thought that if only they brought it on time, all would be well . . . And what have we here?

Perhaps it has arrived on time—the fourth meal of Shabbos is yet to happen, the *melaveh malkeh* meal, that is . . . So I am inviting all the Jews to the table."

The words "all the Jews" and "I am inviting" were spoken stiffly, they sounded stubborn and unpleasant—like words used to address a dead person, like the words of someone pleading for forgiveness.

In a corner of the cell the priest, who had been napping, awoke with a jolt; when he saw there was no cause for worry, he relaxed. The only thing that had happened was that they moved the table on which the priest had been leaning the entire time. The priest crossed himself quietly.

The evening grew darker. In the hallway opposite the door to the cell, worrying steps were now heard—back and forth, steps that couldn't be delayed.

"*O gospodi!* Oh, God!" one of the girls sighed deeply, as if the air was getting pumped out of her lungs.

"'Here, down on earth, a man wouldn't even be able to hurt his own finger if it weren't deemed appropriate in heaven above,' as it is written," Reb Aaron said at the table, swallowing the first piece of challah. "There are four means of punishment: fire, stoning, decapitation, and strangulation. In the Talmud, Rabbi Shimon says: 'By fire, by stoning, by strangulation, and by decapitation' because decapitation is the easiest way to die. And 'they'—the Bolsheviks—here, on earth, 'they' are no more than messengers. I have no complaints—it's quite likely that I deserved this."

"What are you weeping for?" he coldly asked the sobbing clockmaker. "If you are afraid, you should make a confession. Say: 'Let my death be an expiation for my sins.' Because that's what we find in the story of Achan, whom Joshua told: 'My son, show respect for the God of Israel and confess.' And Achan answered Joshua: 'It is true, for I have transgressed.' And how do we know that he was forgiven? Because it is written that Joshua said: 'Achan, why did you lead us into this trouble? Now the Lord is avenging you with the same kind of trouble—but only now; you will not be troubled in the world to come.'"

After this, everyone in the cell sat quietly, listening to what was happening in the hallway, and waited. Reb Aaron, it seemed, was now certain that the silence meant everyone was thinking only about him—him alone. The whole time he kept washing his hands with water from the kettle. Suddenly, with a look on his face that expressed the attempt to recall something, he said to himself:

"How long has this been going on? About ten minutes? . . ."

Only around ten o'clock in the evening, when a guard finally entered the cell, just the names of the two street girls were called. Reb Aaron was instantly persuaded that, after all, he wasn't going to get punished: he, Reb Aaron, couldn't be treated the same as the girls—it simply couldn't be.

So when his name was called after the girls', he remained motionless—the blood drained from his face and he couldn't believe what he had heard.

He couldn't quite get it through his head that everyone in the cell was coming up to say goodbye to him. Suddenly, he saw the young man's grimacing face covered in tears and just as suddenly realized, by looking at that face, that it really was him—Aaron Lemberger—who was being summoned.

"Be well," he said to the young man. "It seems I told the interrogator the truth—that you did no more than running my errands, and that you didn't receive any commission from me. Don't cry. Pray to God. Be well, all of you."

And only after a long stretch of time had passed, during which everyone listened carefully and sat quietly, the inmates recalled how, a minute before he was escorted out of the cell, Aaron Lemberger turned from the door and gave the young man a message for his relatives at home.

The young man's face looked half-dead; he spoke as though he were trying to justify himself:

"What kind of people are you? . . . It's nothing . . . He conveyed a message home . . . Nothing special . . . What is it that you don't understand here? . . . A couple of rubles . . . From his leather business . . . From sales . . . God forbid that this has anything to do with me . . . In foreign currency, of course . . . So what? . . . He sent a message home about where he'd hidden the money."

12

Something awakened them from their sleep, something nameless that ripped pieces of flesh from their bodies and brains.

It happened in the middle of the night.

Yuzi woke up and felt much more alive, much worse, and much simpler, because:

It was simply hunger that had torn pieces of flesh from their bodies and brains.

It sobered them up: yesterday's terror was gone.

Calmer, they could see:

The leftover white challah no longer lay on the table in the middle of the cell. Apparently, one of the prisoners had suddenly forgotten all the laws that Reb Aaron had recited over the challah before his death and, when no one was looking, ate it up—simply because he was hungry, simply because the white challah was tasty . . .

No one knew who had done this, and consequently, the prisoners concluded they all had consumed the challah.

Soon after he woke up and saw that Reb Aaron and the two girls weren't there any more, and then again after two or three hours of sleep, when he and everyone else in the cell ate the remaining white challah, Yuzi sensed his inner emptiness, together with a feeling of derision.

All around him the sleeping prisoners filled the air with their whistling and snoring, just like yesterday.

Only the places where the two girls and Reb Aaron used to sit were empty—until the clockmaker took Reb Aaron's spot near the hot stove. He was sleeping soundly, all the while pressing against the young man who used to work for Reb Aaron. The other prisoners had no better reminder of their suspicions against him than the way he slept: he pressed against one of them so hard that he drenched him with his own sweat.

What came to mind now, more vividly than anything else, was the clockmaker's weeping the day before and Reb Aaron's comforting him. The prisoners also remembered that Reb Aaron, before his death, had asked the young man to give a message to his wife, to tell her where the rubles were hidden—a "couple of rubles"—from his illegal dealings . . .

In the middle of the night it occurred to Yuzi that all this had something to do with him and that it was all very important:

What was this greed for possessions that drove men to their death, notwithstanding all their fine morality and pious speeches?

He remembered how, the night before, the prisoners were talking about another man they had heard of, who died like Reb Aaron. Before his execution he removed his rubber dentures with gold teeth from his mouth and had them sent on to his wife—five gold teeth . . .

Yuzi couldn't fall asleep any more, and that was the worst thing, worse than anything else, because one clear thought was hiding somewhere in a crevice of the emptiness that was his constant companion. He could barely wait until daylight. The absent-minded soldier, the same one who had brought Reb Aaron the white challah the day before, ordered the prisoners to go fetch wood. Yuzi got up first, but without the least servility: he wanted to show his inner emptiness that he didn't care about the "couple of rubles" that Reb Aaron had left—to prove this somehow, even if it meant helping Filipov's cold, iron justice by obeying the soldier's order . . . He was annoyed with the other prisoners' laziness: they made a huge fuss, as if they had to carry armloads of wood.

What everyone else already knew didn't seem to matter to him that much:

The verdict was carried out at around two in the morning. Filipov was standing off to the side, at the edge of the courtyard. Near the fence, someone was smoking a cigarette; you could only see its red ember . . .

People were talking about it in the cell and outside—but quietly and only in snatches—some had their own separate terror of the morning that would come for them, but they weren't complaining, they accepted it, as if it were an impending storm, with thunder and lightning.

More than anything else, they were interested in the red ember glowing from someone's cigarette in the corner of the courtyard near the fence, to them the ember was like a rainbow after a storm that promised there would be no more storms . . .

While they were out exercising, Yuzi kept on trying to distance himself from the groups of prisoners muttering secrets to each other.

His mood:

Depressed, downtrodden, and almost angry with everyone else. Some wanted only to get away and be free of this place. Those who did wouldn't care about the others left behind or the new prisoners who would come later. Some would either return to their smuggling or would be too afraid to. And in any case there would be no one to think all this through properly, except Filipov with his cold, iron justice, and the sailor Igumenko. Guarding the cell yesterday, when the clockmaker was crying, Igumenko gave him a piece of bread and tried to comfort him: "Don't cry, never mind, well, so they're going to shoot . . . never mind."

Remaining on the sidelines would no longer help Yuzi. The whole time the young man clung to him, asking for advice regarding the message for Reb Aaron's wife about the rubles. What should he do if they kept him here longer? How would he let her know?

"Do you understand? They might send me somewhere far away."

Yuzi didn't hear this clearly and wanted to be left alone. He remembered the five gold teeth—the teeth that stuck out of the red rubber dentures; they were all mixed up with Reb Aaron's cache of rubles and would forever weaken and trivialize the fine, pious wisdom that he had recited over the Shabbos challah before dying.

It was around two in the afternoon.

In preparation for Sunday, the prisoners' wives and relatives filled the courtyard as if it was a cemetery on the eve of a holiday and they were visiting the dead.

It was a wintry day and freezing cold outside. The snowy dirt penetrated everywhere: you could feel it in your heart, your soul, and you couldn't tell from the dark, smoky heaven whether it was going to rain or snow.

Boots shuffled in the prickly dampness of the courtyard; they were annoyed at themselves.

In the exercise area, sleepy prisoners exchanged words over the fence that separated them from their relatives; a head with eyes that looked as if they came from the other world asked what was going on at home: "Is Munele going to cheder? . . . Huh? Is he?"

Someone coughed.

"In the office? Eh? Who's there?"

"Three of them."

"'Him' too?" (That meant Filipov.)

From another corner, someone else said, "If he's there, it's bad—but can you come to an understanding with him?"

"You hear? That's what I'm telling you . . . Give it a try, go up to him . . ."

Then the windows of the office suddenly shot out a mean look; this was when the fires were lit; a couple of new prisoners had been summoned very quickly, apparently as witnesses. But they were stopped in the dark corridor just outside the office. Comrade Sasha was running back and forth, her hands full of papers. Agitated bursts of staccato speech could be heard coming from the office, something about a path that people were still using to smuggle contraband across the border. What agent Zubok and investigator Andreyev were saying was interrupted by an angry voice—angry as a fist banging on a table—Filipov's voice. Later, in the exercise area, the prisoners crowded around the frightened witnesses, shoving their way closer to them, interrupting one another:

"What did they ask you?"

"Nothing . . . 'He' was screaming at the agent and the investigator in the office—'You're no better than the prisoners!'"

"I heard, 'We could arrest you and make the prisoners your jailers.'"

"He really laid into them."

"And the woman, Pinke Vayl's mother, the one who was wearing a shawl over her shoulders and crying—he just released her son."

They started pushing toward the fence, closer to the circle of people around Pinke's mother, who was crying.

✦

It was the afternoon of a gray Tuesday or Wednesday.

Yuzi saw that Pinke Vayl was free and easy on the other side of the fence; he was walking around the courtyard in the Red Army uniform that was too big for him. He was wearing a new, high sheepskin hat and black boots; carrying a saddle in his hands, he strode purposefully to the office with a soldier. The soldier had a rifle. Pinke stopped, put the saddle down, and started to roll a cigarette from the cheap tobacco that his friend held out for him.

"Comrade Spivak!" he called out joyfully. "I'm coming to see you! How are you? Comrade Spivak!"

The girlish charm around Pinke's mouth and eyes showed even more.

"I got a haircut," he said, taking off his cap to show Yuzi—who was standing at the fence. "When they released me—very short, close-cropped, you see? And I sent my mother home, oy, did she hear it from me about making an honest living. She didn't even have money for her fare, so I went to Comrade Filipov and asked him for a couple of rubles. 'Well,' he said, I mean Comrade Filipov, 'Money, too—look at all the trouble you make for me. What do you want to do,' he asked me, 'go back to your regiment or stay here?' I had a think, what's so bad about being here? 'I'll stay here. I'll have a horse here. I'll take packages to the new head of the police in Golikhovke and all the other posts far away. Well, and you, Comrade Spivak, what are you thinking of doing?"

Pinke asked the question as warmly and affably as if both he and Yuzi were serving the same cause: he, Pinke, with his honest deliveries to the distant posts, and Yuzi with his honest imprisonment. Only suddenly he noticed something on Yuzi's pale face. The girlish charm around his mouth and eyes quivered.

"Sha," he said unexpectedly. "Maybe you want an apple? . . . Huh? . . . Comrade Spivak . . . My friend here has some . . . I'll just run and bring you one."

He took a drag from his cheap cigarette and puffed out his chest. With the broad cheeriness of some kind of local big shot, he added:

"You know what, Comrade Spivak? . . . Maybe I'll have a word with 'him,' Filipov, about you . . . He was good to me—I swear, it's the truth! You'll see. I heard them saying there was a lot of paperwork in the office, and no one to take care of it . . . There's a lot of work in the office . . ."

It was at dusk at the end of that very week that Yuzi—on his own—was unexpectedly summoned to the office for interrogation.

He saw Filipov for the first time, right next to him. At first he didn't believe it really was Filipov, because in so many ways the boss, Filipov, didn't resemble the Filipov who had to concern himself with the fate of each person who came here, and the fate of all those who would come later. An ordinary person was sitting across from him, with an ordinary appearance and ordinary greased black boots that smelled like any other greased boots . . .

The lamp had just been lit, the floor just washed; the hallway that was always crowded with people—was now empty. Everything was fresh, as if they had deliberately finished their usual work ahead of time, so they could undertake today's task with fresh heads and fresh energy. That task was Yuzi.

The first room was dark; the second, brightly lit—Comrade Sasha was sitting on one side of the two tables that had been pushed together, and investigator Andreyev was on the other side. They began questioning Yuzi hesitantly, as if they were not entitled to ask anything, because of Filipov. He sat completely alone, at another table with his back to everyone; his head and bandaged neck hanging to one side, as if he were asleep, his arms resting on his knees; on the whole, he looked like a person who was not involved, who just happened to be there, because he was bored and had nothing to do in the whole wide world.

✦

The main question was: who did Yuzi do it for? Who did he steal across the border for, with those Socialist Revolutionary documents? Who was he serving?

Yuzi answered honestly:

He was serving the workers.

Comrade Sasha's irritation showed in her voice:

"What workers?"

And suddenly everyone fell silent. At the other table Filipov moved. He was still sitting with his back to them and didn't want to look at Yuzi, as if he, Yuzi, was some kind of repulsive thing. Without warning and in the dissatisfied voice of someone who had just been awakened, he asked, "*A ty kto, rabochii?* Do you take yourself for a worker?"

And with this the first interrogation ended.

Yuzi was shaken by the sound of Filipov's voice. He heard the words in a state of confusion. The feeling remained with him afterward that he owed someone an answer—most of all, himself.

Back in the cell, in his previous spot among the prisoners, he examined his memory for what was wrong with his answer. Suddenly his search took him back to his early years, and he remembered the silken voice of his father, who died young, who used to read Torah, and his mother's Hebrew verses, and his grandfather's unresolved lawsuit against the landowner. His grandfather was gray, big, and strong, and even greater than his size and strength was his piety. He used to wear a long white kittel under his tallis on Yom Kippur and both days of Rosh Hashanah, and would chant the morning prayers with great intensity. Once on Rosh Hashanah his grandfather gave a great cry while exalting God—with such a quaver and in such a loud voice that outside, where Yuzi was playing with the other children, his little brother Muli got so frightened that he fell down the steps of the synagogue . . .

Yuzi remembered all this so clearly that the border of the white holiday tablecloth actually sparkled in his eyes and the fragrance of a piece of watermelon from that distant Rosh Hashanah morning tickled his nose. At the same time he tried to recall the question that he had to answer, and remembered Filipov's sleepy appearance—and his angry voice:

"*A ty kto, rabochii?* Do you take yourself for a worker?"

Again the question confused him:

This was the question that was asked of him and others like him.

The question silenced him. It was like the question a child would ask: "What is the meaning of life?" It was better to speak of other things, more cheerful, less fundamental.

The fact was that others who had given their lives and deaths to the workers' movement could also have experienced Rosh Hashanahs like Yuzi's.

Others were more indifferent toward the movement—they may even have been workers, but to the movement it was all the same.

But it was possible that . . . Nonetheless . . .

The movement could have had an entirely different face—had it been led from the beginning by people like Filipov, a worker from the mines.

Perhaps Filipov was the true face of the movement. This movement would, without hesitation, burst all of Yuzi's tales of his grandfather, or would simply shoot him, without compromising.

It was strange:

Since the age of sixteen, he had been ready to sacrifice his life to the workers' movement. And now the movement was going to shoot him.

They began to summon him for interrogation frequently, almost every day, and always at dusk like the first time. Freshly aired rooms, floor still damp, and freshly lit lamps on tables that had just been cleared off—created a special atmosphere.

It seemed that for his sake they hastily finished their work with other prisoners, because they wanted to hear with fresh ears how he would answer the questions:

"How long have you been a Socialist Revolutionary?"

"Where were you in October 1917?"

One time, he was standing cold and mute in the tidy and bright office across from investigator Andreyev, when Comrade Sasha came running in from Filipov's distant room wearing a white robe.

She ran very quickly.

She was very excited.

She was as pleased as a midwife who had come to say that after a long and difficult labor, she had finally delivered the baby.

She waved her arms, signaling that the interrogation should be broken off—whatever it was that had occurred in Filipov's room was more important. Because she was so excited and so pleased, she forgot that Andreyev was the interrogator and Yuzi the prisoner, and she asked them both at once:

"Who can bandage wounds? Quickly now, quickly, tell me who?"

Her face was red and her eyes sparkled.

The minute he saw her, Yuzi thought that everything that separated people into prisoners and investigators could be made null and void, and he therefore said quickly and uncertainly:

"I can."

And because the emphasis on the word "I" was too strong, he realized what he'd done, and added, "I was a medic during the war."

But Comrade Sasha didn't hear him, and she started dragging him by the sleeve to Filipov's room.

"Quicker . . . quicker . . ."

Thinking he had made a mistake, Yuzi felt dazed all over again when he entered Filipov's room. He felt sick as he glanced at the disorder; the first thing he noticed were the window shutters straight across from him. A strong wind banged them together, but through the crack that remained, he could still see the darkening twilight outside.

A small table stood in the middle of the room. The lamp was lit. Its green shade had been removed and placed on the side. Filipov was standing at the table, wearing pants and boots but not a jacket or shirt.

The strong, muscled, upper half of his body was bent over an earthenware bowl on the table—as if he was going to wash his hair. His bare arms were folded over his chest. Muscles on his shoulders tensed and quivered as if from cold, but his head and face, suffused with blood, bent deeper and deeper over the bowl, and then drop after drop of pus started to drip into the bowl from a couple of swollen wounds on his neck.

He snorted cheerfully, as if in a steambath.

"Get out of me! Here it comes . . . Oozing rot just like the bourgeoisie . . . life in the mines takes everything out of you . . . Now I'll feel better."

With quick, skilled hands Comrade Sasha tore off pieces of gauze in long narrow strips. Yuzi washed his hands, squeezed the swollen wounds, bandaged Filipov's neck, and washed his hands again.

By then Filipov was sitting on a chair in the middle of the room like someone who had had his hair cut at home. He pointed at the bowl with his eyes, signaling Comrade Sasha, "Take it away."

Then Yuzi looked up from under his brow at Filipov—just like that, gave him a look. A certain feeling grew stronger in his breast—compassion for a worker from the mines, who had become the boss of Kamino-Balke, and who thought the bourgeoisie was like pus in his wounds. That was him, Filipov, whose question Yuzi had to answer:

"*A ty kto—rabochii?* Do you take yourself for a worker?"

Yuzi Spivak was still standing there in the room, although no one needed him for anything.

"What are you doing here?" asked Filipov, not understanding why he was still there.

Not recognizing his own voice, Yuzi quietly said:

"*Ne rabochii* . . . I'm not a worker."

"What?"

Spivak turned pale and felt the cold that always accompanied the most difficult moments of his life. He had to remind Filipov that he had asked him several days ago whether he was a worker and he had not answered.

Then Filipov looked at Yuzi's knees, as if noticing for the first time that Spivak's legs were somewhat crooked, and apparently, since childhood.

"Good," he nodded.

And he ordered Yuzi to return to the office so his answer could be entered in the interrogation record.

From that time on, sitting in the cell, Yuzi felt even more undone than before. His last answer tormented him more than a death sentence. That he was not a worker played over and over in his brain, and that they had written it down in the record . . . that was the main thing . . . they had written it down . . .

He felt so sick that it would have been better to die as quickly as possible. However, other thoughts also kept spinning in his brain—that all of them—Filipov, Comrade Sasha, and all the others (not to speak of the hangers-on)—all of them were probably not one hundred percent saints. They concealed their own self-indulgence, the things they did even here at Kamino-Balke . . . Take Comrade Sasha, for example. A few days ago, while waiting in the corridor, Yuzi heard her telling someone in the office that she was going to celebrate her name day with a lot of hoopla—right here at Kamino-Balke . . .

13

The rumor in Golikhovke was:

Insurgents were banding together in the villages along the border.

No one knew whether they were loyal to Petliura or someone else. For a few days a tall, pockmarked man hung around there with papers that showed he was a local. There was no sign that he was going to be arrested. Then he disappeared. At night you could hear someone shooting, not with a rifle, though—with an automatic.

It was Pinke Vayl who carried the report about all this through Golikhovke; he rode his horse all the way from a distant border post.

The day—frozen, slippery, muddy, its eyes half-closed, about to sneeze.

The road, tossing and turning 'til dawn, took five hours. Pinke's young horse was gray and smudgy. When it galloped quickly, it slapped itself on both sides with its short tail as if it were playing. Now it was slowly making its way up one of Golikhovke's streets.

Pinke sat in the saddle like this:

Bent over, with his rifle slung over his back—nodding along with his tired horse. He was happy no one knew the secret he carried.

He looked at the street as he rode and saw wooden houses with whitewashed roofs.

Under his high sheepskin hat Pinke's face with the girlish charm around his mouth overflowed with the curiosity that the curtained windows provoked in him:

"Have a look—the Jews here! "

"Look!"

"They're quite something . . ."

When he had the chance to meet someone, even someone he didn't know at all, he would smile down from his horse, just an ordinary smile at a passerby; the smile meant:

"About those secrets I have, nothing doing, you won't find out from me . . ."

Alongside one house, he got down, dead tired and hungry, and tied up his horse.

He tried the door. It was locked.

Pinke knocked.

Pointless!

The house didn't open, just like a grave doesn't open.

He walked around all four sides, it was a strange house, to say the least. The back door was also locked.

But there he noticed the crooked windows of another wing. On one windowsill he saw strips of fabric, on a second, a tailor's little oil can. From that window you could hear the noise of a sewing machine.

Pinke tried knocking on the window, but at first the sewing machine drowned out the sound because it was focused on sewing. Then it seemed to hear something—it stopped when Pinke knocked a third and fourth time, but it didn't do anything about it, because it was nothing more than a machine.

Pinke was starting to leave, when the door from the other wing opened behind him ever so slightly.

In the dark slit of the open door Pinke saw, instead of a machine, a short Jewish girl in a red kerchief. The girl's eyes looked at him in a friendly, curious way. They were strangely round, black, almost without whites; her nose was small, but very clever, or so it seemed to Pinke. He had never seen such a witty nose.

The girl finally stuck her head out. Her kerchief was embarrassed, it was red, like fire. She asked in Russian: "Who do you need?"

Her smile said in Yiddish, "Who are you looking for?"

"Me, looking for someone?" Pinke's raised shoulders testified it hadn't even occurred to him to be looking for anyone.

"I'm just passing through. I've been on the road since five in the morning. To tell the truth: I'm just plain hungry is all. I'd be grateful if you could show me where I can buy something to eat."

There was silence. The girl, apparently, was getting advice from her clever nose. Her eyes kept looking at Pinke in their friendly, curious way.

"You don't need anything else?" she smiled.

"What else should I?"

"Nothing . . ."

Out of curiosity the girl wanted to know: where Pinke was from, and why he was such a fool to think that someone here would sell him food.

"No, here in Golikhovke no one needs any Red Army soldiers. Imagine: we have better ways of making a living—here they're all cooks."

"Cooks?"

"Yes. Cooks . . . They cook and bake, but not for people like you—here you make 'arrangements' with travelers trying to steal across the border. They grovel in front of the wealthy ones . . . and then lick their chops. Understand? Here it's Sodom."

Pinke kept looking at the girl and seemed very ashamed, that it was Sodom here, and that he was a fool and didn't know it.

"I get it," he said. "What do you think? I'm a six-year old?"

"Well, good for you," but the girl's clever nose still didn't believe him. "As long as you understand . . ."

The girl was surprised at something else: how was it that at Kamino-Balke, which was where Pinke was from, they still didn't know this was Sodom? She was not a local girl, she was not from around here. She had been working all of four weeks for a ladies' tailor.

"But," she said, "what I've managed to see here is quite something. I'll have stories for my great-grandchildren, what else could anyone ask for? My boss is more of a matchmaker than a ladies' tailor; he's always out fixing people up with transportation. Here we have a certain Yokhelzon, an undercover agent, one of the first communists, so he says. All business goes through him lately. There's this blonde, a Christian, she's his second wife, if you get me—what, God forbid, he's not supposed to enjoy himself? They say there's a path between the village of Harne and Belo-Kut. For the right price he'll take you through in broad daylight . . . But wait . . . hold on a minute . . ."

The girl rushed into the house and returned with a big chunk of bread.

"Here," she said to Pinke. "This is my own bread, you can eat it. It's not for the 'matches.'"

"No, many thanks just the same."

Pinke would rather starve a whole day than take her bread.

"What, do you think at Kamino-Balke we have no bread, God forbid!"

He was full of feelings he had never before experienced—not only for this girl, but even for the narrow corridor, the crooked windows of this part of the house, and the foot pedals of the sewing machine, whose sound he had heard—good health to her, to this girl! He was going to regret that he had not stood there with her for at least another minute. He would regret it his whole life. Now, however, he would quickly ride away into the fog that stretched between Golikhovke and Kamino-Balke, and the more quickly he would ride, the more his feelings would grow for that girl's nose, full of wit.

From either gratitude or regret that he hadn't stayed with her a little while longer, he wanted to jump onto his horse as quickly as he could, to do something for the girl, a good thing, a great thing. He would tell Filipov about Yokhelzon and the pathway between the village of Harne and Belo-Kut. But this didn't compare to his regret over leaving the girl so quickly. He would ask Filipov whether he was going to send men—say, fifteen or so—against the insurgents in the far villages along the border. If the answer was yes, Pinke wanted to be one of them.

✦

For several nights, a tall man, not a local, stayed over in Golikhovke with Galaganer the dentist. He wore a gray overcoat, like the Pokras brothers, only he was older, fat, pockmarked, had a thick, blond moustache and small, black eyes—he was a Christian. If you looked in the window, you could see that he had to bend down to leave the house—he had this way of walking . . . like the wind was blowing at him from all four directions even though it was perfectly still outside.

"This is the same man who was seen in the villages along the border. He had the papers of a local on him, and then disappeared."

"It's one of Sofia Pokrovskaya's Socialist Revolutionaries, like the dentist Galaganer."

That's what they were saying in Golikhovke, because the police chief and soldiers from Kamino-Balke had once raided Galaganer: they surrounded the house and searched the attic, the basement, and every room—it wasn't important that they couldn't find anyone because:

That same night Sofia Pokrovskaya could have hidden the stranger somewhere near where she lived.

But if Sofia Pokrovskaya's group was extremely agitated, it also could have been because something had happened to Yuzi Spivak at Kamino-Balke.

"Listen: the Jewish soldier who was at Isaac the tailor's place; he let the girl who worked there know that Spivak sits for days on end with 'them' in the offices at Kamino-Balke and copies out documents."

People in Golikhovke, all worked up, said:

"Well, then, that's a pain for Sofia Pokrovskaya's SRs."

"Who needs them anyway? She's going to bring down the whole city, that Miss Priest."

"If not for them, no one would be inspecting Golikhovke so closely."

Now, because of the story with Aaron Lemberger from the tannery, it got even quieter in Golikhovke than before. But it was still possible to make a living, because people were still trying to get across the border. They paid Yokhelzon big money. Then there were the prisoners' wives who found their way to Golikhovke using paths so hidden as to be almost underground.

People said about these women:

"The rich get anything they want."

"They're stuffed with money."

"Well, yes. You just have to be able to . . . Any idea how much it costs?"

The rich wives came here for the most part at dawn, when people were still asleep in their beds. They paid off the drivers in the fields and arrived in town any which way, one at a time, on foot.

Crowing roosters greeted them at the bottom of the mountain as they hastily and fearfully made their way to town. No lamps were lit anywhere. In their white underclothes people somehow managed to get up from bed and strained their ears until they heard quiet footsteps waking the sleeping windowpanes outside.

Sleepy voices grumbled hoarsely in harsh whispers. Old men, short of breath, coughed out the remainder of the night they had slept poorly.

In the gray darkness the townsmen divvied up the rich wives like a forbidden nighttime gift. They paid their debts using the women; they called them "ladies of the night."

One neighbor would say to the other:

"Be quiet, don't yell! Good: from me you're getting two 'ladies.' I won't, God forbid, bankrupt you."

You spoke to them in a quiet, hoarse snort. You told them to lie low and pay well.

Sighing, you told them about the business with Aaron Lemberger so you could earn a bit more. You winked at the lowered curtains and said something about Filipov.

"Was he there?"

"He was everywhere."

"He can hear everything."

From the winking and the quiet whispering, the wives who weren't from Golikhovke gathered the impression that Filipov was actually somewhere close by—perhaps even sleeping here in the same house, in another room.

What they were afraid of was unclear and secret.

There was still more news, which did not get reported to the rich wives, to keep them from running away. You talked about it quietly in the kitchen, while the "ladies of the night" were sleeping:

"Galaganer's house was surrounded again last night. This time they looked in the neighboring houses, and they took all the 'ladies' that they found back to Kamino-Balke."

14

After the second search on Galaganer's street, Yokhelzon the undercover agent ran to the blonde, the Christian woman staying at Shmuel Voltsis's, and ordered her to get rid of the two heavy cases as quickly as she could. He had learned:

"They'll be searching every house in Golikhovke."

The blonde didn't let him touch her cases. Lazily, she inquired: "Get rid of them where?"

Yokhelzon answered angrily, as if he no longer loved her:

"In the river if you have to . . . Burn them even . . . Lives depend on it . . ."

The blonde stood with her back to Yokhelzon and didn't move an inch. Yokhelzon closed the door behind him and yelled at her loudly.

In Shmuel Voltsis's house they said:

"Just listen to this! They're already quarreling like a kosher married couple!"

Yokhelzon left. But then he came running back again, screaming: if they found her cases during the search—they'd shoot him, too, together with her, because he knew all about it but kept quiet. If she didn't obey him, he'd go tell Kamino-Balke what she had in those cases.

At Shmuel Voltsis's they said:

"Just listen to that! Now it's clear what's hidden in those cases."

Afterwards, the blonde spent the whole night crying—her eyes were swollen and red from regret that she had given her body to a Jew.

When morning came, she wrapped herself in shawls and scarves and stood outside, freezing; she would run to the market whenever she saw a wagon arriving.

At Shmuel Voltsis's they almost died. The wife brought her clenched fists right up to her husband's nose. She had just beaten herself over the head. Gnashing her teeth, she screamed about the blonde:

"*Gevalt!* We're going to die because of her! . . . You, bastard you! . . . Why are you letting her make a run for it?"

Feigning indifference to spite his wife, Shmuel Voltsis just stood there with his hands in the pockets of his trousers. Deep inside, he had already decided: clenching his teeth, he'd take both of the blonde's heavy cases and hurl them into the street and, after that, he'd take the blonde herself and throw her out of the house, too.

"Get out of my house," he'd tell her. "Oh-you-tee, out! Get the hell out! I don't want to have anything to do with you any longer."

He would do all that later in the evening, when it got darker. But when it got darker—the blonde came back with someone else.

She brought a poor man in a torn shirt, patched-up linen pants, and bast shoes laced up around his narrow, nimble feet—a religious, God-fearing peasant from the village of Harne, not far from Yokhel-zon's secret path to the border. He looked dirty and absent-minded, like a dimwit; he answered every question with a vigorous shake of his gray head:

"Yup."

"Yup."

"Could be."

"*A yak zhe?* How else?"

The blonde locked herself in the room with him. Hastily unbuttoning her blouse, she showed him the crucifix on her chest: let him see that she was a real Christian who had nothing to do with these kikes. Then she ordered food for the peasant and launched into a long story. She swore to him. She cried and cried.

After that, she crossed herself and then the peasant—and then spent a long time whispering something to him.

"Yup, yup," the goy answered.

"Could be."

"*A yak zhe?* How else?"

The door to the room swung open.

Laden with the blonde's cases, the peasant, glassy-eyed, shuffled out of the house, as if his feet were shackled. He disappeared into the darkness outside.

In Shmuel Voltsis's house it was suddenly easier to breathe:

"Finally!" they said. "That's the end of that!"

The room, it seemed, was emptied—four bare walls. All that was left to do was open the windows and let the wind blow around. The blonde and her child spent only one more night there—but for Shmuel Voltsis and his wife it was not a night, but a nightmare. In the still of the night they could hear the blonde erupting in tears, again and again. She wailed, deeply repenting that she had slept with Yokhelzon the undercover agent.

She—a devout Christian—had let her body be defiled by a dirty Jew without rhyme or reason. She crossed herself and pleaded with God to forgive her. She suddenly turned holier-than-thou, blessed with the strong faith that God would help her.

✦

In the morning she bundled up the child and put on her furs. She piously closed her eyes and, without saying a word to anyone, as if she were in the middle of a prayer, left the unclean Jewish household.

Avoiding the market, she set out through the snow-covered fields in the direction of Harne, where the peasant had taken her cases the night before. Regardless of what happened, she would trust in God and keep walking toward the village with her child in her arms; there, she would spend the night and then continue on toward the border. She held her child somewhat higher than other mothers. She pressed her head to the child's little head—as if she didn't feel the child's weight. She dashed ahead, her steps light, barely touching the dirty snow—this alone was a sign that God had accepted her prayer and was helping her. Without sensing any effort, she charged ahead with her eyes closed. Peasants passing her in their wagons were frightened of what they saw—astonished, they gave her the right of way.

✦

In the small village of Harne six little houses on one side of the street looked across the way to the three little houses sparsely planted on the other side. These were the only structures in the village; besides them, there was nothing else. All nine houses hibernated the entire winter exposed to the elements—it seemed that the wind blew at them from every side.

Cats and dogs wandered around the nearby fields; they took each step carefully, afraid of sinking deeply into the snow.

Whenever the wind blew, the well crane rattled and wailed its God-fearing supplication for the whole village to hear.

Every screech swore:

"I have no idea whether the border is close or far."

Now it was cold and quiet. The smoke from the chimneys rose through the thin, frosty air like damp incense sent up to the heavens. The thickest smoke billowed from the chimney from the biggest house, in the corner of the village. There wood burned in the stove day and night because the blonde had promised—as if she were in the middle of a prayer—to pay well for the expense.

The spacious room had freshly whitewashed walls covered in icons, an earthen floor, and a pile of cushions on a large bed. It was empty, as if the owners had gone to a fair. Not a soul was in it, save the blonde—and her two cases and the child.

After her journey by foot the previous day, she had spent the night, in paroxysms of devotion, full of God-fearing belief that a miracle would be visited upon her, a sinful woman, who was purifying herself, because miracles were generally visited upon the penitent . . .

Her repentance consisted of accusing and cursing Yokhelzon, the dirty Jew, to whom she had given her body. The more she degraded and besmirched him in her thoughts, the more she felt herself becoming holier and purer. As she knelt, her gaze was fixed on an icon in the corner, right under a rafter: it was the Mother of God, decorated with an embroidered cloth.

The blonde was fasting. Since the early morning she had been kneeling and bowing her forehead to the ground in a stubborn resolve not to move from her place until she prayed her way into a miracle.

A half-miracle had already been visited upon her the day before: she had walked here on foot in broad daylight, and no one had dared to stop her, as if all the passersby she encountered had been blindfolded.

Her strength somehow lasted long enough for her to carry the child ten miles. That's why she spent the morning kneeling and fasting in gratitude and prayer to the Holy Mother:

"Complete your miracle, see it through to the end—to the other side of the border."

After several hours of fasting, pious supplication, and kneeling, the blonde felt decisive. By then she was on such good terms with the Mother of God that she felt they were sisters. So as not to lose this new relative, she kept sighing and praying under her breath even after she finally rose from her knees.

The peasant food, which the landlady had cooked and brought to her, wasn't particularly inviting and didn't elicit the slightest appetite.

This itself—her lack of hunger—was a sign that she was deeply imbued with purity and holy exhaustion. It was easy for her to sit at the table and feed the child as if this were a sacred meal.

She crossed herself again and took a bite of food between her teeth—slowly and all the while continuing to look at the icon of the Mother of God, thinking she didn't have to chew it. It would be consumed by holy fire as if it were an offering. She closed her eyes and recalled the Last Supper, Jesus's final meal.

It was then that the gray-haired peasant entered, wearing his ripped, brown shirt and patched-up pants. He tied the cases to both ends of a short pole hoisted on his shoulders. If anyone asked him anything, he would answer:

"Yup."

"Could be."

"*A yak zhe?* How else?"

It was about two o'clock in the afternoon. The winter day flickered like a short, coarse candle that could go out all of a sudden. This was the right time to set out, so that without rushing, they could reach their destination by nightfall. There, the revolution was no longer in charge—its last strength had flickered and was going out.

The border was a mere five miles away.

The peasant, both cases hoisted on his shoulders, walked along the narrow road that divided the flood of bluish white snow; the blonde, wrapped in shawls and scarves, followed a long distance behind him. Just like the day before, she held the child higher than other mothers, her face brushing up against the child's head. This created the impression that the burden she was carrying wasn't heavy—her steps were light, her whole figure flowing as if she were just about to be blessed with a miracle. Her eyes closed, she kept repeating the same words about the miracle with great devotion, so that every cell of her body would believe it:

"It's coming to pass . . . It must be . . . It must . . ."

Whenever the blonde opened her eyes, she saw the peasant with her two cases getting farther and farther ahead of her. This didn't bother her: after two days of penitential sighs and tears, her previous, sinful life was so far behind that she was necessarily protected against all the misfortunes that could befall a sinner.

The road led into a small forest. By the time she got there, the peasant with the two cases had disappeared from view. But she would not frighten herself—completely assured of her safety, she shut her eyes again and walked farther. The little forest turned out to be a lot bigger than it had seemed, but that, too, didn't bother her.

The main thing was:

To surrender fully—to surrender her entire body—to the miracle and not forget it even for a minute.

"It must happen . . . It must . . . It's coming to pass."

The blonde didn't want to rejoice in her arrival at the end of the forest too soon. Hadn't she believed in her success from the beginning? Why had she ever doubted?

Suddenly, from the edge of the forest, she heard a loud cry. No one answered. It sounded like a shot that hadn't reached its target. But this in no way concerned her—she was, after all, in the middle of her miracle.

The forest was now behind her. For a second, she opened her eyes and saw, from afar, a tall man in a fur coat, empty-handed.

What could this mean?

A sick vision. Apparently—a temptation! When this happened to the saints, they ignored it; they walked by without taking any note.

She quickly shut her eyes again, clung all the more forcefully to her belief in the miracle.

"It must be . . . It's coming to pass . . . Coming to pass . . ."

✦

This happened in the evening, when there was a light wind. It got colder toward nightfall; a cold, translucent fire surrounded the sun setting behind the snow-white mountain.

The wind blew the shawl from the blonde's shoulders and stripped her head bare. The sleeping child leaned her head against her cheek. The blonde walked with a gait that was supposed to frighten anyone coming into yielding to her, as if she were the Mother of God.

But the tall man in the fur coat remained standing in her way. He leaned sideways a little.

He coughed—he coughed for a long time and very matter-of-factly, like a man who had simply caught a cold.

She halted a few steps in front of him, eyes wide open. With her free hand, she covered the child's face and scanned her surroundings in all directions, as if she were looking for a place to hide.

What she saw was this:

The peasant with her cases was disappearing up the second mountain—on the other side of the frozen river that was called "the border."

And suddenly all was clear. The peasant had shown her the place where she should cross the border, and it was precisely there that this ordinary man in his fur coat caught her. This was a man who would never think that the "Mother of God" was considering going over to the other side.

"Are those your cases?" he asked.

With his hand, he gestured in the direction where the peasant had vanished.

Immediately, the blonde felt sinful and ordinary once again— exactly the way she had felt two days earlier. With frightened eyes, she stared at his face—the face of an eternal enemy, who would never believe that the Mother of God had stepped out of an icon frame. This was the face of someone she couldn't bribe, not even with her body.

Because she didn't answer him, his voice hardened:

"I'm asking you, lady: are those your cases?"

She saw the white gauze on his neck.

And, suddenly, something else occurred to her:

This was him—Filipov himself . . . From that place, Kamino-Balke . . .

Her misfortune, her bad luck became clear—it was plain, matter-of-fact, like his cough, and brought her back down to earth. At other border crossings it might have been possible to come to an agreement, work out a deal, but the devil brought her to this stretch of the border, to this man who was now standing across from her and asking her:

"Are you by yourself, or is someone else with you?"

Finally, she answered, in a frightened, quiet voice:

"By myself."

He took a long look at the other side of the border.

"A pity," he said regretfully. "Looks like we'll never find out what was in your cases."

And, once again, he coughed—very matter-of-factly, like a man who'd simply caught a cold.

"Let's go," he said.

A boundless sea of hatred swelled up inside her—hatred toward him and all of his cronies who had installed him at his post. She felt strongly compelled to curse him, swear at him, and tell him they would be torn to pieces—people like them had been ripped to pieces once. Yes. Yes. Torn to pieces.

Her hands trembling, she bundled up her child again.

She followed Filipov only for a minute. Then, suddenly, she halted.

Filipov turned around to look at her.

She was sitting in the snow. She had placed her child on her knee and was crying silently, big tears rolling down her cheeks.

Coughing, he croaked out the words:

"What's wrong?"

Then, suddenly, she became her pious self again and looked at him with new eyes, strange eyes: each pupil revealed another woman inside, and each woman had a crucifix hanging on her breast.

"I have no strength left," she said. "I'm tired. I can't carry the child any farther."

"So that's it?"

His eyes looked around for help in the surrounding nothingness for a couple of minutes.

"There isn't much that can be done," he said. "Give me the child, I'll carry her. And you'll just have to drag yourself there somehow—it's not far."

15

That evening at Kamino-Balke:

Just as they were lighting candles inside, Filipov banged on the door. He was holding a child in his arms. The child's mother—the blonde who had been arrested—was trailing behind.

Filipov looked dissatisfied and annoyed; he was scowling. He didn't say anything, as if everyone was supposed to know. He was sick of having to be everything—the boss and the nanny.

The flames reflected in the office windows were angry. They illuminated the woman's first, long interrogation.

Afterward, when it was late at night, Pinke Vayl and others had to get up—to go to the telegraph station and send dispatches about the documents found on the woman. They were ordered to stop in Golikhovke on the way back and arrest a few people named on a list.

The first name Pinke read on the list was very long and complicated: "Shmuli-Avrom Aaron Volkovitsh Kushnir."

In Golikhovke he was simply called Shmuel Voltsis.

✦

At least in Golikhovke they finally found out who the blonde was:

"She's a courier for the Whites."

"The documents were sewn into the waistband of the child's dress."

"The documents were supposed to be sent abroad to a White general."

"There's a theory that the child isn't even hers—could you know for sure about someone like her?"

One thing was clear:

"The whole town is done for."

"The blonde is a bitch. Hold her feet to the fire, and she'll give the whole town and all us Jews away."

"Shmuel Voltsis first."

"This is just the beginning."

"What a nightmare!"

They put out lights wherever they could. In the neighboring houses people went to bed half-dressed, with their hearts in their throats. Later they heard loud banging on Shmuel Voltsis's door.

In the darkened house next door a terrified woman kept asking her husband, "Who's knocking? Huh? . . . Who's knocking?"

Her husband, all upset, angrily mocked her, "Who's knocking? . . . As if you don't know! Angels are knocking . . . from there, from Kamino-Balke."

His wife lay still, listening.

"They stopped," she said, "maybe they're already inside."

✦

What could Shmuel Voltsis say when they woke him suddenly at night and took him away, under arrest, to Kamino-Balke?

What could he say when Pinke Vayl interrupted his answers, and asked:

"If you're the good guy you swear to be, why did you hide the blonde for two months?"

Shmuel Voltsis had nothing to say to this. He knew that he was done for, and that was it. A great misfortune . . . In his heart and mind it was empty and dark, like the night that surrounded him.

He felt sorry only for his wife, who was crying and lamenting over him as if he were dead, and who didn't want to do anything other than bang her head against the wall.

Out of pity he said to her, "Nekhe, stop . . . stop wailing, you're being told something . . . Well, that's enough, Nekhe . . . They're definitely going to kill me. They already have! . . . Stop whimpering . . . Do you hear what I'm saying to you? . . . I'm going to tear out your innards, Nekhe . . ."

He said all this from great pity toward her—pity without limit: "Nekhe, stop . . . I'd be better off without you, Nekhe."

He gnashed his teeth and tried to kick her.

"You were a cow, like I was, and you and I both kept this misfortune hidden in our house, so what are you bellowing about now, like a calf?"

He kept on lunging at her the whole time, until they removed him from the house. Shmuel Voltsis was being marched off in the middle of the night, surrounded by Red Army soldiers. He was struck dumb, because the answer that he always had at the ready, his excuse—"What do I know, me, Shmuel Voltsis, I'm a simple man"— could no longer serve.

Silenced by his troubles, he allowed himself to be led along.

"That's it," he thought to himself as he considered his position. "Naked and bare you are, Shmuel . . . without shelter, without a wife, without an answer, even—cast out from the world."

The world?

It would be better for the world not to fall into Shmuel Voltsis's hands right that moment, when he was walking with clenched teeth in the middle of the night under guard . . . He would tear it to pieces . . .

He had worked hard at the sawmill since his marriage. But they didn't want to pay him a decent wage. He, Shmuel, knew those people well.

"Those bastards," he used to say about them, "let them catch the plague."

Suddenly the world had become good to him, a pox on it, and begun to shower him with easy money. What'd he know? . . . Nobody believed in God any more, that was for sure. He saw what everyone was doing and did the same . . .

Well? . . . Now it had gone and put his name on the list, it was a fine business, this world, a plague on it.

And was he supposed to have earned this—being taken away in the middle of the night? . . . So he had hidden the blonde whore in his house the whole time . . . So what?

"What am I, a sacrifice or something?"

Shmuel Voltsis wanted only one thing:

If there was justice in the world, all of them, all his fine neighbors—a pox on their throats—should be here next to him! . . . What'd they mean, arresting just him alone? Was he the scapegoat?

It was a good thing they stopped at Yokhelzon the undercover agent's place. They left behind one soldier to guard Shmuel Voltsis and then, checking their weapons, surrounded the building on all sides.

If they caught that wolf in sheep's clothing, there would be no need to take him to Kamino-Balke. It would be enough to hand him over to Shmuel Voltsis right here. He would make mincemeat out of him, the snot, the moldy piece of shit, there would be one less charlatan, one less fop in the world.

Because Yokhelzon, that dolled-up dog, knew what the blonde was and kept quiet.

"I'm telling you, let her stay at your place, it'll be my responsibility, on my shoulders," he had told Shmuel Voltsis.

Where was he now, the dog, with his broad shoulders? . . . Had he managed to sneak off in the middle of the night?

"What a pity!"

"Have you ever heard of such a thing?"

It was good that instead of Yokhelzon, who evaporated, they at least arrested his wife—that hatmaker from Odessa, who had spent half a year wrapped in the silk Turkish shawls that he used to bring her from across the border.

"Come along with us," Shmuel Voltsis said as soon as he saw her. "And where has your fine young man got himself off to? Look here. He left you alone at a time like this—how could he? How is it even possible? He loved you with such great love and slunk off, leaving you in the shit? Come here, come. Let me at least spit in your face exactly the same number of times that he kissed you. Don't run away from me now, you Odessa whore . . . People are saying your Yokhelzon had another wife tucked away somewhere—a wife with two children yet. What? . . . You couldn't just stay in Odessa and keep making hats? You wanted to be a whore in silk Turkish shawls instead?"

The young woman was attractive, her figure lithe even now, in her long, dark shawl that she had thrown over her warm clothes and overcoat—the long, dark shawl that she wore for no reason, unless as a sign that she had been arrested.

In the middle of the night all her quick little steps were imbued with the spiteful dissatisfaction of a wronged woman—each step was an angry expression of her charm.

From minute to minute she quickened her charming gait so as not to hear Shmuel Voltsis's mockery—as if he were a barking dog. She wouldn't look at him.

But Shmuel Voltsis didn't let up and didn't stop flinging dirt at her:

"Listen, where did the Jews get a syphilitic like you?"

"You're an ulcer, you really are."

"A hag."

The young woman couldn't stand it any more. She complained to the soldiers who were taking her and Shmuel Voltsis to Kamino-Balke, and especially to Pinke.

"You're a Jew, right?" she accosted Pinke. "You understand Yiddish. So why are you keeping quiet, you?"

Only Shmuel Voltsis felt that the soldiers actually liked the way he abused her; they were smiling to themselves while they smoked and looked very satisfied. Even at the very minute when she began to complain to Pinke, Shmuel Voltsis's blood was boiling. He lunged at her.

"You there!" he said. "Don't be afraid, I'm not going to hit you. I've only got one more curse . . . Here it is. You and your husband should be struck by lightning, just like you've struck me . . . you and your traitor husband."

"Enough, you," shouted one of the soldiers from behind them, and grabbed Shmuel Voltsis by the back of his neck, "shut up and keep walking!"

Shmuel Voltsis felt that they had tapped him lightly, almost in a friendly way, as if everyone was on his side. He was back at it right away:

"What's wrong with you?" he asked, looking at the woman ferociously, as if he wanted to tear her limb from limb. "What, am I not going, God forbid? Of course, I'm going. Everyone who led me to this fine business should go as nicely as me."

Then everyone walked the last few miles quietly. The final hours of the winter night crept away, and it began to get light. The fields were empty. The rooster's cry could not be heard, even though well-trained ears had long been expecting it.

From far away, from in between the many hills, which lay scattered, one atop the other, the rusty spires of Kamino-Balke's dead monastery came into view. They appeared suddenly on the edge of the horizon, like rusty metal toys, cut from iron or copper. At Kamino-Balke embers still sparkled and glowed from the previous evening, but the fires, it seemed, were cold and still, also awaiting the rooster's cry. These were the fires that would light up the gray day with the judgment handed down that night.

✦

Nekhe, Shmuel Voltsis's wife, was wandering the alleyways behind the houses with the only thing she owned hidden under her shawl: two flasks of alcohol.

This was around three days after her husband's arrest.

If she found a customer for flasks of the ninety-proof, she would send the money to Shmuel at Kamino-Balke. Things were bad there with or without money, people said, because no one was on the take. But without money it was even worse: you should at least have a bit of cash ready in case someone would take it, at least have something to get by.

On the way, Nekhe ran into a few women, she stopped as if to sigh, to keep silent, but there were, after all, a few things to talk about.

"The 'ladies of the night' scattered . . ."

"All of them."

"What are people in Golikhovke going to live on?"

"Rive the slaughterer's wife has one left—her relative."

"Some example! Yesterday she also ran away. She was the last one!"

"We're all going to drop dead from hunger."

"We'll have to scatter, too."

"Where are we going to go?"

They sighed, and looked uneasily in the direction of the farthest villages on the border.

"Maybe we gave in too early?"

"That's what I'm telling you."

"People are saying: Dr. Babitsky . . ."

"Ah, yes. Everyone believes Dr. Babitsky knows something . . . Just a little while ago they came with a wagon to take him to a patient somewhere in a village at the border, he saw something there . . . The deaf-mute went with him. The next day the deaf-mute turned up at the market near the shops. He wanted to say something with his hands, but the doctor came and sent him home."

"The doctor was really angry, he was furious . . ."

"What business is it of his?"

They fell silent for a minute and then started up again about the same thing.

"Something is going on in the villages."

"As if we didn't know."

"I mean Sofia Pokrovskaya and her cell."

"Now they think they're better than everyone."

"They couldn't catch them, though. It's clear no one can."

Not everyone in Golikhovke, however, had lost his head. People believed in a savior who would intercede for them and would not allow them to be harmed, and this was the proof: some people were saying there were disturbances in the area, there was trouble again—something was brewing.

On Sunday Nekhe went to Kamino-Balke to see Shmuel. She took the rubles she got from the sale of the two flasks of the ninety-proof; she had sewn them into a little pocket hidden in her chemise.

At the market, where people were getting on sleighs, the commotion grew by the minute. Peasants were chewing sunflower seeds and laughed at everyone around them. The mothers and fathers of the prisoners threw on fur coats and shawls, and hoisted themselves into wagons—there were only five or six—yelling the whole time, everybody in a great rush, as if expecting looting and killing.

Around twelve o'clock, when Nekhe arrived at the gates of Kamino-Balke, the snow was covered in dirty footprints, and the courtyard was full of wagons that had come from other shtetls nearby.

Looking at the courtyard from a distance, it was possible to imagine that there was a small winter fair taking place. Peasant women from the surrounding villages had gotten cold standing at their booths, so they were warming their hands at fire pans.

From standing in the same place for a long time, the horses pranced of their own accord and kept on dirtying the same spots, just as they would at a fair.

From waiting in the cold for a long time, people stamped their feet and blew into their frozen fists. They warmed themselves at fires scattered here and there.

From the long delay the peephole in the heavy gates yawned with its mouth half-open. The gates opened lazily and then shut. They sleepily grabbed the wife of an arrested man and then ten minutes later spat her out back into the courtyard to make room for another. From the peephole soldiers shouted, "Next in line, keep your places!"

The bunch of people who had been squeezed together, pressing with their bellies against the closed doors, dispersed again. They encircled the woman who had been spat out, their feet leaving footprints all around her in the snow. Their eyes examined her as if there, inside, something extraordinary had taken place. They questioned her:

"Listen here! In the office . . ."

"In the office . . ."

"Who's in charge there?"

Only then the gates found it necessary to discharge a second woman. A shocked, pale female face came out and asked no one in particular:

"How do you like my troubles?"

A little ring formed around her. Her pale, frightened lips told her husband's story:

"A clockmaker . . . he was . . . they're going to shoot him . . . he says they're going to shoot him."

They asked her, "What did they find on him?"

The woman's terrified lips quivered, "Passports . . . twenty. False Polish ones, from the other side . . ."

Someone furrowed his brows in disbelief, "Twenty? . . . Why exactly twenty?"

This was a fattish man in a thick sheepskin coat, unbuttoned—a broad man, with a smooth, shiny stick in his hands; he resembled a cattle-dealer. Bluish red veins covered his face, like the hind parts of a cow that had just been slaughtered. The eyes on that face were diseased; the eyelids were two red, oozing pieces of rotting flesh. He turned away from the woman so that she wouldn't hear him. "Listen: her husband is an informer. He was sent here. I saw my son inside—my son told me."

As he was bombarded with questions, the two pieces of rotting flesh never stopped their coarse winking. Meanwhile, people asked:

"Could it be that your son is lying?"

He looked at the gates and shrugged his shoulders indifferently.

"All right, you've convinced me," he said. "It could be a lie."

He heard more gossip from another bunch of people, not far from the gates; he heard what they were saying.

"Both are in the same cell, as if on purpose. I'm telling you—it's a setup."

"Who do you mean?"

"The Odessa hatmaker and the blonde."

"Because the two of them shared the merit of being Yokhelzon's wives, they'll share the merit of sitting together in paradise."

Then the prison gates lazily opened again to release Nekhe, Shmuel Voltsis's wife. Everyone asked her, "Is it true? He's working in the office? Yuzi Spivak? He's a clerk there? Huh?"

Nekhe's pale lips and glazed eyes couldn't answer, however; she wrung her hands.

"Oy, he's yellow . . . he's so yellow." She twisted her mouth and in a singsong complained, "He is yellow from regret . . ."

It was hard to tell who she was talking about: Yuzi or her husband.

A solid-looking man came through the gates after Nekhe, but he didn't hear what they were talking about and what they were asking him. He was wearing two pairs of glasses with thick lenses and spoke very loudly and deliberately, like someone leading prayers at the synagogue.

"Look," he marveled, "it's still light out, but in the office, they've lit candles, as if it's *neillah*—the end of Yom Kippur."

✦

At that point everyone went home. The news that they would take with them was:

"The blonde and the milliner are together in one cell."

"They tear each other's hair out at least ten times a day."

"The story about Yuzi Spivak is true."

"At night he's with everyone else in the cell."

"During the day he copies out documents in the office."

People got ready to wait for an entire week—an uneventful week—until the following Sunday.

In the middle of its drowsy week, however, one day in Golikhovke roused itself. A couple of coachmen had been released from Kamino-Balke and sent home, and everyone ran over to have a look at them. Their houses were besieged.

"Who let you go?"

"Why?"

It was as if the coachmen had come back from the dead. Their wives shrieked curses in their direction, warding off evil spirits, as if they had been fatally ill and just called back from death:

"Who cares 'why'? What's it to me, 'why'?"

"Thank God!"

"God be praised!"

"As long as they're back home."

The coachmen who had been released suddenly yearned for a new skin after Kamino-Balke; they wanted the bathhouse to be heated in the middle of the week for them, all of them, together. This was the main thing. As far as their hangers-on, who wouldn't stop questioning them, they only wanted for it to be over:

"So, what do you mean 'who'? Well, who else should have ordered our release? Him—Filipov himself. Who else if not Filipov?"

"And 'on what grounds'? God alone knows. No one took any money off us. Anyway, I didn't have any."

For Golikhovke, however, the whole thing remained unclear.

And really, why should they have been released, considering how many other prisoners there were?

One of them was lucky enough to have overheard a few words about Filipov, things weren't so rosy for him there, either, the last few days he had trouble—and from his own people:

"The trouble was with a few Red Army soldiers who were inciting others against him."

"For what?"

"Bad food."

In his dental office, Galaganer's hands shook as he stuffed cotton in the back tooth of one of his patients. Every time he told his patient to rinse his mouth, he rushed over to the window to see whether power had changed hands. He hated the Bolsheviks because he was a Socialist Revolutionary, and had been since he was young. It no longer mattered that much, but he had once been passionately devoted to the cause, and had been imprisoned a few times. But since the war, when he started his dental practice in Golikhovke, it seemed that his passion had been damped down. This was only the way it looked from the outside, however; from the inside the fire was still hot. He burned:

"Fine," he said, "it doesn't matter that they're rebelling over such a trifle—bad food . . ."

And to those for whom a hint was enough, he added, "Every big rebellion can start with something small. We've seen this before . . . yes, on the contrary, even from a small thing."

He was working secretly with Sofia Pokrovskaya's cell in Yanovo and other groups in the border villages, and stubbornly waited for developments. Even if week after week would pass with no news, nonetheless the fire burned in him, he had time. He would stick cotton in his patients' back teeth and wait until a new, quiet day in Golikhovke would rouse itself from its stupor.

16

It was Friday.

The day was like burned food; it smelled like Shabbos cholent that had spoiled. The hours that passed were cold and disgusting—like the cholent itself, like the misfortune in Golikhovke.

"What are we going to live on now?"

The morning hinted at springtime; the sun shone and cheered the white, snow-covered roofs.

The wheels of a wagon made a strangely naked, slapping sound on the far-off dike.

And in the afternoon, when it had become windy and gray again, another prisoner released from Kamino-Balke arrived in town on foot. He was unshaven and very dirty. He was absolutely filthy. He had come alone, taking roundabout paths, circling the town from a distance, slipping behind the houses, and each step he took suggested that he had not really been freed from Kamino-Balke, but driven out. He was a complete orphan and had no one in the entire world; he had nowhere to go.

Yokhelzon's former landlady saw him when she went out the back door to throw out the week's garbage. She swore, "When I spotted him, I was so terrified that I started hiccupping and couldn't stop."

She said this later, when everyone in town already knew that the prisoner was Yuzi Spivak, and that he could be found at his younger brother Muli's, at the pharmacy that had been recently nationalized.

The relatives and wives of the arrested men came running from all over town. Even though Yuzi was known for keeping silent, they hoped to get out of him whatever news they could. The dentist Galaganer also came to have a look, and he said to everyone who stopped him on the way that he wouldn't believe it until he saw Yuzi with his own eyes. But if it really were true, then the reason a few coachmen had been released a couple of days ago was clear:

"They were just a cover for Yuzi, so questions wouldn't be raised as to why they freed only him."

A big crowd stood around the pharmacy. Inside the air was thick with all the people who had come. They wanted to know:

"What's going on at Kamino-Balke?"

Yuzi answered coldly, "What should be going on?"

They asked him, "Well, what about the rebellion? The Red Army uprising?"

He was surprised. "What rebellion?"

"The uprising about the bad food!" was the answer.

They said to each other, "Well, anyway . . . that's the way it is, Yuzi Spivak has stopped understanding what is being said to him."

"There you have it! . . . We've got a new close friend from Kamino-Balke."

A fire burned in Galaganer—the fire that he kept inside. His lips were white with anger, but he restrained himself. He approached Yuzi with narrow eyes, without offering his hand; first he wanted to know for sure whether Yuzi was the kind you didn't give your hand to, ever. He made an effort to prevent his shoulders from quaking in agitation.

"Well, anything bad there?" he asked Yuzi. "You didn't see anything bad there, right? Everything the way it's supposed to be? . . . And who is this Filipov? . . . Is he really a saint? . . . A hundred percent saint?"

Yuzi's response was cold. He wanted Galaganer to change his tone. If he was going to continue to talk to him that way, he, Yuzi, would refuse to answer at all.

"Filipov is a former miner, what of it? . . . Was he a revolutionary? . . . Yes, he was a revolutionary . . . A real one, you ask? Yes, a real one . . . A man of iron? Yes, a man of iron. Are you happy now?"

Galaganer stared at Yuzi, breathing hard through his nose, his lips turning whiter and whiter. Suddenly he gave himself a shake, as if on command, and left the pharmacy.

Outside, however, everyone already knew what Yuzi had said about Filipov: a "revolutionary," a "real one," a "man of iron." Dr. Babitsky emerged from the crowd; smiling with the tip of his nose, he stopped Galaganer.

"Nu, yes," he smiled, 'an iron man and a saint' . . . How's that? I've never met any saint made from iron in my life."

He whispered in Galaganer's ear about Yuzi, "He won't answer the question he's been asked . . ."

Soon he regretted saying this even in a whisper to Galaganer. Why should he, a man on the sidelines, get in the middle of things? After all, his house stood at the edge of town and cared for the surrounding houses exactly as little as he concerned himself with the people around him. It would be better to go home and have a nice, cozy twilight nap, as was his old custom. He would snore, and his snoring would spite the cruel waking hours of the revolution and all its "saints," including the new saint, whose name was Yuzi Spivak; he would snore as a sign that between him and them all bridges had been burned.

✦

Muli Spivak, Yuzi's younger brother, had also belonged to Sofia Pokrovskaya's cell. Muli had participated very quietly, without speaking, because he was generally an extremely quiet and secretive person, who hid his tongue from other people, the way some hide their eyes.

At the beginning of the week he had, as always, worked in the pharmacy in his white lab coat, pouring various powders into small porcelain dishes, adding paper lids to little tubes, writing out prescriptions in his usual nearsighted manner—he was extremely nearsighted.

This time, however, he worked more carefully than usual, afraid that he would make a mistake. This time his nearsightedness was more pronounced, because to his left, on the other side of the curtained glass door, in his cramped bachelor's quarters, his older brother Yuzi was pacing back and forth. He had been there for several days. Sometimes he would read different books in the dim light of the room, while continuing to pace. On those occasions he seemed to be preparing himself for something, as if he had set himself a difficult exam.

Muli had the constant feeling that at any moment his brother would summon him to the dim little room.

From time to time Galaganer would send him angry notes: they all had to do with Yuzi.

Wearing his white coat, Muli separated his powders and sealed glass tubes with paper lids. He had to use his finger to trace the prescriptions that had been written, studying the same lines over and over. While he did this, he read Galaganer's notes, but didn't answer him.

And at the same time Yuzi paced back and forth with measured steps in the dingy room.

He hadn't shaved since his arrest and was growing a wild black beard. Next to the beard, his cheeks looked yellowish, his temples—starkly creased.

His constant pacing either beckoned his brother or saved him the trouble of locking the door. He could be heard clearing his throat, as if it were a fast day.

Muli didn't talk about Yuzi with anyone; he coughed a dry cough, as a pharmacist ought to; only his ears were redder than usual, because of Galaganer's notes and from other reasons.

On the fifteenth or sixteenth day of his pacing Yuzi put on his student's coat—an old, worn coat (it was missing more buttons than all other old coats); and without saying a word, set out on the road for Yanovo.

In town, people were saying:

"He's probably gone to confess to the SRs, to the priest's daughter."

"He's gone to give her an account of himself."

The dentist Galaganer, without stuffing cotton into his patient's mouth—ran over to the window.

"You see, you see!" he said, "Devil take him . . . the lackey, he's become Filipov's lackey . . ."

A few days later practically everyone in Sofia Pokrovskaya's cell gathered in the murky little room at the pharmacy.

The Pokras brothers were there, the dentist Galaganer, a very pockmarked Christian with a blond moustache (the same one who bent over while he walked, as if against the wind, although there was no wind), and also another man, packed tightly into his overcoat, also a Christian, although with a half-Jewish name. They waited for Sofia Pokrovskaya; she hadn't arrived yet.

They sat there the whole night and the next morning and late into the afternoon of the next day. For a long time, they listened to Yuzi, and then spoke against him, separately and as a group. They con-demned him; they put him on trial. Voices were raised against each other, angry voices, and angriest and loudest of all was Galaganer's voice, it burned with the fire he had hidden, which was now re-vealed—a voice that ended with a bang on the table, with a squeak:

"Just a minute! Wait! And the plan? What part of the plan have the Bolsheviks carried out? Wait a minute! . . . Redistributing the land? That's our program!"

And then, as always after Galaganer's hysterical, hoarse outcry, silence would fall, and Yuzi would begin speaking quietly and for a long time until Galaganer's next hysterical, hoarse bang on the table:

"Take that to the Central Committee!"

"Take that to the Central Committee!"

The small room smelled of ashtrays and pungent human sweat. The space was thick with smoke; in the smoke—Yuzi's unwashed, unshaved face, and the unwashed faces of everyone else in the room.

The lamp burned by day. It smoked and smoked. Every now and then Galaganer would drag the Christian with the half-Jewish name into the pharmacy to confer in secret. The latter went reluctantly and spoke hesitantly.

"Well, yes," he said. "I've said it before: there's no question about his treachery; it's clear."

Galaganer got all heated up, his lips grew paler and paler until he could only crank out the words, "Do you hear, this is what's so painful . . . I mean . . ."

"What if he's turned someone in!"

"What if he's denounced us!"

At the beginning of the evening, when lamps were not yet lit, for the most part, but somewhere possibly in some house someone had lit a lamp, everyone emerged from the room, and the last difficult words hovered around Yuzi:

"What have we come to, in fact?"

"Nothing."

"Things are the way they were before."

"Nothing is the way it was."

And everyone went off, each on his separate way, in the dark-ness, into the night that swallowed up the surrounding villages.

The tall, pockmarked man with the blond moustache now had a reason to bend over—a strong nighttime wind was blowing and pushed him to the villages on the border; Filipov had received distressing reports from these places, and then sent them on farther.

✦

Yuzi Spivak spent several nights in the small room at his brother Muli's.

To say he spent the nights was not to say he slept. The nights were leaden and sleepless for both brothers.

Both lay there covered: Yuzi on a small metal bed, Muli on a cot that he put in the room. They put out the lamp. Their eyes were nighttime closed. Their brains—daytime awake.

What was there to talk about if their paths had diverged so widely? Muli later remembered:

"What should you make of your brother's body in the middle of the night, your brother who was distressed and had been judged by his closest comrades, who was lying right next to you the whole night pretending to be asleep—this body that came, like you, from the same father and mother?"

It was in Muli's nature to do this:

One eye remained a little open, even though he had started to fall asleep, and the eye saw in the dark that Yuzi's worn-out student coat lay crumpled on a box—the coat lay there bent over, dejected, as if it had made a long, pointless, idiotic journey.

The coat was missing buttons—many of them.

And a coat loop, too. The lining was reduced to threads stretched over the black wadding, and the material itself was also nothing more than threads, and the whole thing was reminiscent of pains that had been suffered, and an endless new, distant, impending road, whose road? The coat's? His brother's? It was all the same. Let's take, for example, now, in the middle of the night, this coat, and throw it away in the darkness—to hell with everything!

People could knock on the pharmacy door in the middle of the night for a seriously ill family member. Standing amid the medicine cases, next to the lamp he had lit, Muli was ten times more careful than the prescription required. He did everything very quietly so that Yuzi would sleep—if Yuzi was asleep. He was wearing his white coat, Muli was, and coughed very quietly, with his usual cough, the kind of cough that a pharmacist had to have. Let Yuzi do what he wanted, how was this different, if he had already decided, and with such obstinacy . . . He was so stubborn—could anyone get him to change his position even by a hair? . . .

It was quiet now. No one was knocking on the pharmacy door, was Yuzi asleep, or not? What would Yuzi do now? . . . If he planned to leave for the place that everybody expected, he, Muli, wouldn't say anything to him. Yuzi would also no doubt keep quiet until the last minute. Or maybe as he was leaving, perhaps he would say to Muli, "Well?" (while giving him his hand) . . . the hell with it . . . well, anyway, he, Yuzi, would leave . . . he would put on that coat! . . .

The cot under him squeaked as he turned over. If Yuzi were really sleeping now, the squeak would have wakened him. Muli hid his head under the covers. But Yuzi's bed also let out a squeak. From under the covers Muli's ears heard Yuzi say something in the middle of the night—this was a first in the whole time he had stayed with him. Muli's head quickly popped out from under the quilt, then his ears actually heard Yuzi's voice; his ears caught Yuzi's words:

"Also a sinner . . . perhaps."

"Huh?"

"I'm saying perhaps he is also a sinner . . . like all men."

"Who?"

"Filipov."

A pause.

The night was ruined, leaden, the night didn't care.

It was all the same, whether a person like Filipov had given in to temptation, whether he was a sinner deep inside because of what he had done. The thing was, if a group of people were carrying a heavy box, and it fell to one of them to carry it exactly at the heaviest and sharpest part, the place where someone's finger was bound to get cut—that person was not entitled to derive the pleasure called "pity," even for himself, even if he had cut his own finger.

Anyway, someone averse to philosophical inquiry could have concluded that there was one less pleasure in the world.

Only it was Yuzi who just now had said this about Filipov in the middle of the night.

Muli was distressed, and his heart beat very hard, because of what Yuzi said to him in the middle of the night, that alone would have done it, but there was also Yuzi's voice telling him now, in the middle of the night, that Filipov asked at the first interrogation: "*A ty kto—rabochii?* Do you take yourself for a worker?" And how he, Yuzi, remembered: "I remembered our grandfather Mosi's lawsuit against the nobleman . . . And how he shouted the Rosh Hashanah prayers—I remembered, yes . . ."

Muli was listening but didn't understand. "Why is he saying this now, the stubborn fool, when he kept quiet the whole time about more important things?"

And what did grandfather have to do with it?

◆

Because of Yuzi a thin, little horse from Kamino-Balke often stood during the daytime hitched to a post outside the pharmacy. It was saddled and ready. It was Pinke Vayl's horse. The horse looked with almost human eyes at everyone who approached to see if the person would mount it or not. It would shake its head and toss its short tail, as if driving away flies.

At those times, Pinke would sit with Yuzi alone in the small side room of the pharmacy. His huge Red Army overcoat had been altered to fit him and had a long slit up to the waist. He looked sleek in it, and it seemed that he had suddenly gained weight and grown taller.

As he entered the room to see Yuzi, his eyes smiled—they smiled, because he, Pinke, had discovered that he could have certain pleasures in life: whenever he had to travel through Golikhovke on his way to deliver a package, he would stop at the tailor's house and spend a considerable amount of time with the girl in the red kerchief. She smiled at him with her clever nose and told him that her boss, the tailor, had begun little by little to take up his needle again—did he have a choice? People had quit cold turkey—they didn't smuggle anything across the border, she told him, and she and a few other workers here in Golikhovke had started to do other things. The only thing that remained was for them to change the same way that Yuzi Spivak had. Was it true? Everyone was saying that Yuzi had come over . . . Yuzi had come over to our side?

Pinke was very pleased that no matter how long he stayed at the tailor's with her, no matter how many times he asked her whether she was cold, she would always answer no—although her face was blue—her nose was nonetheless clever and would smile at him.

Only this time, while he was with the girl, he felt the need to go see Yuzi at the pharmacy, as a friend, to talk to him privately, and tell him things about Kamino-Balke, things he wouldn't tell anyone else. For example, Kamino-Balke had learned that insurgent groups, led by Socialist Revolutionaries, were forming in the border villages.

"Yup," whispered Pinke, "we know this for a fact."

And to show how firmly they knew this, he pounded on the table with his fist:

"We know, and we've been sent more troops, a small unit, around fifteen men. We have everything, machine guns, grenades. Everyone has a horse. What, you think this is so easy?"

Pinke's brows suddenly looked troubled and he bent closer to Yuzi:

"I should be so lucky as to laze around like some people . . . Yup . . . people are just lazy. Once we had to ride out on patrol, but then it got postponed. Once I even told Filipov, 'What's going to happen? I should be so lucky,' I said to him. I was completely at ease with him. I saw him walking around the courtyard very dejected. I told him so. And he didn't answer me. He had just noticed a bolt—a very rusty bolt from a wagon lying in the dirty snow. He was really angry when he picked it up. 'There it is, damn it,' he said, 'it's lying around in the snow. And later, when they need it, everyone's going to come to me in an uproar, they're going to turn everything upside down.' And he went off to put it away . . . Now you know this, Comrade Spivak, we need more men. I'm telling you this. I'll come back to see you again . . . Are you leaving? Where are you going?"

✦

After Pinke's vist, Muli was frightened all over again that he was going to make a mistake with the prescriptions.

Yuzi could be heard pacing from wall to wall in the dim adjoining room. Sometimes he read books as he walked, and then it would seem once again that he was preparing for a difficult exam.

Perhaps Yuzi really would leave for a long time, even if he had to walk, if not for the fact that he, Muli, had taken his old, worn-out coat to a tailor to mend it and sew on new buttons. Yuzi was waiting, it seemed, for the tailor to bring the coat. Only Muli had made some arrangement in secret with the tailor.

Yuzi himself had gone to see the tailor a few times.

"Maybe tomorrow," the tailor answered. "There's still a lot of work to be done."

And the tailor didn't want to look Yuzi in the eye.

Yuzi cheered up. He put on one jacket on top of another. In the course of a few days he walked around Golikhovke, paraded about as if to show that he wasn't ashamed of the rumors the SRs were spreading about him: he was marching against these rumors.

After that, he stopped waiting for the coat. Wrapping his neck in a scarf, he put one jacket on top of another and ended up back at the pharmacy.

"Well?" he said to Muli (as he gave him his hand).

And he looked at him more cheerfully than usual.

Muli got confused by this alone, because Yuzi looked at him more cheerfully than usual. Only afterward, after Yuzi left the pharmacy, Muli took his new winter coat, the one with the caracul collar, and chased him down the street.

In the street you could see Yuzi changing his second jacket for Muli's coat.

You could see:

Yuzi hesitated for a considerable time, went back to the pharmacy as if he had forgotten something, and then left again, taking the same road as before. He was heading toward Kamino-Balke.

Several days passed. The tailor brought back the old coat in the same condition in which he had received it. The coat remained in Muli's room, an ancient, worn-out thing, without buttons! . . .

17

Sofia Pokrovskaya—in borrowed peasant boots—trudged along the snow-covered fields that were about to thaw and melt. When spring came, the fields would stream into a single river that would flow from Yanovo to Golikhovke.

A damp wind was blowing in her little, dark face, right at the spot where the traces of a moustache made her face look dark and smudgy. The damp wind blew where it liked; it was free, like the spiteful breath of the steppes nearby. It made her close her eyes and stung her whole face up to her ears.

For miles and miles—as far as the two dead windmills above the snow-covered valley—there was no one to be seen.

It seemed as if someone had scattered ash in the valley.

Sofia Pokrovskaya's feet in the borrowed peasant boots sank deeply into the snow. Her gait was crooked, and her shoulders rocked back and forth above her protruding belly, which made her seem unnatural, like a woman in the early days of pregnancy.

She was carrying a package hidden in a sack filled with potatoes and a few eggs, a present for her friend, Dr. Babitsky, who lived in Golikhovke. She breathed very deeply, like a person who was supposed to be moving much more quickly than she was going, but didn't want anyone to know. She cursed with her smudgy-looking, crooked little maw: "The hell with them! They should be torn to bits!"

She reached the first Golikhovke houses around four o'clock and quickly made her way to Dr. Babitsky's. Because of the wind, she looked as though she had been crying; her greed for information peeped out of her wide eyes. She was afraid that something was going to be concealed from her. Her mouth with its moustache grimaced as the pupils of her eyes fixed on Dr. Babitsky.

"Well, what is it, Doctor . . . is there any news?"

She exhaled, instantly driving away both the difficulty of her journey and her shock:

"He's going back there, of all places, back to Kamino-Balke."

Her little nose twitched derisively: "Ccc—comrade . . . Yuzi Spivak . . ."

She sat down and began to smoke, and, waving away the smoke with her nervous fingers, asked, "How do you like that?"

And then again, waving away the smoke: "A helper, eh, Filipov's helper?"

With pleasure the doctor whined, "Yes, yes . . . How, how do you mean?"

"Well, yes. That's what he is—a helper, an assistant. And so quickly, too!"

She added:

"One, two, three, and he's in. There was a trial. No one should laugh. A trial by the comrades. Philosophize all you want about 'who did the Bolsheviks take their program from?' And I said, I'm not going, not going, not going to any trial . . . It's all the same whether he's a provocateur or not, whether he betrayed us or not. Here's what you do: take a revolver and shoot him, because he knows everything about us and is going over to their side. And us? We're in the middle of a war . . ."

And she was off again, pouring out an endless barrage of sharp, polished words, like beads.

The doctor grew bored. He'd already heard the most important news; a few days ago the tip of his nose had uttered its witticism: "A new iron saint!"

The rest of it didn't interest him. He barely managed to stay awake. Only in the first minute did his face suggest that the story he was listening to had cost him his health—he still didn't know whether he would regain his strength soon. He had grown even more jaundiced and lackluster.

He sat in his heavy, worn-out coat across the table from Sofia Pokrovskaya and looked with sleepy eyes at her dark, mobile face, noticing how her mouth opened and shut, and how it became darker and darker and wetter with saliva with each passing moment.

"From speaking," he noted pedantically, "a person could lose his resolve."

The agitation in her pupils—he observed—was fading, it lit up before going out and flamed up again, like a fiery crucifix spread across a mile-wide road. Her even tone cradled him to sleep, embracing his body so long that he felt a tingling up and down his spine.

The doctor felt sorry for her, for her orphaned, lonely fate. He remembered her as a child. He was often summoned to Yanovo because of her. She was all of eleven years old then, and used to have epileptic attacks. Now all her limbs quivered with energy; she was crawling right into the fire. She was bound up with what was taking place in the villages along the border—all the threads stretched from there to her, as a kind of mistress over the entire SR cell in the area. It wasn't so good that she came here to him, the doctor, she wasn't thinking about whether her visit would have consequences for him.

Then the doctor accompanied her out. Her voice had quieted.

The supply of polished, bead-like words had been exhausted, but suddenly, when they were outside, something in her eyes lit up again. She thought for a minute . . . she looked at the dark road she would soon take, the Yanovo road . . . She said:

"You know what, doctor? I've never done this with such passion before . . . I mean, the work in the villages . . . all to spite them . . . they can be damned."

And she trudged off in her borrowed peasant boots.

✦

Several days later, people in Golikhovke found out that Kamino-Balke had dispatched its agents to Sofia Pokrovskaya. They came at night and took her away.

"Now she's sitting in Kamino-Balke, locked up tight, tighter than everyone else."

The priest's wife—perpetually lethargic and swollen—came from Yanovo to see Dr. Babitsky. She drove herself in her wagon.

It was Shabbos. An overcast day. The wind carelessly tossed out snow, tipping it with the color of dark ash. Below the mountain the church bells rang with a heavy, dull sound, they rang for a long time, as if a corpse was to be buried, and that was why people thought that the priest's wife had come to buy a coffin, but it was Shabbos, and nobody would sell her one.

The priest's wife stood in the marketplace next to her wagon, not far from the pharmacy; she cried with a crooked open mouth and fat tears. And in Golikhovke, hearts were cheered, people said, "It's good like this."

"Let them feel it, too."

They stood across from her and looked at her crying face just like that, without mercy. From time to time a mouth would yawn a lazy Shabbos yawn:

"Imagine how good things are for her."

"The priest, they say, was paralyzed."

"Have a good cry, priest's wife!"

The doctor came out of the pharmacy, shoulders raised, arms spread apart, which showed that the last hope had disappeared.

"There's nothing," he said, his lower lip protruding bitterly, "not even a memory."

Then he remembered some pills, which would have helped Filipov two months earlier, when he had been summoned to Kamino-Balke. If he took the pills now it would be a good excuse to go up there. While giving Filipov the pills he could try to intercede for Sofia Pokrovskaya.

He stood for a while with the priest's wife, gave it some thought, made a remark, and set off with shuffling feet toward the row of houses across from the market. He knocked on the door of the house where Yokhelzon the undercover agent lived, and the housewife who opened was greatly surprised, her eyes searching around in fear as she mouthed the name "Yokhelzon."

"Yokhelzon? Evaporated . . . The same night . . . right after they took away the Odessa hatmaker. That very night he went over the border . . . There you have it. People are even saying he's gone to Palestine."

"Right, I completely forgot . . ."

The doctor had to confess that his memory was slipping. As for Yokhelzon, he meant to get the pills through Yokhelzon from the other side—he had no head any more, the doctor.

His lower lip hung even lower; his feet shuffled back more heavily through the mud to the priest's wife. Then he would be exempt, free from them all.

A few days later, however, the priest's wife came to his house again, when he was out. She said nothing. She took a look at the empty walls for an icon, so she could cross herself, and with a deep, pious bow closed her eyes and crossed herself in front of the window instead.

That's what the deaf-mute told the doctor with all kinds of winks when Babitsky got back from tending to a patient in one of the villages.

"Well, good . . . good . . . well, that's enough."

The doctor hated the deaf-mute's habit of relating trivial details in all their minutiae, he hated reminding himself of the pills, because if they had been supplied at the right time, he would have had to take them to Kamino-Balke to intercede for Sofia Pokrovskaya—he, a person who couldn't even ask the smallest favor of all, to be left alone. He needed this like a hole in the head, especially now, when he had just found out while on his way home that it was true: Sofia Pokrovskaya's comrades were planning an uprising in the border villages, and not for some time in the future, but in earnest, today or tomorrow—it would explode . . .

The doctor was not at all tired from his trip, but nonetheless he lay down for his nap—if only to calm the waves of agitation passing over him, so that he could wake up and hear the words: "It has begun."

✦

Somebody outside was banging on the window, waiting, and then starting again.

The doctor, terrified, thought it was a hand without a person. He lit the lamp and after a while went over to the window. From the other side of the windowpane he saw Galaganer's bulging eye. The eye made a demand on him, like a promissory note that demands payment, like a wink you make to your co-conspirator.

The doctor was very upset; he felt that Galaganer was treating him as a member of his own family. He barely restrained himself from asking, "What the hell?"

That same night the chief of the Golikhovke police disappeared. People said:

"I bet you anything that he was also placed here, from them, the SRs."

Now it was obvious why nothing had been found at Galaganer's place.

And on that same night Galaganer disappeared—the last SR.

The word in town was:

"He bought a dentist's office on the other side a long time ago."

"And so? What'd you think, that Galaganer, God forbid, was an idiot?"

"He was idiot enough to rip your skin open when he pulled a tooth . . ."

18

Migrating birds sank in the dawn's fog—milky gray, the color of the sea. They blindly dove into the dirty dampness, their worried shrieks warning the others—birds warming their eggs in their nests—if you fly out even a short distance, you won't find your way back.

To the left of the village of Belo-Kut there was a hidden ravine. The marshy expanse that stretched to the border was enveloped in wet steam. It made you think that Passover was just around the corner. Cold, smoky sweat covered all of the outcroppings of little forests around the vicinity of Moshne, where Pokrovskaya's cell had been preparing for the uprising. The forest was wet and teary with dew, the dew—like drops of crystal, and every sign of a road emerging from the mist appeared mysterious and seductive. A cheerful dog was running after its master as if they were hunting; the dog was following Semenko—the leader of Sofia Pokrovskaya's cell (the one who walked bent over from the wind, even though there was no wind). His moustache was light reddish in color, his coat, fastened with a belt—dirty yellow. He stood still in the foggy depths of the forest, not far from where tree trunks lay. They had been felled recently. He stood and whistled, like a landowner taking in the sight of his estate.

"Varyag! Varyag!" he quietly called out to his dog, who had gotten lost.

"Varyag" was also a password—a signal for Ushak, who was expected to arrive from the other side of the border. To those who knew, this meant:

"I've been standing here since early this morning."

"I'm waiting."

✦

The village of Belo-Kut lay at the edge of the forest, on this side of the border; it smelled pleasantly of warm manure underneath a pregnant cow. The loudest sound in the village was the crowing of a rooster. Its five houses were plopped down helter-skelter; willows surrounded them. The inhabitants lived as if they purposely turned their backs on each other. Everyone in Belo-Kut had the same last name: Lukoyan. This seemed to be the reason that no one in Belo-Kut had any interest in anyone else. If you asked them under oath whether they were relatives, they wouldn't be able to give a straight answer.

The youngest of the Lukoyan offspring, Kuzka, had completed only a few grades of schooling. During the war he was a volunteer recruit of the second rank and a deserter—the kind who lives without a wife or relatives forever. His elder brother Anton, who had lost his right arm in the war, couldn't stand Kuzka.

"You-don't-love-me-'nough," he called him.

Only Anton knew what this phrase meant.

Kuzka stank of shoe polish, empty talk he'd picked up in the city, and a lazy disinterest in household duties. He was friendly with Semenko, the leader of Sofia Pokrovskaya's cell, and was also a member of the cell. Since the middle of the winter he had been sheltering Semenko in his half of the house. Together they'd been smoking real, good-quality tobacco—Kuzka had been living well on his lodger's dime. But now someone else found his way into Kuzka's half of the house: the elder of the Pokras brothers. He arrived there at night to wait for Semenko, who had gone off to the forest to meet up with Ushak. He didn't feel all that good about it: after all, he was a Jew, while Ushak had been mixed up in pogroms—a lot of pogroms, the worst and bloodiest in the region. Ushak had had to flee to the other side of the border several months earlier. His gang—thirty-odd people who took off with him—worked for wealthy Polish landowners on the other side. But that was an insignificant detail, according to Ushak, who said that his gang was armed and always at the ready.

"It's not necessarily a good thing that he carried out pogroms—but, in any case, it's worth hearing him out to see what kind of plan he has," the cell decided.

✦

Anton's wife—an angry, snub-nosed peasant woman—had spent the entire morning kicking her eldest shiksa of a daughter. Her younger child, a two-year-old, got tangled up in the hem of her maternity dress—she hit this one with her fist, all the while hissing at Anton:

"Not much longer left to wait . . . He's going to get himself caught, your good-for-nothing Kuzka! They've got wind of it at Kamino-Balke. One of their patrols swept through Harne—just last night . . ."

Anton wouldn't have protested if Kuzka got picked up. He cursed under his breath—though he didn't know who he was cursing, maybe Kuzka, but maybe also, while he was at it, his wife, that fool who didn't understand that it would be this way . . . Let them come here from Kamino-Balke and shoot Kuzka . . . Who cared, anyway? . . . He threw on his undershirt and left the house in anger. In reality, however, he was going to survey his property, especially the fields: if Kuzka were to get shot, they would all belong to him. The fields had been fertilized, the soil was rich, and everything was ready for springtime sowing—the fields were filled with longing for Anton and were running out of patience from all the waiting . . .

From there he continued farther down the road. Near the freshly fertilized fields around the village of Harne, Anton spotted the middle-aged madman, Fedka, who had climbed high on top of a pile of manure to keep an eye on the nets he'd set up to catch wild doves. Fedka's eyes were shut, as if he were praying, his lips whispering an incantation aimed at the doves—let them fly into his nets as soon as possible. Anton learned from Fedka about the patrol Kamino-Balke had sent to Harne the night before:

"Yes, they rode in—and then rode away."

"In which direction, Fedka?"

"You're going to spook the doves."

Fedka shut his eyes again and started whispering once more. He lost his mind only three months a year, in the summer. At that time, he would pop up at marketplaces all over the area with a cow's bone hidden deep in the pocket of his pants—swearing that the bone was actually a human's. Now, however, he was poorly but neatly dressed, as he always was in springtime, and ready to earn his keep in any and all ways—both kosher and not. Anton sat down next to him on the manure pile, rested a little, sighed, reminisced about the fields that were longing for him and, like him, were running out of patience from all the waiting . . .

"Listen," he said. "They would pay well for this at Kamino-Balke . . . If you went there and told them—that, say, you saw it yourself, that you know everything because you come from the place where it's all happening . . ."

And so he relayed everything he knew: about what was going on in Kuzka's half of the house, and also everything he knew about Moshne, about the capture of the local peasant brigade.

"That'd be a good place to pick up a nice, fatty bone." Anton tugged on Fedka's elbow from behind. "A lot better than sitting here and muttering at doves . . . You idiot!"

Anton scanned his surroundings:

Fedka's lips had stopped whispering, his eyes stared at the faraway field and blinked and blinked.

✦

Ushak's arrival from the other side of the border contained an element of surprise: instead of walking over on foot to the place where Semenko was waiting for him, he rode in on horseback. His black felt cloak was majestically draped over his horse as far as its tail. His caracul hat was cocked on the side of his head—adding to his nonchalant, devil-may-care appearance. His long, wet moustache, which hung down the sides of his mouth, moved slightly as he attempted to form a smile, but his droopy girlish-pink lips barely managed to open, making him look like a fish. Only his two pupils, as dark as pinheads, burrowed deep beneath his charmingly bushy eyebrows, managed to smile:

"So, how goes it?"

The smiling eyebrows together with this "So, how goes it?" meant the following:

"Are you saying that I am afraid of 'your' side of the border? That I'm shaking with fright? Me? Afraid? If I say I'm going to come, it means I'm coming. And what about you? Still getting warmed up, isn't that so? You only know how to do one thing: talk and talk . . ."

The sealed letter that Ushak brought with him from the SR cell on the other side of the border was brief:

He considers himself an SR. A former teacher. He has offered to collaborate several times before. He was asked then—'on what conditions?' And he answered: 'We'll figure it out later, we'll agree somehow.' His most recent suggestion: attack Kamino-Balke in the middle of the night.

From the letter's brevity and dry, objective style, Semenko sensed the honesty of his co-conspirators on the "other side," and, moreover, he felt his own reliability as the leader of the cell on "this side." And, guided by this realization, he was certain he could reliably size up Ushak:

"Your hands are covered with blood, brother—it seems that a little too much blood is on your hands even for this civil war."

As he thought this, he felt superior to Ushak and purer. As a result of this realization, another thought immediately occurred to him:

"The way you carry yourself reminds me of a criminal—from long, long ago."

He took Ushak over to Kuzka's half of the house—a spacious room with a stove in the corner, all heated up the way it should be just before Passover. The room had a dark, short hallway leading to the other side of the door.

When he got to Kuzka's, Ushak asked:

"And could someone get me some booze?"

Kuzka answered cheerfully, like an army officer's orderly:

"In Harne . . . They've got moonshine there."

And he was off to get some alcohol.

Semenko looked at Pokras: this was supposed to convey the reliability of Semenko's judgment, a glance to let Pokras know what he was thinking:

"My impression is . . . well . . . so-so."

"Well, yes," he answered Ushak sternly and coldly. "We're getting ready. No point rushing. We must proceed in an orderly fashion, according to plan."

"Well, well, well."

Removing his hat, Ushak almost hit his hand against the low ceiling.

"In an orderly fashion," he sighed. "Nice words! But that's precisely where you've got it wrong. That's how you get yourself finished—even if you are Petliura! During a civil war—what kind of 'order' are you talking about? This isn't some kind of strategy-driven war against the Germans! The Bolsheviks—devil take them—understand this very well: the main thing is not to let the enemy get accustomed to any sort of 'order' for any reasonable length of time—because, if the enemy organizes according to this 'orderly fashion,' that's a terrible thing for them. Get this through your head already."

He suddenly halted, squinted, and looked at Semenko.

"Booze . . . will there be any?" he whispered into his ear. "It'd be nice if I had some."

Semenko suddenly felt that Ushak held himself in higher regard than Semenko's entire cell, higher than Semenko's sense of his own reliability. It became obvious—quite quickly—that Ushak had no special secrets to share, no specific plans to put forward. In the darkened hallway Semenko whispered to Pokras:

"This isn't quite what we thought . . ."

He fell silent for a second, then waved his hand in resignation:

"A criminal . . . I'm not even sure he has any men behind him."

They lingered in the darkness.

Pokras inquired:

"Then why do we need him here?"

A pause.

Semenko answered:

"Let him head back."

They returned from the little hallway with a new plan. Pokras was now going to travel to Brozhe and Pidvesoke—to meet with the peasants who had promised to join the uprising there.

✦

Around midnight someone knocked on Kuzka's door—weapons were delivered in two separate wagons. The hours raced ahead. The remaining hours of sleep—there were few of them—turned to the morning's events:

"By this time tomorrow, the peasant brigade in Moshne will have been taken."

The next day, however, time moved quickly, and the first half of the day was gone in an instant. Suddenly, it was one o'clock in the afternoon. Kuzka was yet to return from a remote spot in the forest, where a group of armed men was supposed to assemble at dawn. In the meanwhile, from the early morning on, Ushak downed one shot after another in Kuzka's half of the house. It didn't even occur to him that the others wanted him gone. He kept assuring everyone about his consistently good fortune:

"Nothing bad ever happens to me, brothers."

But, at the same time, his narrowed eyes hinted that something was being kept from him, that he stood to be offended. This, however, wasn't advisable:

"Anyone thinking of not doing right by me is going to come to a bad end. What?" He stopped Semenko in his tracks and embraced him. "You think I'm wrong? Oh, well. I didn't say anything."

His shirt unbuttoned, he was beaming with the healthy strength of a man who had no outlet for his desire. Lustfully, as if they were women, he would press himself against every male in the room—as if lying with a man was something he was keen on doing.

"Laughable!"

Around three o'clock the elder of the Pokras brothers returned from Brozhe with bad news:

"Their answer: 'Let those in Moshne go first—we'll rise up after them.'"

Kuzka returned from the forest—there were a lot fewer people with him than expected.

Semenko advised Ushak to leave—to go back to "the other side" where he came from. He said Ushak would be sent for if his help was needed.

Ushak didn't hear him: he was completely drunk. His dark pupils—like two pinheads—stuck out from underneath his swollen eyebrows; they peered out, bloodshot, before his eyelids finally concealed them. Drowsy, his body stiffened and slid off the chair. His head—the hair partially covering his face, his wet mouth in the middle—craned to the side. He wheezed:

"Laughable!"

No one could pay attention to him any longer. It was already twilight outside. Heavy, wet snow—the kind that falls shortly before Passover—was falling. It was time to set out in order to have at least a modest chance of covering the ten miles to the middle of the forest on the way to Moshne. Then they could arrive on time at the place where another cell, led by a former policeman from Golikhovke, would be waiting for them.

They traveled through the forest, their heavy wagons screeching. When darkness fell, somewhere deep in the middle of the forest a string of gunshots rang out—one after another, continuing for a long time, as if submerged in thought. In the wagons, they discussed the gunfire:

"Maybe it's Ushak's gang? They are bent on protecting him."

"Oh, yes, he's precious to them . . ."

"Whenever he travels across the border, two or three others follow him—that's the rumor, anyway . . ."

The following morning Ushak awoke in Kuzka's half of the house; sober, he realized he had been left on his own. He started yelling, but no one came in. He went out and then back inside the room, slamming the door each time. In the other half of the house, Anton's snub-nosed wife was laying into her husband:

"Go check on him, may the cholera take you! He's going to tear apart the house in there!"

Anton was very angry that this woman stuck her nose everywhere like it was her business. Finally, he punched her a couple of times, right there at the stove where she was busy with steaming pots. Afterward, he snuck into the barn, shut the gate behind him, and peered into the yard through the gap in the fence. He saw Ushak run out of the house time after time, open the flaps of his coat, and, like all drunkards, answer the call of nature—from all the alcohol he had consumed the day before, and all the while swearing up and down at the SRs who had so offended and fooled him:

"You just wait!" he'd say, taking aim higher and higher. "You'll hear from me yet, sons of bitches! I'll show you yet! You'll remember me for a long, long time!"

Night began to fall. Ushak put on his long felt coat, mounted his horse, and rattling off one curse after another, set out for the other side of the border.

"Wait, you just wait! I'll show you yet, sons of bitches!"

19

As evening fell, fiery sparks stained the distant storm clouds at the border blood-red—the flames of war.

At the marketplace in Golikhovke, people gaped at the fiery skies. The deaf-mute came running into the house from the street. Bending over, huffing and puffing, he winked to the doctor every which way:

"There, in a village . . ."

Possibly, what he meant was:

"Fires!"

Or, perhaps:

"A fight! That's what people are saying . . ."

And another one of the deaf-mute's grunts:

"The SRs . . ."

The doctor's face became a sour grimace: the deaf-mute was going to be the end of him with these cursed SRs.

"Well, " the doctor begged him. "Well, that's enough, enough."

His hands trembling, the doctor put on his coat. Slowly and with great excitement, as if he were heading to a celebration, to assist a woman in labor on the eve of a long-awaited birth, he threaded his arms through his coat's old sleeves and left the house to take a look at the bloody stains of war.

He muttered to himself:

"So it's getting under way. It has begun."

✦

Two artillery cannons were brought to Golikhovke from Kamino-Balke. Many horses were used to drag them along—like a heavy threshing machine. They were positioned just outside town, at the edge of the little bridge. Everyone who came running to look at them out of curiosity got pushed back. Eli the klezmer musician—he used to serve in an artillery unit—even earned himself a few heavy punches from the sailor Igumenko for loitering around too long.

The cannons' muzzles—black, fat, and eyeless—stared longingly in the direction of the forests around Moshne, toward the distant corner of the border where the red blaze had been seen the night before.

In the marketplace, the crowd gathered around the wagon drivers who weren't successful in finding buyers for the horses they could no longer ride to the border. Hatskel Shpak said something many people heard:

"The same exact thing must be done in Golikhovke . . . to our own fat cats."

Haykel Berezovsky—formerly Golikhovke's richest timber merchant—followed up with an inquiry:

"To which fat cats, eh? Hatskel?"

Hatskel answered:

"To you, for one."

Berezovsky said:

"So, what are you waiting for then, Hatskel?"

Hatskel looked at him provokingly:

"It'll happen . . . It'll happen . . . You think anybody's going to be shy about it?"

On the other side of the bridge the two cannons started firing, and everyone at the marketplace promptly dispersed; Hatskel Shpak darted off together with Berezovsky, even though he had threatened him just a few seconds earlier:

"It'll get done . . . It'll get done . . . You think anybody's going to be shy about it?"

Longing for home, the doctor headed back. A boundless desire to wrap himself inside his house consumed him, as if it were a warm blanket that could cover his entire body and head.

Let the pills get to his house on their own: now, of course, he had no intention of taking them to Kamino-Balke—the uprising had, after all, begun, and not very far off, too . . . The uneasiness that had spent long winter evenings waiting in the haunting rustle of leafy trees had awakened from slumber.

A policeman was killed in the big village of Moshne, which lay about ten miles from Harne and Belo-Kut, and the most powerful peasant brigade in the area was disbanded.

Golikhovke lay in wait, as if preparing to draw a number in a lottery—would it win or lose?

"Aha, that's where Pokrovskaya's gang chose to get started!"

There was much whispering outside back doors:

"Before the Bolsheviks retreat, they release prisoners."

"Rumor has it that they do this everywhere."

The villagers counted out the days:

"Monday, Tuesday, Wednesday . . ."

There was sighing, too:

"In the meanwhile, it's neither here nor there."

A guest arrived at Dr. Babitsky's house—the lame priest from Yanovo. He stayed at the doctor's house for several days: if things got stirred up in Yanovo, too, he wanted everyone to know that he hadn't been at home then. In Yanovo he would tell time not according to the clock but according to his old habit as a priest—all of a sudden, with an expression on his face suggesting that he had heard something somewhere, he'd holler:

"Oh! Time for midday mass!"

Or, in the evening, in the middle of yawning uncontrollably, he'd get startled:

"Oh, oh, oh! It's late! Way past the evening service."

Both of them, the doctor and the priest, spent the entire day at home playing checkers. They felt as if they were passengers on a train that had halted for a long while in the middle of a field somewhere and that they had no way of figuring out what to do with their lives before the train delivered them to their intended destination. From time to time they'd sit still and try catching some distant sound:

"Are the cannons still firing close by, or are they farther away now?"

In addition to everything, the priest was not very bright: a fat village sack reeking of fish oil, with a heavy tongue good for not much more than "Lord-have-mercy-on-us," and not quite up to figuring out the revolutionary events taking place. Without any enjoyment, the doctor kept winning time after time, while the priest counted on his fingers:

"Moshne."

"Great Tsebermonove."

"Brozhe."

"Podvesoke."

"Well, so," he urged the doctor. "Your turn to go now, your turn."

The doctor looked at the piece that the priest had moved a moment ago and considered both his next move in the game and the meaning of the events that were taking place:

"So a big revolution with little revolutions on the side," he said with a sneer. "Like a bit of a breeze blowing alongside a gale—into the nooks and crannies where the gale can't reach, the breeze certainly would . . . The little checker piece here, stuck in the corner—that's also something. Like Filipov, eh? What's Filipov's next move going to be now?"

Finally, the doctor moved the checker and looked at the priest, astonished that his opponent didn't seem to notice that he was about to lose the game. The doctor watched the priest looking at the pieces on the board. He was in a daze and kept on mumbling slowly:

"And in Yanovo—still not a sound . . . What? . . . Yanovo is too close . . ."

In town the same villages were also the topic of conversation:

"The SRs have always maintained a strong organization in the Moshne area."

"Which SRs do you mean? The ones in charge have long gone to the other side, all that's left here is small fry."

"Are they really all on their own, though? Who, then, threw this business their way?"

"Listen up! Berezovsky has it right: it's all been arranged with the British and the French!"

The Red cavalrymen took up positions in the marketplace. Not a soul was out in the streets, except for a few young workers and the girl in the red kerchief. Beaming with joy, they acted like new bosses in town:

"They drove them off!"

"Pushed them back!"

In town there was talk about them:

"They are saying so themselves: the SRs just got chased away, they didn't succeed in taking Moshne."

News came knocking on Haykel Berezovsky's door:

"That girl in her red kerchief together with that lad from Brozhe who works at the smith's by the bridge—they are prancing around boasting to anyone who'll listen: 'We'll take Berezovsky's house— for a club!'"

It was Sunday.

The two heavy cannons were returned to Kamino-Balke.

Nekhe, Shmuel Voltsis's wife, also returned from Kamino-Balke, all alone. She was wrapped in layers of shawls and had such a severe cold that others had trouble recognizing her face and voice.

"Shmuel—like death warmed over," she said. "They plan to inter-rogate him face to face with the blonde. He's going to take his life!"

She didn't understand the questions that others kept asking her and continued to wail:

"I tell him: 'You said so yourself—they are going to let you out.' And he answers: 'Yes, but I'm not going to be able to handle it . . . on account of that whore . . .'"

Toward nighttime, the last mounted patrol passed through Go-likhovke on its way back to Kamino-Balke: there were twelve riders in total, excluding Pinke Vayl, who stopped for a bit at the tailor's to visit his girl. The sailor Igumenko was at the helm, and Yuzi Spivak was also spotted. People said:

"A simple Red Army soldier . . ."

"Poor thing, how wretched . . ."

"Apparently he didn't wish for anything better for himself than this."

"What's so hard to see here? It's impossible to achieve a higher rank so quickly!"

The deaf-mute brought this latest news from the marketplace home to the doctor. The doctor smiled with the tip of his nose and barely had time to say:

"More Catholic than the Pope . . ."

He was about to beat the priest again in another round of checkers.

✦

The patrol slowly made its way through town. Silently, they rode uphill, looking at the houses: each house—a grave for some old and cold unbelief. The graves kept quiet. Only the restless windows stuck out, tracking the horsemen:

"You are leaving, aren't you? Forever?"

They blessed the riders:

"May you have a happy-ever-after . . ."

For this reason, the men tried to restrain their horses as much as possible—as if out of spite, they slowly rode into the open field.

Pinke Vayl, charging out of town and all aglow, caught up with them and rode up to Yuzi Spivak:

"Comrade Spivak!"

It occurred to Pinke that he was, in fact, fighting for the happiness of all mankind with every movement of his horse, with every particle of his love for the girl at the tailor's. He was content that there was work for him to do, happy about the answer he gave to the Jews at the tailor's:

"I told them: 'What, you think they are going to hesitate about what to do with you? Just let them find any of you sheltering an SR—then you'll see.'"

He noticed that Yuzi's face froze at the word "SR"—he realized that he shouldn't have said it, but it was too late, so he fell quiet.

Precisely then, he wanted to say something warm and kind to Yuzi, for the sake of the happiness of all mankind. For example, at the tailor's, his girl told him about eight young men from around there—all of them workers—who wanted to join the fight, and about others like them in shtetls farther afield who were ripe for doing the same and could be pushed along with the help of a little political education.

"Of all of us, there is no one better than you for the job!" he appealed to Yuzi wholeheartedly. "I know what I'm talking about."

Suddenly, he realized he hadn't fully expressed his happiness, the realization that there was work for him to do, and all the warmth he felt for Yuzi. He was riding alongside Yuzi, very close to him—their feet touched each other from time to time.

"Comrade Spivak!" he petted the mane of Yuzi's horse with his free hand. "Oy, what a silent man you are! . . . Why do you stay so silent, huh? When you have the word at meetings, you speak straight to the point . . . But about yourself—nothing! What a silent man you are!"

Wanting to smile, Yuzi's face grimaced as if it were about to weep. Where was he supposed to begin telling Pinke about himself: with the story of his grandfather Mosi? . . . Or his mother's quotations in the holy tongue? Or should he tell him about his years of work with the SRs, the enemy he was presently setting out to fight? It would have been truthful for him to say: "I keep to myself because I have a lot, a lot to say—a lot more than anyone else from our unit." But when he glanced at Pinke, these words were even more difficult for him to utter. He saw that Pinke was looking at him with tears in his happy, sparkling eyes, which didn't stop begging him for a minute: "Speak, speak, Comrade Spivak . . ." He reached out to Pinke with his left hand and pulled him close. Suddenly, he understood what it was that he wanted to say:

"All right," Yuzi said. "We will prevail."

And he started explaining to Pinke how the world was going to look later—after they prevailed.

20

A few days later.

A second patrol—at least, another one, with different uniforms and weapons—arrived in Golikhovke as if through its back door.

This was around ten o'clock at night.

The patrol stopped at the pharmacy, the only building with lights on. The men stood quietly, heads lowered modestly, as if in dignified mourning.

From across the way Haykel Berezovsky's darkened windows looked at the pharmacy. His solid house stood on a stone foundation and was just like Haykel Berezovsky himself, either afraid, or dying for everyone to know:

"He was the greatest timber trader in Golikhovke."

From Berezovsky's darkened windows a couple of people could be seen dismounting from their horses and entering the pharmacy, where they remained. At Berezovsky's they were watching with bated breath. No lamps were lit, and it felt as though you had to keep everything inside, like a mute "mazel-tov" for a woman who had just given birth. In the house no one dared to speak; Haykel Berezovsky kept everyone quiet with a cough, "Sha!"

What he meant was his wife shouldn't make any predictions. It was an old rule—when she foretold anything, it came out exactly the opposite.

He, however, was convinced, like everyone else:

"Who was it, then?"

"Apparently, them, the SRs."

At Haykel Berezovsky's, where there were few men (in all, just Haykel), Moyshe Volovnik, his former steward, had spent the night, just as he did every night—for the sake of coziness. He was a tall, yellow, sickly man, very asthmatic, but nonetheless a heavy smoker. He also looked out the window. He was upset and badly wanted a smoke, but didn't have any tobacco.

Agitated, he tried flattering Berezovsky, "Maybe we'll be able to resume the trips to the forest again . . . The SRs will give us back the forests, right? . . . Mr. Haykel . . . give me a smoke . . . with good tobacco . . ."

And the minute he said it—in that instant . . .

This is how Moyshe Volovnik told the story afterward.

✦

In that instant someone banged on Haykel Berezovsky's door—loudly and crudely. At first, it seemed to Volovnik that he was the cause, because he had been too free with his boss, he had said all in a rush, "Give me a smoke, Mr. Haykel."

Three people suddenly entered the house, commanding gruffly that no one was to move; they were to give them all the cash, gold, silver, and jewels, and food, the best food—a roast turkey—and if it turned out that they were hiding something . . .

Berezovsky's daughter began talking to them (the daughter who got stuck here, whose husband had married her for her beauty, and to this day was a rich man living somewhere else)—and they took one look at her . . .

Moyshe Volovnik told it like this afterward: "It's better not to remember how they looked at her . . . But then they noticed there was cherry brandy on the sideboard, in bottles, well, and then they had a wild time all night long!"

This is what he said the next morning. None of "them" remained in the town.

Moyshe Volovnik said, "All hell broke loose!"

Muli, beaten up, was lying on the floor of the pharmacy.

They had taken everything in the cash register and all the cocaine. They left a note on the cash register:

> Ushak says all the SRs who hurt him and mocked him can go
> fuck themselves. He is showing that before they can make a
> move, he and his men can be in Golikhovke and even Kamino-
> Balke. He's waiting with his men on this side of the border—get
> ready for a meeting.

At the market all kinds of hidden troubles got raked up:

"They were in other houses, too."

"A lot of other houses."

"At poor people's, too."

"At the blacksmith's next to the bridge they killed a worker—the son of Naftali from Brozhe . . . They found everything on him . . . The banner also."

"The banner? . . . The banner was put up there only this week . . ."

"He bragged just yesterday, this boy—'We'll take Haykel Berezovsky's house for a club.'"

He was killed in the morning, at sunrise.

✦

In the light pre-Passover frost it smelled of sleepy, girlish lust; there was a honey-sweet fragrance in the air, but no one knew where it came from. The whole town had become a swamp covered in the frozen glass of broken windowpanes that cracked with a clang under running feet. A sharp clap from a back door could be heard; a voice said:

"You idiot!"

"What SRs are you talking about?!"

The girl in the red kerchief darted out from the tailor's shop, a chilly breath of air tickling her nose and face. Her eyes were ready to catch anything out of the ordinary. Her clever nose had no time to smile; her red kerchief teased the town:

"A-ha!"

"Longing for SRs, are you?"

She was off to see the body of her murdered friend at the blacksmith's near the bridge. She found that they were preparing the comrade's funeral with aplomb, with a new banner, with everything necessary . . . and they were speaking against the SRs.

In the huge crowd of people near the pharmacy, voices were getting louder:

"Who?!"

"That girl?!"

"You're joking."

"It's all her doing, her in the red kerchief."

Haykel Berezovsky's daughter's face was wrinkled—the traces of how they looked at her last night—or so it seemed. She approached the crowd.

"Why are they letting them come?" she asked. "The SRs will be here today or tomorrow."

The sun grew warmer, as if it were spring. The ice, like broken glass, melted under their feet—the pure blue sky extended over the muddy earth. The air was imbued with young desire, with a honey-sweet fragrance, and no one knew where it came from.

✦

This is how affairs stood with Haykel Berezovsky:

"Every enterprise costs a great deal, and there is no such thing as a good business that can't earn a profit at least for a little while."

Haykel Berezovsky's cheeks were practically unshaved, on the contrary, little patches of beard remained under his mouth, each hair was precious—that's what kind of man he was; he was already gray. He paced around the entire day at home in his robe and slippers and thought, "What does it matter . . ."

If all this did, indeed, originate with the English or the French, the SRs' return would be a sure thing, once and for all . . . That meant he could go back to the forests and start up the sawmill again like before, with Shmuel Voltsis as woods supervisor, Moyshe Volovnik as steward, the goyim as workers, and him, Haykel Berezovsky, as the boss. Ridiculous! The price of timber was even higher than before. Because of this, what happened last night was nothing, robbing them and taking everything, practically without a shirt on their back—was nothing more than a pinch of tobacco . . .

On the other hand . . .

If all these rumors were worthless, and there were no SRs, only their hangers-on, he might as well be six feet under, and he wouldn't survive—either an apocalypse, or the same fate as Haim Rothoyz, the timber merchant from near Zhitomir—who ended up with a noose around his neck . . . Or he would have to hear in his old age what people would say, "Haykel Berezovsky is a beggar," which was exactly the same thing as, "Haykel Berezovsky is a thief, a charlatan . . . he robbed the entire world."

He suddenly saw Volovnik coming in and asked him, without stopping his pacing:

"Well? Moyshe, what do you think?"

Moyshe Volovnik was tall, yellow, asthmatic, and always wanted tobacco, like a heavy smoker, and was also upset—and as the days got longer and more beautiful, closer to Passover, he grew all the more upset. The skin on his dry lips was peeling, as if he were fasting, and his lower lip was covered in pimples, each one a dry sore.

"It's like a wedding over there at the blacksmith's . . . They let Kamino-Balke know, the 'comrades' of the murdered boy. They want to have a funeral with all the bells and whistles, with red banners and klezmers and speeches . . . against the SRs."

Haykel Berezovsky's beard smiled:

"Like for a pious Jew, huh?"

He scratched himself under his collar, without ceasing his pacing.

"And did he know how to sign his name, this boy from Brozhe? Huh?"

He decided, anyway, that Volovnik would quietly summon a couple of wealthy men, and they would figure out what to do:

"First, it could be better to pay the klezmers not to play, and second . . . As soon as night falls, and we still don't know whether Ushak is coming back . . . and whether the SRs aren't far away somewhere across the seas . . ."

They figured out a plan, which Haykel Berezovsky couldn't bring himself for anything to say out loud, "You understand who to call, Moyshe?"

✦

Too many people gathered at Berezovsky's, not only the ones he had summoned on the quiet. Many wanted to know what sort of plan Haykel had.

"Maybe it's true what they say: he once had a lot of luck . . ."

After a day of warm spring sunshine they had made their way to the house, carefully finding dry patches in the mud. As if arriving at an inn, they entered through both the back and front doors. They filled the whole house to the brim, asked each other for cigars, smoked like crazy, sprawled on the floor, and listened, delirious, as Haykel Berezovsky twisted and turned, spoke in incomplete sentences—as far as his plan went, let them guess it.

They asked, "So tell us, what are we supposed to do? And if the SRs really are close by?"

Haykel began again from the beginning:

"I'm saying: I'm a merchant. I know warming yourself at the stove gets nothing done; have you seen anyone earn money from sitting at the stove? I'm saying: If you want to be a partner, you have to put something into the business, and what are you afraid of? What's life worth, if you have no livelihood? I'm saying this because I've heard the SRs are close by . . ."

Suddenly someone ran in from the street, as if from a fire:

"Oy, they're taking him now . . . with red banners, with klezmers!"

Everyone poured into the street.

It was a lie.

No klezmers were playing. They were carrying the dead boy only with two banners: one had just been sewn, and the other was old, the one they had put up earlier in the week, but at the marketplace there was a big crowd. Filipov had come with a whole squad, people had come running from the surrounding villages where he had agitated against the SRs. Various remarks were made off to the side:

"See how angry he is!"

"He's completely hoarse."

"And how!"

"Look at his face!"

The evening had darkened; the air was fresh and chilly, sweet with the fragrance of honey. No one knew where it came from. The funeral procession had long since passed by. In the surrounding darkness only the place where the sun had set remained transparent and blood-red. Filipov was sitting on his horse in the middle of the market; a big crowd had gathered around him. His eyes flashed as he shouted:

"It's all the same to us, whether it's Ushak or SRs, or all of them, whether the SRs are hiding here waiting . . . *Chto vy, shutite?* What, are you joking?"

Afterward he listened in the darkness to the young workers and the girl.

"See? He's even gentler with them."

"They're heading for Haykel Berezovsky's."

"Filipov is giving them a paper that says they can turn the house into a club."

✦

On Sunday, in honor of the new club, Red Army soldiers arrived from Kamino-Balke.

A brand-new banner had hung on Haykel Berezovsky's house since the day before. Inside there were Red Army soldiers, the girl in the red kerchief, young workers, and others who lived on the blacksmith's street, near the bridge. They bustled about, plastering posters everywhere, and prepared a wall newspaper. Haykel Berezovsky could not bear to remain hidden in the back three rooms, allotted for his living quarters, and snuck outside, where a crowd had gathered. With a cutting look, he said:

"You rats . . . But it's only for a few days. Then we'll see."

He saw a few familiar people and smiled into his thin strip of a beard.

"Here you are . . . We don't even say thank you."

From early morning on the sun worked quickly to dry the paths in preparation for Passover, and under the sun workers got the porch ready. Next to it, they hammered together a viewing stand from wood they had sawed and hacked.

People said about them:

"They're fearless."

"The SRs are right under their noses . . . wouldn't it be smarter to give this some thought?"

Young and old eyes in the crowd were preoccupied with watching what was going on, and the tall, exhausted Moyshe Volovnik was among them; as a former timber supervisor, he couldn't restrain himself and began to explain that they had set the posts next to the porch the wrong way.

"It's going to come out crooked and bent, the platform . . . Idiots!"

Little by little, from nothing better to do, he came closer and closer, until he himself began to hold the post steady, while others poured dirt and tamped it with their feet. The young workers asked him, "Is it even?"

"We can hammer it in now, right? Volovnik?"

Hatskel Shpak, a former coachman, felt even closer to the work.

This was because Filipov had once said to him, "If you don't stop going to the border, I'll shoot you." He could not forget that Filipov had said it to him and not anyone else, although it wasn't true: Filipov threatened not only him, but also Bunem the Red. But still this made Hatskel feel close to the whole young group. It was also because he had quit being a coachman a long time ago, returning to his old profession—he was a dyer and dyed white cloth all kinds of different colors, green, blue, yellow, gray, and sometimes all of these together—no big deal. What he said was:

"As long as the peasant women grab it up and pay with potatoes, flour, or eggs, or even a chicken or pig bristles."

He was the one who had dyed a few sheets red for the workers' club. Some were drying at his house. One was fluttering cheerfully on the roof of the club. He was standing there and enjoying it.

"Bright red," he said. "Ah? It's pretty! The rest will be even better, they'll be deep, deep red."

"Hatskel!" someone shouted to him through the window from the club, "where are the klezmers? You said you would bring them . . ."

Hatskel snapped to attention like a young man falling in step.

"I swear," he said, "I went over there three times . . . I'll run over right now. I'll bring them here dead or alive . . . I'll bring them on a stretcher . . ."

"What do you have against them, poor things! They've never played at a wedding like this."

"We're making a wedding for the whole city—don't they see that?"

Hatskel dragged the klezmers to the club one by one.

"I almost had to give them grief," Hatskel said.

As soon as he brought the last one, the first one, in the meantime, ran out—he had a yellowish beard, short hair, and blue glasses that made him look worried, and he smelled of smoked fish, although there was none to be bought since before the war.

Hatskel, covered in sweat, ran off again after him.

"He's their leader," he panted. "I'll knock his teeth out."

The "leader" was standing outside with Haykel Berezovsky, smelling of smoked fish, and looking at Haykel with his worried glasses, answering him as if Haykel were the wealthiest boss—as if what he paid for a wedding was worth ten weddings elsewhere:

"What, then, you think I wouldn't be happy if they would leave me in peace?"

At that point people in the club started singing, the sound carrying right through the open window. Everyone came running. The day became even newer than the banner on the roof; the sky was brighter. Golikhovke stood still for a minute, looking into the club window; it saw a lot of uncovered heads inside, and listened to the song. It was an unfamiliar song, blasphemous and not so sure of itself, but heartfelt, stubborn, and free—these were the sounds that came from the open window.

To the accompaniment of this song Haykel Berezovsky recalled with great regret that he used to be a big shot, who had owned this house, a sawmill, the woods between Brozhe and Podvesoke—he had been a lucky man, and wherever he went, people used to say good things about him. The louder the song grew, the more surprised and irritated he became that the situation didn't bother anyone else:

"You see?! . . . They're not even stopping."

"Look at that! They're enjoying themselves . . ."

21

A poor peasant came to see Filipov—from the Moshne peasant brigade that had been forced to disband.

Filipov wasn't there; he had taken some men to patrol the villages and was making speeches against the SRs to groups of peasants.

The peasant hung around the office and ate everything offered him.

Between one dish and the next he chomped away at bread as if he were famished—he had made his way here stealthily, through the swampy woods of Moshne, and had not eaten for a few days.

Several times when he was summoned for a new interrogation, he didn't waste time, but continued to gnaw on the bread.

He kept on blinking, because he had been poor from the time he had left his parents' house and because he had night blindness—this is what he said:

"When it's night, I can't see more than a step ahead."

The first piece of information they got from him:

"It took the SRs from Thursday night to Friday to capture Moshne. They weren't alone. Kotsak and his gang joined them from the other side of the border."

"Were there a lot of them?"

He stopped chewing for a minute:

"Let's see . . . About . . . a few hundred."

He blinked:

"They had automatics, rifles, all those kind of things . . . They arrested a few people from the peasant brigade."

He was asked:

"Decrees . . . Did they put up any proclamations around the village?"

He stopped chewing again.

"People read—if Kamino-Balke shot anyone of theirs, they would shoot the entire peasant brigade."

The sailor Igumenko, who was in command of Kamino-Balke's soldiers, had a sour, sleepy expression on his face, but his heart grew heavy.

"So, here's what's going on: who was right, Filipov or me?"

Earlier he had said, "It's ridiculous, you don't ride out against Moshne with thirty-eight men from Kamino-Balke: Moshne is in the forest—you couldn't manage even with a whole regiment."

Filipov had begun shouting, "Regiments! As if you only have to say the word, and they're at the ready for you!"

"Let Filipov squirm—if he's such a great leader straight out of the mines . . . let him become the commander of the brigade and let him try—the hotshot—he shouldn't mix in when he knows nothing."

✦

To set the scene:

Igumenko and Filipov—were like oil and water. From the first day they couldn't get along. Igumenko had ridden out to the distant city a few times and hotly declared:

"That's it! It's either him or me."

On each of those occasions he was answered cold-bloodedly, so he would know:

"Both of you are good for nothing."

With this, he was supposed to understand that no one was going to be treated with kid gloves.

Something happened in the early days, when the blonde was first arrested. In the middle of the night her child started crying, screaming loudly, as only a child can. Like a madwoman, the blonde started banging on the door of the cell with both hands—she hammered away in a rage that lasted a long time. In the middle of the night, she terrified the prisoners, she railed against Kamino-Balke and all the authorities, demanding a bottle of milk instantly, that very minute, for the child.

Filipov, ill and in pain, was lying in bed. He ordered:

"Someone go to the closest village for milk."

Igumenko answered for everyone:

"There are no more nannies for the gentry . . . Let him go if he wants to. We aren't running a nursery!"

In the middle of the night, Filipov—who was in great pain—got up from his bed.

The end of the story was that Pinke Vayl went to find the milk.

At dawn, he brought back a bottle of milk and two bottles of alcohol—so that no one would remain offended, and he and Igumenko drank late into the day. They became fast friends. Igumenko's complaint against Filipov became more painful as he drank. When he banged his fist on the table, he sensed that he wasn't merely correct but profound:

"If I've got to shoot counterrevolutionaries, I can't nurse children!"

But Pinke was also drunk and quite certain that the words he spoke as he embraced Igumenko were wiser and even more profound:

"Well, fine . . . You can't . . . You have to . . . do you have a choice? You'll learn how!"

The matter would not have been resolved so quickly had it not been revealed at the blonde's second or third interrogation that the child was not hers. They removed the child from her, and Igumenko played with her more than the others as she ran around the office on her swift little feet; Igumenko liked to sit down next to the three-and-a-half-year-old girl, smile at her, stick out his tongue, and ask:

"*Skazhi-ka,* tell me, little miss, where did you go?"

He was strangely pleased, and made everyone watch whenever the child poked her finger at his snub nose and said in a doll's voice, "*Tak tebe,* you deserved it, ha-ha!"

Now, however, Igumenko had something else against Filipov that he could take to the authorities in the big city—and this was no small thing:

"They would see! Filipov was making trouble for them by interfering. He should admit it. Who was right? The peasant is a living witness."

◆

As soon as Filipov got back from visiting the surrounding villages late at night, the first thing he did in the morning was to call the peasant for another interrogation.

"Explain it from the beginning," he said to the peasant, "everything you know."

The peasant stopped chewing and explained again that the SRs took Moshne Thursday night, Kotsak and his gang came from the other side of the border to join them, and there were a lot of them, a lot.

Filipov interrupted him:

"Maybe it wasn't Kotsak, but Ushak?"

He looked sharply at the peasant, who squinted in confusion:

"Yeah, it probably was him . . . Ushak . . ."

The whole story didn't jive with the note Ushak had left in the pharmacy, the one saying he was on the outs with the SRs.

Filipov left the office and ordered the gates of Kamino-Balke to be guarded carefully. The peasant was not to be allowed to go anywhere without his order. This is what he commanded:

"Keep him under watch as he wanders around the courtyard."

As soon as Igumenko heard this, he turned red and gnashed his teeth—not only from pity for the peasant. The thing was that Filipov had thrown suspicion on the peasant indirectly, by sleight of hand: maybe he was a plant, from them, from the SRs. They had no one on their side and had sent the peasant to have a look around and frighten people.

"Aha! He's a clever one, that Filipov."

"He's wise to their tricks!"

"If that's the way it is, let him try on his own . . ."

◆

Every time Igumenko saw a Red Army soldier in the courtyard, his heart knocked in his chest, as he shouted that he was no longer the commander of the detachment.

"Let 'him,' the great leader himself, take over the command!"

"Son of a bitch!"

"Let the son of a bitch show off all the tricks he learned in the mines . . ."

There was chaos among the soldiers in the courtyard.

The mood was like before a strike; no one would do anything.

The poor peasant from the peasant brigade strode about chewing bread, blinking, and listened to every shout and everything that was being said.

The morning unfolding before them began to look different from other mornings; it seemed new, as if there had never been a morning before. In one of the buildings they were hammering together a crate, as if packing to go home; from above, the sun seemed to respond to the hammering by shining cheerfully, in its usual pre-Passover way, on Kamino-Balke's rusty spires.

Around eleven o'clock Filipov came out of the office, dressed as always in his fur coat and sheepskin hat; only this time, he had shaved, as if for a holiday known only to him. He coughed, turned around, looked where Igumenko was standing and complaining to the soldiers. He saw the peasant wander around with his mouth chewing and ordered his arrest. He waited until they brought him the key from the separate cell where they put him, turned around and went back into the office, and bawled everyone out because it was already eleven and no one was getting the tables ready for work. He especially scolded the tall investigator:

"Precisely you, only you, my friend, have to be more diligent than others . . . you alone know why . . ."

Comrade Sasha's face broke out in red spots. They began setting out documents and calling prisoners for interrogation. Then, breathing hard, Igumenko came in so upset that he couldn't say more than a few words:

"I've served from the first day . . . served the revolution . . . I demand his release, the Moshne peasant . . . to my custody . . ."

But Filipov's stubbornness had no limits. He didn't answer Igumenko, didn't even look at him. He was absorbed by what was happening in the office: near Comrade Sasha's table Shmuel Voltsis and the blonde were standing eye to eye. This was the blonde that Voltsis had hidden for more than two months in his house.

"Later," Filipov finally answered Igumenko. "Don't bother me . . . you might end up ruining things, like two months ago, when you had her in hand, this one here, and you let her go."

He showed with his hand the one he was talking about.

Igumenko clenched his jaw and ground his teeth. He left. The work in the office continued.

✦

Shmuel Voltsis stared peevishly in the blonde's face. He looked like someone who just got up from a nap after a heavy Shabbos dinner.

Her cheeks flaming, she looked like a drop-dead gorgeous, stubborn hussy, who was ready for divorce—but wouldn't allow herself to be abandoned just like that.

How Shmuel Voltsis felt:

Like the blonde was pretending to be his wife. For him it was a matter of life and death. He had to be free of her right here, in this place. He looked at her with hatred, as if she was a great sin. The marrow of his bones cursed her. He asked:

"I rented a wagon for your journey? . . . When did I do this?"

The blonde cleared her throat; when she answered him, she used a voice that masked deception: even if she was lying, you'd be damned if you could tell.

"You did more than rent it for me . . . You wanted to make a profit off me, all of you did, the whole shtetl of yours."

Shmuel Voltsis's eyes wanted to pierce her. Look—she was seething with hatred toward Jews . . . she wanted to denounce all of Golikhovke . . . And if there was a bit of truth in what she said: so what? . . . People didn't use a piece of merchandise like her? . . . Only Shmuel Voltsis thought that even when he made money off her, he did it in a more refined way than anyone else in Golikhovke—everyone else snorted over her like pigs, but he, Shmuel, thought from the very beginning: "They're going to pay a price for this."

He asked, "When you came back from the border, didn't I ask you to find another place? Didn't I refuse your money?"

The blonde closed one eye. Her nostrils expanded with air.

"When I came back from the border," she said, "you were delighted to see me: you and your wife ran out to meet me."

Someone at the table asked:

"And her letter? . . . Didn't you bring her letter to someone?"

Shmuel Voltsis's heart sank. The blonde had got Dr. Babitsky mixed up in this, too . . .

He began to explain that neither he nor the doctor wanted to get involved in her "business"; he described how he had accompanied the doctor out of his house through the back way with a lamp in his hands; he had asked, "Who is she?" and the doctor had answered:

"These days . . . If you knew someone yesterday, it doesn't mean that you know him today."

From the stillness around the table, from the pious velvet eyes that looked at him, Shmuel Voltsis gathered that they believed his statement more than the blonde's. He explained that, until the "misfortune," he had worked hard at Haykel Berezovsky's sawmill, and then, when people like us started to get some respect . . . Only, as if in a fever, he had to break off. What had happened? The blonde wanted to say straight to his face that he was lying. Shmuel Voltsis looked at her with true anger:

"Do you see or not? She's a brazen-faced liar!"

If that's how it was going to be, he'd have her in the shit; he asked her:

"You pestered us to death: didn't you want us to take you to Filipov?"

"Sha! . . . Didn't you boast that Filipov would fall in love with you?"

The room was quiet.

Everyone's eyes grew still.

Filipov asked, "*Kto*? Who? . . . Me?"

Everyone around the table laughed, as if to show how relaxed they were, as if to say "the parents are away," but they felt strongly that Filipov was the parent.

"*Khorosho*, fine," Filipov stopped the laughter, "maybe we'll get married."

He walked across the room to have a look at her.

"I guess," he suggested, "if it's for the sake of the motherland . . ."

He was about to leave the office annoyed, as if in truth they were committing him to a very bad match, when he stopped at the door and attacked Shmuel Voltsis all over again:

"It doesn't matter who you were before," and he waved his hand in the air. "You hid this piece of work in your house, now you're going to pay for it . . . you're going to spend a couple of months in a concentration camp . . . *Chto vy, shutite?* What, are you joking?"

For him, there was a lot more in "what, are you joking?" than these words implied: each person that he had to deal with had his own rotten sense of justice, and believed that he was right to harm the Bolsheviks and try to stop them. And there was the great rectitude of the revolution that trampled down and burned these petty, rotten pieces of justice in merciless fires. And lo! it was burning even now with all its might, the great justice:

"*Chto vy, shutite?* What, are you joking?"

He ran into Yuzi Spivak in the courtyard, had a look at him, and stopped, had a friendly chat with him for the first time, as if he were from here, asked him whether he knew the peasant from Moshne:

"Well, you know, from before, from your work with the SRs."

Yuzi turned pale and answered slowly and reluctantly:

"He doesn't look familiar."

He got even paler and added:

"It's suspicious, though."

"Exactly."

It was clear that Filipov's conviction grew stronger, because he wasn't the only one to think so. He approached the soldiers still standing around Igumenko and began persuading them, gesturing with his arm in the air:

"What's going on here? Are we nervous? To go for a ride and then have a stroll, then come back? It's eight miles to Moshne, and you were afraid to enter those villages there? . . . You had the poverty of the countryside in your favor . . . I've just come from there . . . their poverty puts them on our side! Just one example and nothing more, that's all you had to show them . . ."

Several times he walked away, upset.

But each time he came back:

"What, were you expecting entire regiments to show up and assist you?"

"Entire regiments, huh?"

"That would stand at the ready waiting for your orders?"

"Where are they supposed to come from?"

As he was leaving, he heard a voice shouting at him:

"Why didn't you go yourself, Comrade Boss?"

"There, in fact, to Moshne . . ."

"You searched for an easier destination! . . . The villages that were close by . . . Where you knew you'd be welcomed with open arms, that's where you went . . ."

He turned around.

"Me?" His face flushed, and he beat his breast. "So that's it?! I'm the one duping you?"

He no longer wanted to approach the group of men. On the way back to the office, he spotted Yuzi again, stopped, and breathing hard, as if his head were still over there, in the group of men, managed a few unclear words:

"Maybe you'll drop in later . . . Comrade Sasha also . . . Maybe we can talk things over."

Yuzi stared at him: this was the first time this person had said 'maybe' . . . until this point he had always known everything for sure.

In the afternoon, the prisoners were let out for a walk. A group of them (including Shmuel Voltsis) were told to get ready: they were going to be sent with a convoy to a concentration camp that day.

During the exercise period, they learned everything: SRs were in Moshne, Ushak in Golikhovke, a goy nobody had heard of was here in Kamino-Balke; apparently, people were deeply divided. The prisoners looked over the fence with watchful eyes, with hope:

"Nothing has been said yet . . . Maybe the whole thing will collapse?"

The eyes that looked at the courtyard were full of expectation.

"Would it take that much? . . . One little flare-up . . ."

The "little flare-up," however, did not occur.

A few hours later, when the spring weather suddenly turned, when it again grew gray and cloudy, a new cold wind blew from the north, and heavy, wet snowflakes started falling.

A bunch of people, around fifteen—a mix of Jews and non-Jews—stumbled their way out of the gates. They were bent over, wrapped in tattered scarves and shawls, and from a distance looked like a funeral procession that had been thrown together. They turned quickly to the right, to the muddy road that went around Golikhovke. They went with the feeling that all this happened—a long, long time ago—they had once traveled like this, and moreover, they had to, and nothing could prevent it: not the mud, the cold, northern wind, the big soft snowflakes falling on their bent shoulders, moistening their faces, their arms, and even their eyes—they went not because they had earned their destruction, for their bad deeds, but because this was their fate.

People long known to each other were in this bunch: the young man who had served Reb Aaron in the tannery, Yokhelzon's wife, who had faded, but was still beautiful, with all her layers of clothing on top and underneath. She kept powdering herself and spraying herself from a bottle of cologne she had hidden. There was the clockmaker, who had become more talkative and lively than the others, but only because at least there was an end, he was free from all the talk that he was an informer, because he was being sent to the camp by a big official, the investigator himself . . .

Shmuel Voltsis seemed to be all alone in the middle of this group, he was completely silent and withdrawn into himself. He experienced a kind of inner squeamishness when it came to the other prisoners, as if they were the lowest of the low, and he, Shmuel Voltsis, out of his own superiority had ordered himself to go with this crowd and suffer punishment.

He didn't forget that they were taking him to a concentration camp, and with great bitterness unceasingly thought the same thing:

"I worked hard all those years for Berezovsky at the sawmill, and now, suddenly, when our kind of people are finally getting a bit of respect . . ."

22

"There you have it!"

"Done for . . ."

"Ushak turned up near the Verminsky forest."

"They attacked two peasant wagons between Tatarovke and Lyuban."

"A bandit's trick."

"He left a note, 'I'll be back,' and kept his word . . ."

It was not yet dawn and still dark outside. The commotion awakened Kamino-Balke.

Four peasants had come from Lyuban and Tatarovke, two poverty-stricken villages. At first, when Filipov spoke against the SRs, the peasants sympathized with him. But now, these four—from the peasant brigades—came to lodge complaints:

"This is it."

"Done for."

Filipov, who had given a speech there a few days earlier, was responsible for all this.

He was out in the courtyard at the first rooster's crowing. Dressed in his fur coat over his undershirt, he saw people running from one building to the other with the news—joyfully, convinced that he, Filipov alone, was to blame for everything . . .

He was grumpy and sleepy as he listened to the peasants; every sour breath he took combined disgust for the enemy and the grumblers. Angry, he said to the peasants:

"And what did you do, you, the 'peasant brigade'?"

Exasperated, he turned to go back to his room.

The courtyard darkened.

The peasants stuck to their complaints. The Red Army soldiers heard them out, listening to every detail: on their way to Kamino-Balke, Ushak searched their wagons and took everything they had.

"We had to take our boots off; we're down to our undershirts."

"He ordered us to tell everyone that he was coming to the villages to butcher everyone who had anything to do with the communists."

Upset, Filipov went back out to the courtyard to make the peasants go home. They began complaining again, but he interrupted them:

"Fine. You said so already."

"Measures will be taken."

Filipov looked as though he had to restrain his anger with all his might.

Even after the peasants left, he continued to pace around, and his cough found its way to the corners of the courtyard. The cough was dry and hoarse, it was an ordinary cough that said:

"It's your funeral . . ."

Then there was a pause, and the second cough finished the sentence:

"It's your funeral . . ."

He summoned Comrade Sasha and Yuzi Spivak.

Their opinions:

"It's clear . . . There's no danger . . . A bunch of bandits made camp not far from the woods . . . But on the other hand . . . From the rear . . . The Moshne SRs . . . They don't have the strength to leave Moshne . . . They're going to fade away."

To prove to herself that she was not afraid for Filipov, Comrade Sasha asked, "What if we asked headquarters for backup?"

Filipov ordered her to remain alone with him and unhappily removed a packet of documents from their hiding place and showed her that he had written to headquarters twice seeking help; both times the answer came back marked "secret":

> There are too many fronts as it is; we ourselves have few forces
> left at our disposal. No government could hold out with as little
> manpower as we have.

The second time headquarters answered:

> Do as we do: maintain your positions with your own forces.

"What?" Filipov said to Comrade Sasha in an offended tone. "Are you joking?"

And he moved away to the window to look outside. The weather was like his mood—twilight all day long. There had been summertime rain alternating with wintertime snow. Big, soft, cottony snow-flakes plunged their clear whiteness into muddy puddles—a sign that this was happening in life also.

◆

At around ten o'clock in the morning.

The same muck that was underfoot outside weighed on their hearts; it seemed that it was going to last a long time. Ushak's arrival in the area had spoiled the springtime completely and for good. Everyone recalled the roads around the Verminsky forest, where Ushak was hiding—they were also muddy, dark, and dirty, like the courtyard. Filipov would have to order a group of soldiers to the forest:

"Get ready! Six of you, mount your horses!"

But yesterday's complaints echoed in his ears:

"You looked for an easier assignment."

"You went where a soft bed was waiting for you."

And everything grated on his nerves and drove him to distraction.

As though it were an ordinary day, the soldiers led the horses to the well, washed and groomed them, and yelled when they wouldn't stand still. Comrade Sasha ran from one building to another, carrying two frying pans, as if getting ready for a party . . . Even she had become an ordinary woman:

Why wasn't she reporting for work in the office?

Around ten-thirty.

Once again, Filipov headed for the stables, where the soldiers were puttering about—to rebuke and exhort them. His anger drove him there, pulling him along. His feet trod firmly in that direction. Halfway, however, he stopped. Inwardly his anger turned right and left, and then his iron resolve—which came from the revolution—emerged. It hardened and supported him always, in all his difficult moments, prompting him to do what was necessary and right, but now, after yesterday's conflict, he saw something like a veil before his eyes, like a fog blocking his mind . . .

He remembered the answers he had received from headquarters, but to take them to the soldiers meant divulging them, making

known that which he alone was supposed to know. It meant showing off, justifying himself, salvaging the shred of integrity he had
left . . . From that very thought he burned with all his inner fire. He
inwardly shouted at himself:

"*Chto vy, shutite?* What, are you joking?"

This "what, are you joking?" dispersed the veil and fog that had
enveloped his mind since the previous day, making them disappear.
His feet steadfastly began to tread back to the office. There he was
imbued with the revolution's judgment, and was as cold to everyone else as he was to himself. In the office he asked: "Whose papers
come first?"

Anna Arkadevna Morzovitsky's were at the top of the pile. She
was the former wife of Yesaul Zharov, a tsarist officer who had deserted (in Golikhovke she was simply called "the blonde"). Filipov
was asked: "Her first, or someone else?"

He didn't answer. It didn't matter, because the merciless resolve
he felt toward others was the same as his feeling toward himself.
Yuzi Spivak came into the office to pass along the information that
around four miles from there, near the little woods, someone had
seen four or five bandits from Ushak's gang. Filipov, however, interrupted as soon as he began speaking:

"Leave me alone," he said. "Don't bother me."

✦

It was afternoon; the sky was just about to clear up when it became
overcast once again.

After working in the office, Filipov went for a walk down the
middle path, holding his arms behind him and his head with his
bandaged neck a little to one side. Yuzi Spivak approached him and
wanted to say something, but Filipov waved him away with his hand.
He wanted to be left alone. He seemed to be on the verge of saying:

"You won't accomplish anything by talking—you have to do
something."

And he walked farther away.

He turned left near the stables, where every burst of laughter and
every shove reminded him that cheerfulness was unhealthy. He dis-

appeared into a corner that was blocked off, where reserve horses, neglected, wandered about, and re-emerged with the black nag he had ridden before his last illness—it was a skinny little thing with sleepy eyes and a long, uncombed tail. She ate together with all the other horses, but it didn't do her any good—she grew thinner every day.

"Stand still!" he shouted to her.

The mare with her horsey sigh opened her drowsy eyes and looked at him joyfully. He began to bridle and saddle her. He did this without hurrying, sure of himself, pleased that nobody was doing anything to assist him; his own steady, even movements helped him keep his thoughts focused on the Verminsky forest, where Ushak was hiding:

"You'll get there—first, figure out how many of them are over there . . ."

"Of course . . . should have made the trip first thing in the morning . . ."

Tense to the point of clenching his teeth, he ran the strap under the horse's belly and finished saddling her with the thought:

"Six or so of them . . ."

Then he heard someone calling very uncertainly from behind his back. The weak voice tried to become stronger but remained weak. His eyes looked around very slowly, as if not believing what they saw, first lots of red spots on Comrade Sasha's face, then Comrade Sasha herself, and then the red calico blouse she was wearing. Her lips were pale. Her eyes squinted and blinked as they always did when she sensed that Filipov was upset.

"I," she said, narrowing her eyes, "I wanted to invite you . . . to stop by, Comrade Filipov . . . today is my name day . . ."

Her shoulders remained raised in confusion from not finishing the question, while her head hung down, eyes and face twitching: "What will come of it? What's going to happen?"

"So that's what it is," he said. "Your name day . . ."

Once again he turned his back to her and examined his horse, making sure that the saddle was properly fastened. Somewhere deep inside, under a veneer of decisiveness, a feeling stirred in him—a feeling of pity for all the months they'd worked together. What was happening to her now? Had she really lost her mind, celebrating her name day in these circumstances? Or was she planning to facilitate a truce around the table—a woman's diplomacy?

"Fine," he answered without looking at her. "I'll stop by. And in any case—my rifle is there, at your place . . . I'm going to need it."

✦

They had sugar, for a change. They smiled broadly as they poured it into their hot tea, taking every additional spoonful for an act of revenge on the world bourgeoisie:

"That's how they used to do it—a plague in their bellies."

Investigator Andreyev became the butt of everyone's jokes:

"Keep pouring . . . keep pouring . . ."

"Don't be selfish, brother."

"Show us how you used to do it in the good old days . . ."

Sticking it to her, Filipov answered Comrade Sasha:

"I don't know when my name day is. Like I was actually born in October."

Across from him, Igumenko's eyes lit up:

"Always about himself . . . He only talks about himself!"

Filipov called someone out of the room for a private consultation, then went back in and called another person, and then someone else as well. There was a grudge heating up inside Filipov—a grudge at Comrade Sasha: "What did she bring me here for?" Then, an image of his saddled horse all ready behind the stables flashed before his eyes. The swampy, dirty roads around the Verminsky forest beckoned to him as lightly as a wind caressing his eyes and brow with its freshness.

"And the boy . . . he was a good boy," he reminded himself about the question that Comrade Sasha had asked him.

He began telling the story about his life at his grandmother's, about their poverty. She was a strange, fanatically religious woman. They lived at the edge of a big city, in a neighborhood near some coal mines. He didn't have a mother; it seemed that his grandmother, without ever having children, somehow got herself a grandson in her old age. He remembered: red, teary eyes, a sunken mouth that reeked of stale ashes, stubbornly upright shoulders, and a bony, dry hand hitting him for not kneeling properly before the icons. The last of her three deceased husbands was Catholic, and she no longer knew whether she was Catholic or Russian Orthodox. She lit candles at both churches, dragging him with her, so that he would kneel next to her in prayer. What he noticed, however, were the beggars asking for alms at the entrances to the churches. He wanted to lead one of them—a blind man—away from the steps of the church, to wander the world with him. That was the best thing: to lead a blind man while looking at passersby for their reactions—both tears and laughter.

"And the boy . . . he was a good boy."

He had no shoes and no hat until the age of twelve. As a result, his friends always hoisted him up on their shoulders to help him climb over the tall fence behind Dementyev's large garden to swipe the fruit—if he got caught, what was there to take from him, anyway?

But this was not at all what he wanted to tell them about.

His grandmother's bony, dry hand woke him up early one morning—only a fanatically pious grandmother could wake a child so pitilessly. The young muscles around his eyes strained painfully, and his eyes opened. In the neighborhood doors opened as quietly as the night. A sleepy lamp went out in one house and lit up in another—the inhabitants were heading out for their shifts in the mines. The gray drizzle of early morning moistened everyone. A great mass of people was walking—and he was with them, led by his grandmother. On the way, in the middle of the city, on a hill, all the church and monastery bells were tolling at once: it was time for morning prayers. Their noise brought his grandmother down to her knees right in the middle of the dirty sidewalk—to cross herself.

"Kneel!" she yelled at him, while making the sign of the cross.

It was then that he realized, in fright and for the first time, that she was taking him to work at the factory near the mines.

Except for Comrade Sasha, there was no one left at the table. Her face covered in red blotches, her squinting eyes and her protruding upper lip kept on asking:

"What's going to happen? . . . What's going to happen? . . ."

A longing that sprang from reminiscences about his childhood once again pulled him outside to his waiting horse, and to the muddy roads near the Verminsky forest.

"Wait," he recalled. "My small rifle—I once left it here someplace..."

Later Comrade Sasha recounted that when she took the rifle from a corner of the room to give to Filipov, he said:

"'You've chosen the easiest task for yourself, eh?' someone yelled to me yesterday. Is that a justification? Is that why nobody actually does anything?"

✦

Out in the fields the wind blew, damp as an open cellar.

It seemed that Passover was still a long time coming: hard, frozen grains of ice blew across the fields, shaking the air like some gray medicine inside a bottle. For a moment, the hail stopped. The wind subsided, and mist descended from above—it was raining and snowing, making Filipov's hands and face wet and the horse underneath him sweaty. The smell of rotten vegetation came from the nearest marsh. Hoarsely, as if it had caught a cold, a bird called its evening cry, and in response, his heart jolted in his breast:

"'You've chosen the easiest task for yourself, eh?' someone yelled to me yesterday. Is that a justification?"

Out of spite he turned left, toward the forest where four or five of Ushak's men had been spotted earlier that day. As he shook in his saddle, the words he spoke when telling his story to Comrade Sasha reverberated in his mind—mechanically, without emotion. He seemed to spur his horse on with the same words:

"And the boy . . . he was a good boy."

The fields around the forest were empty. He dashed to the left and to the right but didn't notice anyone. Like smoke from damp fuel that wasn't of good quality to begin with, the fog first thickened and then thinned again, spreading low at the tree trunks. Night was falling. He stopped his horse and listened carefully:

"No one's here . . . They can all go to hell . . ."

The stillness spread around every tree from one end of the forest to the other. It filled Filipov with painful regret: to return just then to Kamino-Balke, alive, to return there with nothing would have meant leaving everyone with the excuse, "You've chosen the easiest task for yourself, eh?" This would have meant: Moshne and Ushak all over again, people from nearby villages coming once more with their complaints . . .

From this thought alone—the thought of returning to Kamino-Balke with nothing—Filipov became disgusted with himself and the predicament closing in on him. He climbed down from his horse and stood, as if waiting for something that had been decided ahead of time. Then he proceeded along the edge of the forest.

The night grew darker. The condition of the road improved as it wound its way up the hill. Filipov's horse ran a little faster, jostling the irritation right out of him, although by then he had stopped giving it much thought. Not a trace remained of the heartless feelings he had experienced earlier in the day when he saddled his horse behind the stables—the sense that he was setting out to solve an insoluble problem. He sat in the saddle as if he had been forced to, implacable and merciless, his eyes lowered, with his neck bandaged, and a voice that would have sounded hoarse were he to begin speaking. He listened to the silence around the forest, which threatened him with death. He was feeling drowsy, his head fell lower and lower. His sense of himself as Anastasyev grew duller and faded under the pressure of the great thing for which he had labored his entire life, ever since his grandmother had taken him to the factory that morning. He had worked in the coal mines, wandered from prison to prison in Siberia, fought against Kolchak and other enemies, had served at Kamino-Balke. He wasn't thinking about any of this. He simply waited, filled with a deep, drowsy yearning, for the end of his service, with the awareness that it could be and had to be the end of him as well, the end of Filipov who used to be called Anastasyev before the revolution. But it would still be Filipov who would inspire everyone to set out against Moshne, after they brought him back to Kamino-Balke, a dead man, murdered by criminals. He had barely thought of this before, but now, with all his drowsy senses, he felt that the cause he served demanded it—not from him personally. It wasn't personal, either, when he, the final arbiter, ordered someone to be shot. The heaviness he felt in his head and in all his limbs made him feel that he faced the same suffering and death—there was nothing that could be done about it, because that was his lot.

"Ya!" he spurred his horse on and turned toward the Verminsky forest.

✦

In Tatarovke only the villagers whose houses bordered the Verminsky forest heard the shots—in the middle of the night, as some later reported, or, according to others, by the gray light of dawn.

Early in the morning, several of Ushak's men rode into the village requesting fresh towels to use for bandaging; they also inquired whether there was a pharmacy in Tatarovke. From this, the villagers concluded that a couple of Ushak's men were wounded. From Bezkrenyuk, the peasant who gave them fresh towels, they also took a copper samovar, two sheep, and a young calf—while they were at it. They boasted:

"Last night we took down the big shot himself!"

Kamino-Balke was notified of this development.

23

The cell where Sofia Pokrovskaya and the blonde were locked up—a roomy, rectangular cell with a clay floor—had a different smell from the other cells. It smelled like a nighttime train journey, a sleepy railway car reserved exclusively for proper folk—each passenger so proper as to be exceedingly polite even when answering nature's call. The only thing missing from the picture: wheels turning rapidly under the floor. It was hard to say whether anybody was actually asleep: once evening arrived, everyone inside would be lying down, eyes closed. The air inside the cell was also snoozing; all that was lacking was the scent of lemons and oranges.

It was hard to discern faces in the nocturnal darkness. In opposite corners, the two women lay like passengers in third class, each on her own mattress, barely acknowledging the other's presence. It seemed that every conversation ended with the women souring on each other and insulting the ideas that had gotten them locked up: Sofia Pokrovskaya's Socialist Revolutionary doctrine and the blonde's religious monarchism.

As for quarrels, well, they had a grand total of two—but they were serious.

Quarrel number one:

Yokhelzon's missus had been locked up with them in the same cell. The blonde and Yokhelzon's wife were like two widows who had been married to the same man—at each other's throats several times a day. The blonde had grievances against Pokrovskaya: why was she, another Christian woman, silent?

"Look at her!" the blonde pointed at Yokhelzon's wife. "Look at her putting on airs! Look at her daring to defend the communists . . . They're the ones who got her locked up, and she wants to defend them. A dirty kike! Watch out: all yids are exactly like her!"

Sofia Pokrovskaya, full of hatred toward both her cellmates, let the blonde know that she was not on her side.

"No, my dear," she said to the blonde, her pupils dark as pinheads in her eyes. "I am what I am, but I am not in the Black Hundreds like you!"

The blonde's response was no less caustic:

"Well, yes, so you say, of course. Those SRs, the devil take them! The Bolsheviks would never have come to power if not for you!"

"That's enough," Sofia Pokrovskaya cut her off. "No more talking."

With this, she meant to let the blonde know that she had not the slightest interest in continuing this debate.

Quarrel number two:

By then Yokhelzon's wife was no longer in the cell with them—only Sofia Pokrovskaya and the blonde were still there, having resigned themselves to remaining silent forever. Sofia Pokrovskaya, however, was teaching the blonde how to behave by her own insolent example. As a provocation, she would throw the food that was brought to her back in the guards' faces and demand better meals; she caused a ruckus asking why the cell wasn't heated on time, and screamed day in and day out:

"Why aren't you giving us bedding?"

In general, she found ways to demonstrate that there was no reason to either fear or respect "them," even though she was in their hands. All this was supposed to tell them:

"Usurpers—that's what you are!"

Only the blonde had her own charming rules: she'd blow a kiss to every soldier around, ready to play lovey-dovey and repay every favor with everything she had. This behavior elicited endless anger from Pokrovskaya.

"Not quite sure how to put this politely," she said to the blonde. "It's like you're washing their feet and drinking the dirty water . . ."

The blonde had been waiting for this comment all along. Her hands trembling in excitement, she adjusted her dress and spat out:

"So, well, what a joke! . . . Who can possibly compare to you? Ugh! You, the SRs—you are the privileged ones here! You really do belong. They never have your kind shot—the most they do to you is exile you like little children who've gotten lost . . . They are even grateful to you—for the favors you served up to them in the past . . ."

Instead of answering the blonde, Sofia Pokrovskaya picked a fight with the officials: why did they put her in the same cell with smugglers and prostitutes? She screamed:

"You're doing this to spite me!"

She demanded to be moved to a different cell:

"Immediately! No excuses! Right this minute!"

When the prisoners were allowed out for the exercise period, they talked about the uprising in Moshne. There were also rumors about the new prisoner—a goy, who had clearly been sent by someone on the inside to pretend to be a member of the Moshne peasant brigade. There were also conversations about Pokrovskaya—how they were taking her in for interrogation for no good reason because hadn't she told them:

"I'm not going to answer a single one of your questions."

Pokrovskaya looked like she was fasting. Her heart raced from not knowing whether she was going to be sentenced before the uprisings in the nearby villages would reach Kamino-Balke. Her mattress distanced itself by what seemed like miles from the blonde's mattress in the opposite corner of the cell. It seemed that the events unfolding around them were winking at her:

"What do you have to do with that blonde? Why do you even have to look in her direction?"

✦

Sofia Pokrovskaya spent her days sitting in her corner of the cell half-asleep—little, angry, her face green and her health failing. Her dark, wet little mouth was created for the purpose of nonstop talking. At that moment it wasn't finding any listeners. She wrapped herself up in her village shawls, swaying from side to side as if she had a persistent toothache; only one of her cheeks was visible—red and swollen all the way to her nose, her short pug nose like all the other noses in her family . . .

She barely moved and hardly made a sound. Her heart pounding, her eyes shut, she kept thinking about the developments in Moshne, which were quickly spreading to Kamino-Balke. Before her arrest, she had laid the groundwork for what was taking place: it would be a struggle, a struggle for a just cause . . . A lot of blood would be spilled—so be it. Let "them" know they weren't dealing with milksops or wretches like that Spivak and his ilk who surrendered the moment the wind shifted direction . . . Many would be killed—so be it, this was a matter of life and death.

From time to time and seemingly on their own her thoughts circled back to the goy, who was also locked up here like any other prisoner—in the very same building, even. Who was he? Nobody knew. First she thought: he was someone from her political cell on this side of the border, or from the group on the other side. But during the exercise period the other prisoners concluded that in fact he was a simple man—a peasant. And, indeed, when she was confronted with him at an interrogation, it was immediately obvious that she didn't know who he was—though it also was clear that he would either set her free or die with her. She had trouble understanding only one thing:

"Who sent him?"

All day, seemingly on their own, her thoughts—half-awake—circled around this question, but in the middle of the night, when it was pitch black, it felt different. Thoughts about the end—intensified by her sleepiness—crawled into her heart like living creatures. In complete darkness, all wrapped in her shawls, she sat up on her mattress and felt, in her entire body, a longing for him—for that peasant:

"*On zdes'* . . . He's here."

An extraordinary religious feeling filled her heart with submissive devotion and coursed through her entire lethargic body. It was like the pious mood that comes over obedient nuns when they say their *moyde ani*—their morning prayers—still in bed with their eyes closed. She was drawn toward "him" as if he were a saint. He was not one of her relatives—not her father or brother. He came from the people—someone completely unlike her, someone from the depths of the village; it was in his name and in the name of his fellow villagers that the SRs had spent several decades risking their necks on too many gallows. He had come quietly, his steps barely heard—a symbol of gratitude, a miracle from the lower depths that had always been oppressed by terrible backwardness and ignorance. He arrived quietly to redeem the suffering of death with his own sacrifice—and just as quietly he kept calming her in a paternal way from the other side of the wall where he was kept under lock and key:

"Shhh . . . Quiet . . . No need to be hysterical."

That was why her cheek turned pale only for a moment when the list brought into the cell made it clear that one of them—either her or the blonde—had her fate sealed. Wrapped in her shawls from head to toe, she sat petrified atop the mattress in her own little corner, her cheek swollen and protruding from her shawls. Her teeth made a quick clattering sound as if from fever but, more likely, only because the guard who arrived with the list had mispronounced her name:

Why did he say Mokrovskaya, not Pokrovskaya? . . .

After that, she lowered her head even more and remained still—nothing else could concern her at all.

✦

The blonde, on the other hand, took these developments in a different way: the fact that someone had come in with the list of names left her so calm that she was almost ready to yawn.

After the guard left the cell, she was entirely certain she wasn't the one they had in mind. She lay down on her mattress, sprawled on her back as if completely at ease, stretched her arms behind her head, shut her eyes, and, with all of her inner feeling, queried her hands, her feet, and her breast whether she was right. The answer her robust limbs promptly gave made her feel calm. All the muscles in her body presented their report together:

"We feel the same way—we aren't the ones they have in mind . . ."

As a result, her sense of certainty grew even stronger. So as to forget entirely that someone from the prison administration had even been there with the list in the first place, she lay down with her eyes shut and her arms stretched out behind her head and imagined a scene. She was sunning herself in the nude on some beach at the edge of the sea, and right away, as per usual, this fantasy made her feel attracted to the good-looking men who appeared to be standing close by, looking at her naked body. Lust spread from all over her body toward her breast, where it gnawed and gnawed at her, bringing her greater and greater ecstasy—this, too, had a calming effect: her body's passion was the opposite of death and was in itself further proof that it wasn't her they had in mind.

At this point there was no reason to be deceitful any longer. The blonde suddenly sat up and saw Sofia Pokrovskaya, who was sitting across from her in her corner of the cell, slowly and sleepily withdrawing her gaze. The blonde barely managed to hold onto the edge of that gaze, to the tiny bit that remained, but even that insignificant remainder was sufficient to jolt her heart—it made her feel that Sofia Pokrovskaya had spent that entire time looking at her, thinking that it was her, the blonde, whom they had in mind when the list was read out. For the first time, she felt she had been gravely insulted—it was as if Pokrovskaya had called her the most shameful names. She wanted to curse. At the very same time, however, for the sake of her inner sense of calm, it was also of the utmost importance that the thought—in that list of names, it was her, the blonde, that they had in mind—not occur to anyone else, not even her sworn enemy, the woman from the SRs. As a result she immediately let go of all the quarrels and mutual recriminations they had made against each other and started to pace the cell, back and forth, back and forth, talking nonstop:

"Me? Of course, not me! She was bragging, wasn't she? Me?"

She moved rapidly about the cell—almost running—and kept blabbing about what a great believer she was:

"I feel it with my entire body, even with my hair and nails I feel it, too . . . I can always sense the tiniest bit of danger from a mile away . . . But now, I'm calm . . . I'm a very passionate creature . . . Now, right this minute, I want a man . . . I want a man very much . . . And this, too, is a sign . . . Me? That can't possibly be . . . If only you saw me naked, you would surely agree . . . I've never imagined and would never consent to the thought that I will die—everyone else will die but not me, not even many years from now when I'll be old and decrepit . . . And God will not allow that unimaginable thing, so nothing can possibly happen . . . I see a lot—a whole lot—of sunny summer days for myself in the future: they are mine, mine, those days are mine . . . Nobody can take them away from me, not even "they"—their arms are too short for that . . ."

Dashing back and forth, her face aflame and her eyes glistening, the blonde blabbered on for a long, long time until she saw: Pokrovskaya, petrified, was sitting in her own corner of the cell with her head bowed—not listening to her. The blonde sat on her own mattress in the other corner. Her wide-open eyes, their muscles all tensed up, fixated on something as if wishing to shatter it. Suddenly she erupted in hysterics:

"I don't need it . . ."

"I don't want it!"

She tore the hair on her head. All of a sudden, her hands reached around her neck to squeeze it with great force—they were at it for a long time. Her face turned red, her bulging eyes popped out of their sockets. Then, just as suddenly, she fell silent and let go of her neck. Like an automaton, with no trace of inner preparation, she fell on her knees in the corner, crossed herself, and began to pray.

After that, time in the cell barely moved . . .

When Sofia Pokrovskaya had to lift her head out of her shawls at dusk, she saw: having been strengthened, apparently, by her renewed faith, the blonde stood with her head bent toward her, whispering in her believer's voice that "he" . . . that "he" was not going to allow it . . .

"He will make himself known at the last moment . . . That's why he was sent here on account of me—by the Whites from the other side . . ."

Sofia Pokrovskaya felt as if cold frogs were crawling all over her naked body. Her open eyes noticed: the blonde was certain that the peasant was sent here by her "Whites"; she felt no less certain about that than Pokrovskaya herself, who was certain that "he" was sent here by her SRs . . .

She didn't want to see the blonde's face any longer and recoiled from her. But the blonde continued standing next to her, stubbornly repeating:

"You'll see . . ."

✦

The following afternoon, it seemed at first that the blonde's "you'll see" was coming true.

Gusts of wind swept into the cell from the distant corner of the courtyard. Loud wails mixed with the soldiers' curses hastened the wind that carried them forward. A sorrowful commotion accompanied by the sound of people running wheeled around from one building to the next, spun with the force of a whirlwind, and then stopped in the courtyard out of breath.

Concealed hands tapped on the prison windows, and immediately the inmates felt that they had been left all alone, without anyone keeping watch—the last of the guards was summoned from his post so loudly that everyone could hear. Joy at the thought that perhaps they all had been freed switched to fear with the swiftness of an arrow. The building where they were locked up was burning on all sides; they were done for, everyone was going to die.

In the cell, the blonde was the first to begin shrieking and pounding at the door.

With teeth clenched and eyes shut, she threw the whole weight of her body at the door with all the strength she could muster, banging on it with her fists and both feet. And, just like that—and just as savagely as the blonde—other prisoners in the neighboring cells took up pounding on their locked doors. In one of the cells, out of sheer panic, someone broke the glass of the high barred window, perched on another inmate's shoulders and saw:

In the middle of the courtyard an assembly was coming to an end—Yuzi Spivak was giving a speech. The sailor Igumenko, his voice hoarse, issued an order—and from the middle of the courtyard, the soldiers, taking their rifles, dashed over to their horses; after that, the guards' steps became audible in the jail's hallway. The guards opened the door of one cell after another, yelling more angrily than the prisoners:

"What do you think you're doing? . . ."

"Have you lost your minds? . . ."

They yelled at the blonde more angrily than at anyone else.

"What are you rejoicing for? This is not some celebration!"

But the blonde managed to get her claws on one of the soldiers yelling at her; she pulled him in close and gave him a kiss. She shimmied, trembled, and vamped—all with such passion that the soldier could barely get away from her.

"Nothing's the matter," he said, pushing her back into her cell.

"So, they killed him . . . Filipov . . . What's it to you?"

A wave of joy rolled over the blonde inside the locked cell—she danced and skipped about the room. Her arms open, she rushed over to Pokrovskaya in her corner:

"Did you hear that?! . . . And what did I say? . . ."

But suddenly, she collected herself. In great excitement she went back to her corner and kneeled again to pray and cross herself in gratitude.

This time around, the praying lasted several hours.

Once again, night fell.

Once again, the cell smelled like a sleepy railway car carrying refined people; the air dreamed up a fragrance of lemons and oranges. The blonde finished praying.

Tired from saying her prayers, crossing herself, and bowing, she crawled over to Pokrovskaya and, in quiet piety, started to whisper in her ear about the "miracle" she hadn't stopped believing in even for a moment, ever since she set out for the border with a child in her arms:

"Now it's really coming—the miracle . . . It's coming, it's almost here . . ."

Full of God-fearing piety, she kept speaking about "him," the peasant who was arrested—it was all his doing, he arranged Filipov's murder . . .

Still more submissively and quietly she leaned toward Pokrovskaya and piously whispered in her ear:

"He's a holy man . . . Put your faith in him . . . He will save you, too . . ."

✦

By the gray light of dawn, they led the blonde out of the cell to hear the judgment against her: she was convicted of espionage, shuttling stolen papers from Red Army headquarters to White generals on the other side. Filipov had signed the order several hours before he was killed.

In Golikhovke, this is how they talked about it:

"Oh, did she raise a holler! . . ."

"Oh, did she not want to die! . . ."

"What is there to say? . . . What a piece of work! . . ."

"That's the blonde for you! . . ."

After he was set free from Kamino-Balke, the poor goy wandered around the marketplace in rags. He stopped passersby and, eyes blinking, asked to be given a piece of bread on credit—he swore that he would pay in wild doves.

Market vendors recognized him:

"That's Fedka, the village idiot from Harne."

"He was pretending to be a member of the Moshne peasant brigade."

"They say someone convinced him this would get him paid well at Kamino-Balke."

Haykel Berezovsky's former timber steward Moyshe Volovnik showed up at Berezovsky's house—dirt poor and full of worries, his lips all chapped. He longed for a smoke. His appearance: as if the whole world was good for nothing.

"So, you see," he said. "We made such a mistake with that goy."

24

Without his overcoat or rifle, Pinke Vayl rode from Kamino-Balke to Golikhovke fast—as fast as he could.

The horse's mane was sweaty.

Pinke's mane was sweaty.

How Pinke looked: both he and his horse might as well have exploded from their wild ride—it wouldn't have mattered at all. The main thing was:

"They murdered Filipov . . ."

He, Pinke, didn't know anything about the whole affair—he was part of a convoy bringing a group of prisoners to a concentration camp. It took two and a half days to get there, and on the way he caught a cold and lost his voice. Even when he yelled at the top of his lungs, it was as if he was just moving his lips, and his voice was barely audible. But that wasn't the issue. Quite the opposite—it was because he was sick and wasn't taking care of himself that Filipov's death affected him so strongly.

"Onward!" He gritted his clenched teeth and spurred his horse on.

It seemed to him that he kept repeating:

"You're going to explode . . . explode . . ."

The horse flew, its belly elongated and muscular, its neck outstretched. They were just about to reach Golikhovke. From behind, the sun warmed the horse's neck and back. Pinke looked at his galloping shadow flying across the ground and saw lives flitting past even more quickly than the shadow. Whose? . . . His, Filipov's, everyone's: those who had fallen like Filipov and those who would fall like him . . .

Pinke thought:

The wagon that brought Filipov's murdered body to Kamino-Balke sat outside the office for much too long. Both courtyards were empty. For a long time, no one approached the wagon—as if some deliberation were necessary, as if the living Filipov needed to be consulted about what to do with the dead one. Pinke saw Comrade Sasha starting to carry benches and tables out of the office—

her nose showed signs of crying, even though her eyes were dry; Pinke helped her. Filipov was laid out on the couch in the office and was covered with a red cloth; the walls were also decked out in red—they gathered up whatever banners they could find in Kamino-Balke, even though there weren't enough. Pinke pondered the situation: this wasn't the proper way to honor Filipov—whole swaths of wall remained white, and besides, Filipov was lying in the office all alone, with no one coming to pay their respects. So he remained with the body in the office. Pinke observed: Filipov was shot multiple times—perhaps five or six bullets. Besides that, there was a deep, bloody slash on his face reaching all the way to his forehead. His eyebrows, however, were raised in anger, so that it seemed he was ready—even more now than when he was alive—to say:

"*Chto vy? Shutite?* What, are you joking?"

Pinke thought:

It took a long time before the soldiers began arriving, one by one. The first was the sailor Igumenko: he stalled at the door, as if ready to leave as soon as he walked in, but then he stayed awhile and looked and looked at the angry eyebrows on Filipov's face, and suddenly let out a wail:

"*To-vaaaa-rrrrishch!* Commm-rade! . . ."

And right after that, shrieking, he darted out into the courtyard. All the soldiers stood assembled. Yuzi Spivak gave a speech, Comrade Sasha spoke; Igumenko, swinging his fist in the air, sensed that Yuzi wasn't finishing his speech the way Filipov used to:

"*Chto vy? Shutite?* . . . What, are you joking? . . ."

In the name of Comrade Filipov, it was decided:

"Today, before nightfall—attack Moshne."

Yuzi Spivak set out to the far-flung shtetls to recruit workers willing to join the effort, while he, Pinke, was off to carry out a similar task in Golikhovke, to assemble the eight or nine young workers he had met through his girlfriend—the one in the red kerchief—at the club. If necessary, he was prepared to give a speech there. He spurred his horse on. He rode faster than the wind; it seemed to him that it wasn't just his horse that was flying but he also—his mind kept circling back endlessly to the same thought:

"You're going to explode . . . explode . . ."

◆

When Pinke arrived at the tailor's, the girl—home by herself—met him in the entryway. There was complete silence. It was as if the tailor and his family had gone away to a fair. The girl stood up from the sewing machine where she had been working; seeing him made her think more highly of herself—at least, that's what it looked like to Pinke. Her nose had forgotten to smile and be witty. Her small breasts bounced, while her eyes—round and like little black buttons that were alive—took him in from a distance. This assured Pinke that he, too, should remain standing and take her in from a distance, at least for a while. She had already learned of Filipov's death; something in her heart had told her that Pinke was about to arrive. Her gaze appeared to be saying, at once, two different things that joined together in one much larger truth that grew and grew to such an extent that Pinke's heart started racing, too. Something prodded him to approach her, to take her hand in his, to utter her name:

"Basya . . ."

While he was holding her hand, he again experienced the strong desire to approach her and take her hand. As he attempted to speak, his voice sounded even more hoarse than earlier.

"Filipov has been killed," he said to her, his voice barely audible.

He looked at her and saw her eyes closing.

"I know," she whispered quietly without opening her eyes. "Filipov was killed."

Both of them felt their chests heaving—why? Because Filipov had been killed? Because they were in love? Everything at once . . . Both these reasons seemed to be one and the same thing—and it moved them both greatly.

There was a knock on the door. A comrade arrived, one of those young workers who were ready and knew all the facts, and couldn't sit still and wait but, instead, were running back and forth—what sort of a question was it whether they would go or not? What was there even to ask? Were they really going to sit around and wait until others came and stabbed them one by one, the way that worker from Brozhe got stabbed a week earlier? So there he was, the young worker, running out the door to bring all the other comrades to the house.

At that moment Pinke felt intensely that he had plenty to be angry about: his rage about Filipov's murder grew by the minute.

His comrades assembled outside, Pinke gave a speech—for the first time in his life; he wanted to explain what Filipov had given his blood and life for. It didn't bother him that his voice was so hoarse. Chills running down their spines, his comrades saw the blood flowing to his face from straining to speak with all his might; they saw his lips moving without hearing a single word—the wind outside was much too strong—but, in any case, there were no words to describe what Filipov had given his life for, and maybe it was actually for the best that Pinke's voice was so hoarse while he spoke . . .

Then Pinke remembered that there were patches of exposed white wall in the office where Filipov's body was laid out—not honoring him properly.

"Give me your banners," he said, his voice even hoarser. "Surrender your banners, all of them, for him—to put on the walls . . ."

Pinke meant this straightforwardly, simply—but what came out brought shivers to the spines of everyone assembled there. His face flushed even redder than before; it seemed that he was on fire, screaming with all his might:

"Surrender your banners, all of them, for him—to put on the walls!!!"

3 **Special Section** Unit in the Cheka (the secret police of the new Bolshevik state) that monitored counterrevolutionary activity and identified instances of espionage and treason, among other activities.

7 **"Like a Jew circling the synagogue on Simchas Torah"** Refers to *hakofes* (or, in Hebrew, *hakafot*), the ritual procession of the male congregants with the Torah scrolls in the synagogue service on Simchas Torah (in Hebrew, Simchat Torah). Simchas Torah, the joyful holiday at the beginning of the Jewish new year (in the autumn), marks the moment when the annual cycle of reading Torah (the first five books of Hebrew Bible) starts anew from the beginning of the text.

6–7 **"Over the earth a storm is prowling, / Bringing whirling, blinding snow. / Like a beast I hear it howling, / Like an infant wailing low . . ."** Opening lines of Alexander Pushkin's poem "A Winter Evening"; in the original text of the novel, these lines are spoken in Russian transcribed in Yiddish characters. Our translation is based on that of I. Zheleznova.

7 **Junker** Military rank for junior officers from the nobility in Imperial Russia's armed forces.

14 **Pani** Polish polite form of address for a woman, similar to the English-language "Ms." or "Mrs."

15 **"Hasidic Jews with their rebbes"** Hasidism is a movement in Judaism that emerged in in the eighteenth century in Eastern Europe, particularly in the area corresponding to the territory of modern Ukraine. Hasidism places emphasis on spiritual fulfillment as opposed to Torah study alone, to be achieved through prayer, singing, and dance. The leadership of Hasidic communities centers on the figure of the rebbe, a charismatic spiritual teacher in each community. The founder of Hasidism was Rabbi Yisroel ben Eliezer, also known as the Baal Shem Tov (1700–1760).

16 **Tolstoyan** Follower of the social movement identified with the religious and ethical teachings of the Russian writer Leo Tolstoy (1828–1910). Rooted in the moral teachings of Jesus Christ and critical of the established teachings of the Russian Orthodox Church, the movement was characterized by asceticism, a life of simplicity, vegetarianism, and pacifism.

16 **Shtundists** Sectarian evangelical Protestant groups that emerged among Ukrainian peasants in southern regions of the Russian empire (present-day Ukraine) in the second half of the nineteenth century, influenced by the Baptists, Pietists, and Mennonites who settled in the area. From the German word for "hour," referring to the practice of setting aside an hour a day for Bible study.

17 *havdole* The ceremony marking the end of the Sabbath and the beginning of the work week, celebrated at sundown on Saturday nights. In Hebrew, *havdalah*. The word means "separation," referring to the distinction Judaism makes between the holy time of the Sabbath and the everyday time of the work week.

17 **Shabbos** The Sabbath, the day of rest in Judaism, during which commerce and other forms of work are forbidden. Shabbos begins on Friday night and ends Saturday night.

25 **"A simple girl—the bride of a condemned revolutionary—made the former tsar change his mind"** Refers to Nicholas II's pardoning of a tubercular student involved in revolutionary activity, following a plea from his bride in 1908.

30 **Socialist Revolutionary (SR)** A member of the Socialist Revolutionary Party, founded in 1902, which was a major player in the Russian Revolution. The SR Party won the plurality of votes for the Constituent Assembly following the 1917 October Revolution. After the Constituent Assembly was disbanded by the Bolsheviks in 1918, the SRs split, with some fighting against the Bolsheviks on the side of the Whites. Ultimately defeated, the SRs were put on show trial by Lenin in 1922.

36 **black flannel shirt** Flannel was the common material for clothing for typhus patients, because it was believed to contain the spread of the infection.

68–69 **"The doctor . . . put one end of a stethoscope to his ear and the opposite end on the patient's chest"** An older version of the stethoscope, which had the shape of a tube. One end was placed against the patient's chest, while the physician listened through the other opening.

77 *Realschule* Secondary school in the Russian empire and Western Europe, in which general education was geared toward technical subjects.

91 **Reb Aaron** An honorific term, a polite form of addressing a man in Yiddish, similar to the English-language "Mr." "Reb" is not the same as

"rebbe" or "rabbi" and does not impute rabbinic authority to the person addressed.

91 **kapote** Long coat worn by male Hasidic Jews.

94 **"Reb Aaron started pouring water over his fingers right onto the floor near him—three times over the tips of his fingers, one hand at a time."** In Judaism, the ritual washing of the hands immediately upon waking. In Yiddish, the custom is known as *negl-vaser*—literally, "nail water."

94 **tallis** In Judaism, a ritual prayer shawl traditionally worn by males starting at thirteen years of age. The tallis is worn over other clothing during certain synagogue services and when performing certain prayers alone.

95 **kulak** In the late Russian empire, a relatively affluent peasant. From the Russian word for "fist," distinct from later Stalin-era use of the word.

96 **Petliura** Semyon Petliura (1879–1926), a Ukrainian nationalist leader who led the struggle for Ukrainian independence in the aftermath of the Bolshevik Revolution. Petliura was assassinated in 1926 by Sholem Schwarzbard, a Jewish refugee in Paris, who held him responsible for widespread pogroms against Jews in Ukraine during the civil war.

97 **Mishnah** Compilation of rabbinic interpretations and commentary collected by the third century C.E., aimed at supplementing, explaining, and clarifying the commandments of the Torah (the first five books of the Hebrew Bible). The Mishnah forms part of the traditional curriculum for Jewish males.

97 **"Four paces away from the place where [the criminal] is to be stoned"** Description of the process of executing a criminal found in the Mishnah (Mishnah Sanhedrin 6:3).

99 *melaveh malkeh* Literally "Escorting the Queen," the meal held immediately at the conclusion of the Sabbath, which is referred to as "the Queen" in Judaism.

99 **"In the Talmud, Rabbi Shimon says: 'By fire, by stoning, by strangulation, and by decapitation'"** The full quotation from the Talmud reads: "Four punishments were permitted to the supreme court, stoning, fire, beheading, and strangulation. Rabbi Shimon says: 'By fire, by stoning, by strangulation, and by decapitation'" (Mishnah Sanhedrin 7:1).

99   **story of Achan**   In the book of Joshua, Achan was considered responsible for the Israelites' initial failure to capture the Canaanite city of Ai, and was subsequently stoned (Joshua 7).

107   **kittel**   A white linen robe worn by male Jews at their wedding and by married male Jews during Yom Kippur services and, in some instances, on Rosh Hashanah. The *kittel* also serves as a burial shroud when the man dies.

118   **bast shoes**   Footwear, made of straw, worn by Russian peasants.

128   **"Naked and bare you are, Shmuel . . ."**   "Naked and bare" is the description of the people of Israel in exile in Babylonia after the destruction of the First Temple, as attributed to God who compares the people of Israel to a destitute and ragged young woman, in Ezekiel 16:7.

137   **cholent**   Stew that usually contains beans, potatoes, and meat, eaten during the Jewish Sabbath. Because of the prohibition on kindling fire during the Sabbath, cholent is prepared before the start of the Sabbath and is kept continuously warm on low fire.

141   **Central Committee**   Of the Communist Party, the highest decision-making authority of the new Bolshevik state.

156   **peasant brigade**   In Russian, *kombed*, an abbreviation of *komitet bednoty* (Committee of Poor Peasants). Established in 1918 as local institutions bringing together impoverished peasants to advance government policy, these brigades were primarily responsible for requisitioning grain on behalf of the Soviet state and distributing manufactured goods.

165   **"it's all been arranged with the British and the French!"**   Reference to the foreign intervention in the Russian civil war, during which the Allied forces, after victory in World War I, supported the Whites against the Reds.

169   **"like a mute 'mazel-tov' for a woman who had just given birth"**   Loudly announcing the birth of the baby by congratulating the mother would have made the baby's presence known to the evil eye, hence the "mute" congratulations, or "mazel-tov."

175   **wall newspaper**   Newspapers displayed in public spaces that became widespread after the 1917 revolution and during the civil war, in part due to the shortage of paper. Wall newspapers were used to disseminate government information as well as ideological propaganda.

180 **three-and-a-half-year-old girl** Bergelson gives different ages for the girl.

184 **you're going to spend a couple of months in a concentration camp...** The first concentration camp for political prisoners in postrevolutionary Russia was established in 1919 on the White Sea island of Solovki. The term "concentration camp" in English gained currency during the Second Boer War (1899–1902) and referred to internment camps set up by the British.

199 **Black Hundreds** An ultra-nationalist movement in the Russian empire at the beginning of the twentieth century. Opposed to any retreat from the monarchy, the Black Hundreds espoused xenophobia and antisemitism, and instigated pogroms against Jews.

201 ***moyde ani*** In Hebrew, *modeh ani* for men and *modah ani* for women; literally, "I give thanks." The first words of a prayer in Judaism that is traditionally recited upon waking, while still in bed, to thank God for renewing each person as a new creation every morning.

The original title of Bergelson's novel is *Mides-hadin*. This transliteration into Latin characters reflects one of several ways this Hebrew phrase is spelled in Yiddish (transliterated into Latin characters as, for example, *mides ha-din*; *midas ha-din*; *midas-hadin*; *mides ha"din*). We used this transliteration in our introduction to reflect Bergelson's chosen Yiddish spelling and to be consistent with the bibliographic information in the original publication of the novel. However, we used YIVO transliteration standards for the other terms that contain the Hebrew definite article *ha-* (*mides ha-rakhamim* and *yom ha-din*).

We have transliterated Hebrew words as they would be spoken in Yiddish. We transliterated Yiddish using the YIVO system, except in cases when these terms already entered English under a different spelling. The other exception is proper names: we tried to make proper names in Yiddish easier to pronounce, which meant abandoning YIVO rules when necessary.

We are grateful to the Yiddish Book Center for awarding us a translation fellowship that permitted us to complete this project, for our wonderful translation mentor Susan Bernofsky, and for the cohort of our fellow translators. Sebastian Schulman, then in charge of the fellowship program and a skilled translator in his own right, offered invaluable advice and assistance. We are grateful to Michael Levine for bringing this book to Northwestern University Press, and to the editorial team that took over after his departure.

Dr. Marina Raskin Bergelson graciously permitted the translation of this text and more than generously spent many hours talking about her grandfather and her own experience after his death. In addition, her fine sense of the nuances of Bergelson's prose style pointed us in the right direction.

Harriet would like to thank Sissela Murav, Sam Lavigne, and Lisa Rosenthal for reading drafts of the translation. The Slavic Reference Service at the University of Illinois at Urbana-Champaign provided useful tips for working with Bergelson's archive in Moscow, and Olga Borovaya offered warm and generous hospitality and moral support. Bruce Rosenstock had many invaluable suggestions about our working method, and his ear for English and knowledge of Hebrew and German enabled him to answer any number of queries. Harriet is grateful to Sasha for his terrific sense of humor.

Sasha would like to thank the Center for the Humanities and the Arts at the University of Colorado Boulder for awarding him a travel grant in the summer of 2015, which made possible the necessary in-person work with Harriet, and to Liora Halperin for reading drafts of multiple chapters of this translation. He is grateful to Harriet for supplying many a joke, particularly when she would break into impromptu dramatic readings of various drafts to sound out a particular word or phrase.

As we worked on this translation separately and together during visits at each other's homes in Champaign and Boulder as well as during other get-togethers in Amherst, San Antonio, Brooklyn, and Chicago, we grew to appreciate the collaborative spirit that can productively shape translation and scholarship alike.

Joseph Sherman, who translated David Bergelson's novels *Descent* and *The End of Everything*, planned to translate *Judgment* as well. He was unable to see this project through before his untimely death in 2009. We dedicate our work to his memory.